U0093870

環遊世界一本通

Travel around the World

背包客
一定要會的
英文便利句

MP3

英語名師 **張翔** / 編著

使用說明

1 各篇章抬頭清晰，讀者好翻好查。

Unit **5-1** 詢問銀行服務
機票和攜帶的錢財

🔊 MP3 026

救急情境演練 Situation

2 外師親錄 **102**場情境，讀者隨聽隨學。

Ⓐ：Where's the bank in the airport?
請問機場內的銀行在哪裡？

Ⓑ：In the lobby of the 1st floor.
一樓大廳。

Ⓐ：I want to change Australian dollars.
我要換澳幣。

Ⓑ：Please fill in this form first.
請先填寫這張表格。

Ⓐ：How should I fill it out?
我該如何填寫？

KEY SENTENCES
關鍵句 （完→完整句‧順→順口句）

3 完整、順口關鍵句，滿足讀者正式會話與輕鬆口語需求。

5-01 ▶ 這附近有銀行嗎？
完：Is there any bank around here?
順：Any bank here?

5-02 ▶ 這車站附近有銀行嗎？
完：Are there any banks around the station?
順：Any banks here?

5-03 ▶ 請問匯兌窗口在哪裡？
完：Excuse me. Where's the exchange window?
順：Exchange, please?

4 背包客旅遊筆記，每篇章尾聲分享背包客經驗談和旅遊資訊，給讀者安全感。

✕ 旅客服務篇 Part.**5**

背包客旅遊筆記 BON VOYAGE!

蒐集行前資料是背包客該做的首要功課。在此要推薦一個實用的旅遊資訊網頁，「背包客棧旅遊網」：http://www.backpackers.com.tw/forum/（臉書專頁連結：https://www.facebook.com/#!/backpackers.com.tw）。這是匯集各地背包客旅遊資訊的交流空間與論壇，你可以在此遇到許多「前輩」背包客，並能上傳旅遊心情文章與相片；如果想「揪團」自助旅行，也可貼文徵求同好，例如該站的「志工旅行」專區，非常歡迎滿腔熱血的旅人起義來歸；旅人們也會在這個空間張貼提醒公告，要全球各地的背包客注意自身安

訂房

5 全書共有**13**個主題，搭配主題圖標，篇章分明好找。

單字片語維他命 Useful Vocabulary 📷

- **bank** [bæŋk] **n** 銀行
- **account** [ə`kaunt] **n** 帳戶；戶頭
- **deposit** [dɪ`pazɪt] **v** 存款
- **withdraw** [wɪð`drɔ] **v** 提款
- **transfer** [`trænsfɚ] **v** 轉帳
- **remit** [rɪ`mɪt] **v** 匯款
- **wire** [waɪr] **v** 電匯
- **remittance** [rɪ`mɪtn̩s] **v** 匯款；匯款額
- **exchange window** 匯兌窗口
- **foreign exchange rate difference** 外幣匯差

6 單字片語維他命，補充字彙能量，不怕單字片語不夠用！

輕鬆說英文，開心玩世界

　　許多人羨慕瀟灑自由行的背包客，說走就走，到嚮往的國度展開精采旅程，卻因自己的英語口說能力卻步。

　　某家知名英語教學雜誌的電視廣告，隨機訪問街頭的路人：「你會說英語嗎？」只見被問到的人們如驚弓之鳥，紛紛四散走避；最後問到一位歐巴桑時，她反而微笑著搜索腦海裡出現在生活中的英文單字，侃侃脫口而出。

　　雖然學習英語已是全民運動，但每當真正遇到必須說英語的場合，很多人就像廣告中大多數的路人一樣選擇逃避，或默默站在一旁拉長耳朵，暗忖自己到底聽懂了多少。想想看，我們從小到大接觸了那麼久的英文，對這種語言有或多或少的認識，但為何還是有那麼多人不會說呢？其實，關鍵原因不在於「不會」說、而是「不敢」說。很多人害怕說錯了會被取笑，乾脆選擇沉默以對，甚至「催眠」自己對英語一竅不通。

　　事實上，跟外國人溝通的時候，沒有想像中那樣困難。就像廣告中那位瞇眼微笑的歐巴桑，只要能掌握想要敘述的對象、主題，再加上肢體語言從旁輔助，以比手劃腳加上五官

表情，絕對能輕鬆擁有以英語和他人溝通的能力，這也是本書特別規劃旅遊英語便利句的目的。

　　不管是自助旅行或跟團，本書依照旅遊情境，挑選出最常用的一千三百句英語，並細分各種小插曲，為讀者呈現紙上實況，在第一時間內迅速找到所需要的一句話；在內容上則採第一句是完整句、第二句是順口句的編排原則，讓讀者能用簡單、少少的幾個字，達到十倍速的溝通效果。

　　別擔心單字片語不夠用，本書會為讀者補充足夠的字彙能量，讓旅行不再「字」到用時方恨少！想知道青年旅館有哪些設備嗎？如何在外「方便」不出糗？每個單元的尾聲，都會分享背包客的經驗談，並提供實用的旅遊資訊，讓讀者擁有安全感。

　　讀者可收聽隨書奉送的MP3光碟，由外籍老師以清晰的口語錄製，包管聽得懂、講得通；加碼附贈的「必殺單字」與「旅遊補充包」，除了提供實用字彙外，也告知各國機場網站、我國旅外救急專線等好用資訊。

　　盼望本書能成為旅行良伴，讓旅人們暢所欲言、通行無礙。現在就輕鬆帶著這本小書，開心地朝目的地出發吧，Bon Voyage！

張翔

目錄

使用說明 …………………………………………… 002

作者序 ……………………………………………… 004

Part 1 準備篇

Unit 1-1 **機票與劃位** …………………………… 014

Unit 1-2 **飛行資訊** ……………………………… 020

Unit 1-3 **確定航班** ……………………………… 024

Unit 1-4 **變更預約** ……………………………… 028

　　訂餐筆記 ……………………………………… 031

Part 2 機場篇

Unit 2-1 **詢問機場內的場所** …………………… 034

Unit 2-2 **說明座位喜好及行李託運** …………… 038

Unit 2-3 **詢問其他飛行資訊** …………………… 042

Unit 2-4 **免稅商店** ……………………………… 046

Unit 2-5 **登機** …………………………………… 050

　　優惠筆記 ……………………………………… 053

Part 3 機上篇

Unit 3-1 **座位** …………………………………… 056

Unit 3-2 **行李** …………………………………… 060

Unit 3-3 **飲料** ························ 064
Unit 3-4 **機內用餐** ···················· 068
Unit 3-5 **詢問其他服務** ················ 072
Unit 3-6 **機內購物** ···················· 076
Unit 3-7 **不舒服時** ···················· 080
Unit 3-8 **與鄰座應對** ·················· 084
Unit 3-9 **飛機抵達前** ·················· 088
　　健康筆記 ························ 091

Part 4　入境篇

Unit 4-1 **入境審查：說明目的** ········· 094
Unit 4-2 **入境審查：說明住宿** ········· 100
Unit 4-3 **入境審查：機票和攜帶的錢財**··· 104
Unit 4-4 **行李提領** ···················· 108
Unit 4-5 **行李遺失** ···················· 112
Unit 4-6 **海關** ························ 116
　　行李筆記 ························ 121

Part 5　旅客服務篇

Unit 5-1 **詢問銀行服務** ················ 124
Unit 5-2 **詢問匯率與貨幣** ·············· 128
Unit 5-3 **旅客服務中心** ················ 132
　　網站筆記 ························ 138

目錄

Part 6　住宿篇

Unit 6-1　預約訂房 …………………… 140
Unit 6-2　登記住宿：有預約 …………… 144
Unit 6-3　登記住宿：未預約 …………… 148
Unit 6-4　詢問住宿費用 ………………… 152
Unit 6-5　詢問房間設備 ………………… 156
Unit 6-6　預定住宿天數 ………………… 160
Unit 6-7　詢問飯店設施 ………………… 164
Unit 6-8　詢問飯店設施的營業時間 …… 168
Unit 6-9　寄放行李 ……………………… 172
　　　「方便」筆記 …………………… 175

Part 7　飯店篇

Unit 7-1　客房服務：餐飲 ……………… 178
Unit 7-2　客房服務：送洗 ……………… 182
Unit 7-3　客房服務：其他 ……………… 186
Unit 7-4　飯店內的商店 ………………… 190
Unit 7-5　住宿抱怨 ……………………… 194
Unit 7-6　留言 …………………………… 198
Unit 7-7　飯店附屬設施 ………………… 202
Unit 7-8　使用飯店設施 ………………… 206
Unit 7-9　改變行程 ……………………… 210
Unit 7-10　退房 ………………………… 214
　　　青年之家筆記 …………………… 217

Part 8 異地用餐篇 🍽️

Unit 8-1 詢問餐廳 …………………………… 220
Unit 8-2 預約餐廳 …………………………… 224
Unit 8-3 進入餐廳 …………………………… 228
Unit 8-4 點菜 ………………………………… 232
Unit 8-5 點酒 ………………………………… 236
Unit 8-6 用餐 ………………………………… 240
Unit 8-7 談論菜色 …………………………… 244
Unit 8-8 餐後 ………………………………… 248
Unit 8-9 速食店 ……………………………… 252
　　　飲食筆記 …………………………… 256

Part 9 購物篇 🛒

Unit 9-1 營業場所和營業時間 ……………… 258
Unit 9-2 樓層詢問 …………………………… 262
Unit 9-3 顧客服務中心：店內服務 ………… 266
Unit 9-4 顧客服務中心：店內設施 ………… 270
Unit 9-5 詢問尺寸 …………………………… 274
Unit 9-6 詢問顏色 …………………………… 278
Unit 9-7 詢問商品 …………………………… 282
Unit 9-8 詢問店員意見 ……………………… 286
Unit 9-9 修改 ………………………………… 290
Unit 9-10 詢問價格 …………………………… 294

目 錄

Unit 9-11 **決定購買** ················ 298
Unit 9-12 **決定不買** ················ 302
Unit 9-12 **詢問維修** ················ 306
Unit 9-17 **換退貨** ················ 310

　「血拼」筆記 ················ 313

Part 10 觀光篇 📷

Unit 10-1 **詢問遊覽行程** ················ 316
Unit 10-2 **詢問遊覽內容** ················ 320
Unit 10-3 **詢問遊覽費用** ················ 324
Unit 10-4 **旅途用餐** ················ 328
Unit 10-5 **變更行程** ················ 332

　生態旅遊筆記 ················ 335

Part 11 交通篇 🚇

Unit 11-1 **問路** ················ 338
Unit 11-2 **搭計程車** ················ 354
Unit 11-3 **搭公車** ················ 358
Unit 11-4 **搭地鐵** ················ 362
Unit 11-5 **搭火車** ················ 366
Unit 11-6 **租車** ················ 370
Unit 11-7 **加油** ················ 374

Unit 11-8 **汽車故障** ……………………… 388

🔖 **美國公路筆記** ……………………… 391

Part 12 電信聯絡篇 📱

Unit 12-1 **國際電話** ……………………… 394
Unit 12-2 **國內電話** ……………………… 398
Unit 12-3 **郵局** ……………………… 404

🔖 **手機漫遊筆記** ……………………… 415

Part 13 意外狀況篇 🚑

Unit 13-1 **遺失** ……………………… 418
Unit 13-2 **遭竊** ……………………… 422
Unit 13-3 **交通事故** ……………………… 426
Unit 13-4 **生病受傷** ……………………… 430

🔖 **預防時差筆記** ……………………… 435

附錄

必殺單字

✔ 十二星座 ……………………… 438
✔ 數字 ……………………… 439
✔ 顏色 ……………………… 440

✔ 菜單 …………………………… 441
✔ 飲料 …………………………… 442
✔ 甜點 …………………………… 443
✔ 紀念品 ………………………… 444
✔ 住宿 …………………………… 445
✔ 飯店服務 ……………………… 446
✔ 搭機 …………………………… 447
✔ 機上小物 ……………………… 448
✔ 交通好幫手 …………………… 449
✔ 汽車種類 ……………………… 450
✔ 郵局單字 ……………………… 451

旅遊補充包

✔ 國際電話怎麼撥？ ………… 452
✔ 國人旅外救急小幫手 ……… 456
✔ 各國駐臺機構 ………………… 458
✔ 國際機場網頁連結 ………… 469
✔ 各國國名 ……………………… 475
✔ 各國貨幣代碼 ………………… 479
✔ 各國紀念日 …………………… 480

Part. 1

準備篇

Unit 1-1 機票與劃位

Unit 1-2 飛行資訊

Unit 1-3 確定航班

Unit 1-4 變更預約

* 訂餐筆記

救急情境演練 Situation

A: I want to check in.
我要辦理登機。

B: Yes, I'm at your service.
好的，我馬上為您服務。

A: I've booked the tickets.
我已訂了機票。

B: Please tell me your name.
請告訴我您的大名。

A: Rebbeca Owen. I'm a VIP of your airline.
瑞貝卡‧歐文，我是你們航空公司的貴賓。

B: Your VIP card, please.
請出示您的貴賓卡。

A: Here you are. May I upgrade to the first-class cabin?
這是貴賓卡，我可以升等到頭等艙嗎？

B: No problem, I'll upgrade you to it.
沒問題，我將為您升等。

A: Could you get me a window seat?
你能幫我劃靠窗的位子嗎？

B: Of course, wait a second, please.
當然，請稍候。

B: This is your VIP card. Have a nice trip!
這是您的貴賓卡，祝您旅途愉快！

014

A : Thank you very much.
　非常謝謝你。

KEY SENTENCES
關鍵句 （完→完整句・順→順口句）

1-01 ▶ 我想訂一月三十日飛往洛杉磯的機票。
完 : I'd like to book a flight ticket to Los Angeles on January 30.
順 : To L.A. on January 30, please.

1-02 ▶ 什麼時候有飛往倫敦的班機？
完 : When do you have a flight to London?
順 : To London, when?

1-03 ▶ 最早飛往雪梨的班機是什麼時候？
完 : What time would be the earliest flight to Sidney?
順 : The earliest flight to Sidney, please?

1-04 ▶ 週二有飛往東京的班機嗎？
完 : Do you have a Tokyo flight on Tuesday?
順 : Any flight to Tokyo on Tuesday?

1-05 ▶ 週一飛往雪梨的班機還有機位嗎？
完 : Is there any space on Monday's flight to Sidney?
順 : Any space to Sidney on Monday?

1-06 ▶ 有飛經芝加哥的班機嗎？

完：Is there a flight that stops at Chicago?
順：Any flight that stops at Chicago?

1-07 ▶ 抱歉，這班班機已額滿了。
完：Sorry, the flight is full.
順：Full, sorry.

1-08 ▶ 下一班飛機是什麼時候？
完：When is the next flight?
順：Next flight, please?

單字片語維他命 Useful Vocabulary

- **flight** [flaɪt] **n** 班機
- **airline** [`ɛr. laɪn] **n** 航空公司
- **airport** [`ɛr. port] **n** 機場；航空站
- **upgrade** [`ʌp`gred] **v** 升等
- **VIP** 貴賓(= Very Important Person)
- **the first-class cabin** 頭等艙
- **business class cabin** 商務艙
- **economy class cabin** 經濟艙
- **check in** 登機報到
- **at sb.'s service** 聽候…差遣；為…服務

MP3 002

救急情境演練 Situation

A : I'd like to make a flight reservation. Can you help me?
我要預約班機,你可以幫我嗎?

B : Yes, I can.
是的,可以的。

A : Please give me two business class tickets.
請給我兩張商務艙的機票。

B : Sorry, we have only economy class tickets.
不好意思,只剩經濟艙的機票了。

A : Well, two economy class tickets, please.
那麼,請給我兩張經濟艙的機票。

B : Yes, I'm finding seating for you.
好的,我順便為您劃位。

A : Please give me seats at the front.
請給我前面一點的位子。

B : Yes, I'll query it for you.
好的,我為您查詢。

A : How long will the flight be delayed?
班機會延誤多久呢?

B : Because of the fog, the flight will be delayed about 2 hours.
因為起霧,班機大概會延誤兩個小時。

B : Excuse me, sir. There're no seats at the front. How about seats in the middle?
先生,不好意思,前面沒有位子了,中間的位子可以嗎?

A：Well, that's OK.
好吧,中間的可以。

KEY SENTENCES

關鍵句

(完→完整句・順→順口句)

1-09 ▶ 機票多少錢?

完：How much is the flight ticket?

順：How much is it?

1-10 ▶ 我要兩張六點的機票。

完：I'd like two tickets on the six o'clock flight.

順：Two for six o'clock.

1-11 ▶ 可以刷卡付費嗎?

完：May I pay by credit card?

順：Credit card, OK?

1-12 ▶ 我需要另外付機場稅嗎?

完：Do I have to pay airport tax separately?

順：Airport tax separately?

1-13 ▶ 不用,機場稅已內含。

完：No, the airport tax is included.

順：No.

1-14 ▶ 我要訂素食餐。

完：I'd like to order vegetarian food during the flight.

順：Vegetarian food, please.

1-15 ▶ 我要訂特別餐。

完：I'd like to order a special meal during the flight.

順：Special meal, please.

1-16 ▶ 我要訂一份兒童餐。

完：I'd like to order one special meal for a child.

順：One special meal for a child, please.

1-17 ▶ 我需要年長者的關懷服務。

完：I need special care for aged men / women.

順：Special care for the elder, please.

單字片語維他命 Useful Vocabulary

- **reservation** [ˌrɛzəˋveʃən] **n** 預約
- **query** [ˋkwɪrɪ] **v** 查詢；詢問
- **delay** [dɪˋle] **v** 誤點；耽擱
- **fog** [fɑg] **n** 霧
- **snow** [sno] **n** 雪
- **tsunami** [tsuˋnɑmɪ] **n** 海嘯
- **earthquake** [ˋɝθˌkwek] **n** 地震
- **volcanic ash** 火山灰
- **because of** 由於；因為
- **make a flight reservation** 預約機位

🔊 MP3 003

救急情境演練 Situation

Ⓐ：Could you tell me the flying hours?
請問飛行時數是？

Ⓑ：It takes 3 hours and 40 minutes.
三個小時又四十分鐘。

Ⓐ：Do I need to transfer flights?
我還需要轉機嗎？

Ⓑ：Yes, please wait in the hall for a moment.
是的，請在大廳稍待片刻。

Ⓐ：Where do we transfer the flights?
我們要在何處轉機？

Ⓑ：You transfer in Tokyo.
您們將到東京轉機。

Ⓐ：Where should we take the flight transferring to New York?
到紐約去哪裡轉機？

Ⓑ：You need to make a stop at Hong Kong.
會在香港停留。

Ⓐ：Where's the flight transferring counter?
轉機櫃檯在哪？

Ⓑ：The first one at the front.
最前面第一個就是。

Ⓐ：When will BR-802 depart?
長榮航空802號班機何時出發？

B : In about one hour.
　　約一小時後。

KEY SENTENCES
關鍵句 （完 →完整句．順 →順口句）

1-18 ▶ 長榮航空705號班機什麼時候出發？
完 : What time will BR-705 depart?
順 : BR-705, when does it leave?

1-19 ▶ 國泰航空435號班機何時起飛？
完 : When is the departure time for CX-435?
順 : CX-435, when does it depart?

1-20 ▶ 中華航空736號班機何時抵達？
完 : When is the arrival time for CI-736?
順 : When does CI-736 arrive?

1-21 ▶ 達美航空827號班機何時抵達？
完 : What is the arrival time for DL-827?
順 : When does the time DL-827 arrive?

1-22 ▶ 何時會起飛？
完 : When will it depart?
順 : When does it depart?

1-23 ▶ 何時會抵達？
完 : When will it arrive?
順 : When does it arrive?

1-24 ▶ 飛行全程要多久？

完：How long does it take for the whole journey?

順：Time for the whole journey, please?

1-25 ▶ 到新加坡要飛多久？

完：How long does the flight to Singapore take?

順：Total flying time to Singapore, please?

1-26 ▶ 這班飛機直飛巴黎嗎？

完：Is it a direct flight to Paris?

順：Direct to Paris?

1-27 ▶ 需要轉機嗎？

完：Do I need to transfer?

順：Any transfer?

1-28 ▶ 我們會停在檀香山嗎？

完：Do we stop over in Honolulu?

順：Stop over in Honolulu?

1-29 ▶ 我在香港轉機需要多久時間？

完：How long do I have to stay in Hong Kong for the connecting flight?

順：Time in Hong Kong, please?

單字片語維他命 Useful Vocabulary

- **journey** [`dʒɜnɪ] **n** 旅程
- **depart** [dɪ`part] **v** 出發
- **departure** [dɪ`partʃɚ] **n** 啟程
- **arrive** [ə`raɪv] **v** 抵達
- **transfer** [træns`fɜ] **v** 轉機
- **airport tax** 機場稅
- **flight transferring counter** 轉機櫃檯
- **flying hour** 飛行時數
- **wait for a moment** 稍候片刻
- **make a stop** 停留

Travel NEWS

　　想從事自助旅遊者，可自行設計旅遊行程；想從事半自助旅遊者，可委託旅行社或社團代為安排當地的交通及住宿。

🔊 MP3 004

救急情境演練 Situation

A : I'd like to reconfirm my flight.
我想再確認我的機位。

B : Please give me your flight number.
請給我您的班機號碼。

A : Sorry, may I give you my booking code?
抱歉,我可以給你訂位代碼嗎?

B : Yes, you can.
好,可以的。

A : My booking code is CI-88363.
我的訂位代碼是CI-88363。

B : Booking name is Mary Chen.
訂位大名是陳瑪麗。

A : Yes, it is.
是的。

B : Ms. Chen, your flight is BR-324 for Japan, at 8:30 p.m., Feb. 17.
陳小姐,您訂的是二月十七號晚上八點半,飛往日本的長榮航空324號班機。

A : Yes, I also ordered vegetarian food during the flight.
是的,我還訂了素食餐。

B : Yes. Do you also need special care for the elder, Ms. Chen?
有的。陳小姐,您還需要年長者關懷服務是嗎?

🅰 : Yes, for my mother.
要，是幫家母申請的。

🅱 : OK, Ms. Chen, your ticket is confirmed.
好的，陳小姐，您的機位已確認無誤。

KEY SENTENCES
關鍵句 （完→完整句・順→順口句）

1-30 ▶ 我要再確認我的機位。

完 : I'd like to reconfirm my flight.

順 : Reconfirm flight, please.

1-31 ▶ 我想再確認下週一去紐約的機位。

完 : I want to reconfirm my flight to New York for next Monday.

順 : Reconfirm next Monday flight to New York, please.

1-32 ▶ 我想再確認下週六去洛杉磯的機位。

完 : I want to reconfirm my flight to Los Angeles for next Saturday.

順 : Reconfirm next Saturday flight to Los Angeles, please.

1-33 ▶ 我想再確認下週三去舊金山的機位。

完 : I want to reconfirm my flight to San Francisco for next Wednesday.

順 : Reconfirm next Wednesday flight to San Francisco, please.

1-34 ▶ 我想再確認下週五去那霸的機位。

完 : I want to reconfirm my flight to Naha for next Friday.

順 : Reconfirm next Friday flight to Naha, please.

1-35 ▶ 我想再確認星期日飛往馬尼拉的預約班機。

完 : I'd like to reconfirm a reservation to Manila on Sunday.

順 : Reconfirm Sunday flight to Manila, please.

1-36 ▶ 我想再確認星期四飛往臺北的預約班機。

完 : I'd like to reconfirm a reservation to Taipei on Thursday.

順 : Reconfirm Thursday flight to Taipei, please.

1-37 ▶ 請問您的姓名和班機號碼？

完 : What's your name and flight number?

順 : Your name and flight number, please?

1-38 ▶ 您的機位確認已完成無誤。

完 : Your ticket is confirmed.

順 : It's OK.

1-39 ▶ 您必須在班機起飛前至少二小時報到登機。

完 : You must check in at least two hours

before.
順 : Check in two hours before.

單字片語雜他命 Useful Vocabulary

- **confirm** [kən`fɜm] **V** 確認
- **reconfirm** [ˏrikən`fɜm] **V** 再確認
- **flight number** 班機號碼
- **booking code** 訂位代碼
- **booking name** 訂位名稱
- **red-eye flight** 夜航班機
- **the elder** 年長者;長輩
- **special meal** 特別餐
- **special care** 特殊服務
- **special demand** 特殊要求

To see is to believe.

★　★　★　★

百聞不如一見。

🔊 **MP3 005**

救急情境演練 Situation

🅐 : I'd like to change my flight.
我想更改班機。

🅑 : Please give me your flight number.
請給我您的班機號碼。

🅐 : Sorry, I can't remember my flight number.
抱歉，我想不起班機號碼是幾號。

🅑 : Well, give me your booking code, please.
那麼，請給我您的訂位代碼。

🅐 : FD-24583.
是FD-24583。

🅑 : Booking name is Harriet Wang.
訂位大名是王涵莉。

🅐 : Yes, I am Harriet Wang.
是的，我是王涵莉。

🅑 : Ms. Wang, your ticket is to Los Angeles on May 24.
王小姐，您的機票是五月二十四日飛往洛杉磯。

🅐 : Yes, I want to postpone the date to Aug. 20.
是的，我想把日期延到八月二十日。

🅑 : Let me check, to Los Angeles on Aug. 20....
讓我查一下，八月二十日飛往洛杉磯…。

🅐 : May I upgrade to business class?
我可以升等至商務艙嗎？

B : Yes, please wait a moment. OK, it's done.
可以，請稍候片刻。好，更改完成了。

KEY SENTENCES
關鍵句 （完→完整句・順→順口句）

1-40 ▶ 麻煩你，我想變更預約。

完 : I'd like to change my reservation, please.
順 : Change reservation, please.

1-41 ▶ 我想把出發日延到星期日。

完 : I'd like to postpone my departure until Sunday.
順 : Postpone to Sunday, please.

1-42 ▶ 我想把出發日延到下週五。

完 : I'd like to postpone my departure until next Friday.
順 : Postpone to next Friday, please.

1-43 ▶ 我想搭晚一點的班機。

完 : I want to take a later flight.
順 : Later flight, please.

1-44 ▶ 我可以把我的預約提前為稍早的班機嗎？

完 : Can I change my reservation to an earlier flight?
順 : Earlier flight, OK?

1-45 ▶ 我想把經濟艙的票改成商務艙的票。

完 : I'd like to change my ticket from economy class to business class.

順 : Change to business class ticket, please.

1-46 ▶ 我要取消機位。

完 : I would like to cancel my flight.

順 : Cancel my flight, please.

單字片語雜他命 Useful Vocabulary

❧ **change** [tʃendʒ] **v** 變更

❧ **date** [det] **n** 日期；日子

❧ **check** [tʃɛk] **v** 核對；檢查

❧ **postpone** [post`pon] **v** 使延期；延遲

❧ **later** [`letə] **a** 較晚的

❧ **earlier** [`ɜlɪr] **a** 較早的

❧ **cancel** [`kænsḷ] **v** 取消

❧ **separately** [`sɛpərɪtlɪ] **ad** 個別地

❧ **extra** [`ɛkstrə] **a** 額外的；外加的

❧ **at least** 至少

背包客旅遊筆記 BON VOYAGE！

　　搭乘飛機前，許多人會因為宗教或健康因素，預訂特別餐，旅客可在買票時說明特別餐點的需求，像是伊斯蘭教徒的清真餐、糖尿病患者的低糖餐、素食者的齋菜、嬰幼兒的離乳餐等餐點。通常航空公司會希望旅客在四十八至七十二小時(二到三天)前，就預訂好特別餐，以便空廚有充裕的時間做準備。

　　基本上，歐美的航空公司會供應一般素食(vegetarian)、或亞洲素食 (Asian vegetarian)。歐美跟亞洲對於素食的定義不同：歐美除了不吃地上的動物外，其他像是海鮮、雞蛋、牛奶、乳酪都可食用；而亞洲的素食，則完全不吃任何肉類、甚至還有辛香料的禁忌。如果有茹素的乘客，一定要在訂餐時特別說明自己不吃哪些食物。

　　訂了特別餐，在飛行途中是無法更改的。如果有人要轉好幾趟班機，就得考慮是否要一路都吃同樣的餐點。我就碰過有人只吃早齋，其他時間想換別的餐點，但那天的班機客滿，餐點份數剛剛好、沒有多餘的份量，其他乘客也不願意換，結果就只好一路吃素，直到目的地。建議：如果只有一餐需要吃特別餐，最好別訂特別餐，先準備好自己那餐要吃的特別食物，那麼其他時間就能享用一般的餐點了。

　　一般來說，特別餐會按照訂位時的座號來派送。有時候，一班飛機上會有五、六十份、或更多份數的特別餐，如果沒有照原來的位子坐，空服員很難將特別餐送到指定乘客的手上；若有更換座位，最好提早通知空服員。

　　到底飛機上的餐點都是在哪裡製作的呢？飛機上的餐點都是由地面的廚房工廠製作的，也就是「空中廚房」，簡稱「空廚」。通常航空公司會投資旗下的子公司建立空中廚房，以確保供餐品質。

　　製作飛機餐點的廚師們完成餐點後，會先放入餐車，再以大貨車運送至飛機，工作人員再將貨車內的餐點運至飛機內，接下來，就是我們所熟知在機上與空服員點餐的流程了。

　　因為飛機上的餐點都是在起飛前做好，並保存於冷藏庫內的。所以在用餐前，要先由空服員將餐點送入蒸烤箱加熱，為避免烤乾，蒸烤箱是以蒸氣加熱的。約加熱十五至十八分鐘，空服員會將主菜與搭配好的甜點，放進餐車裡的托盤上，就能將餐車推出，開始服務旅客。目前，新型飛機擁有現代化的廚房配備，像是微波爐、烤麵包機與電鍋，讓空服員在機上為乘客準備餐點。

Part. 2

機 場 篇

Unit 2-1 詢問機場內的場所

Unit 2-2 說明座位喜好及行李託運

Unit 2-3 詢問其他飛行資訊

Unit 2-4 免稅商店

Unit 2-5 登機

＊ 優惠筆記

🔊 MP3 006

救急情境演練 Situation

A : Could you tell me where the counter of UAL is?
請問聯合航空的櫃檯在哪裡？

B : The third one at the front.
最前面第三個就是。

A : Is this the check-in counter for HX-154 flight?
這是香港航空154號班機的登機櫃檯嗎？

B : Yes, it is.
是的，沒錯。

A : Where's the service counter?
請問服務櫃檯在哪裡？

B : It's in front of the entrance.
在入口處的前面。

A : Where's the taxi stand?
計程車招呼站在哪裡？

B : Exit No. 5.
在5號門出口。

A : Where's the carousel?
行李轉盤在哪裡？

B : I'll show you, follow me, please.
我帶你去，請跟我來。

A : Could you tell me where the restroom is?
你可以告訴我洗手間在哪裡？

B：It's just at the corner.
就在轉角處。

KEY SENTENCES
關鍵句 （完→完整句‧順→順口句）

2-01 ▶ 長榮航空的登機櫃檯在哪裡？

完：Where's the check-in counter for EVA Airways?

順：EVA's counter, please?

2-02 ▶ 阿聯航空的登機櫃台在哪裡？

完：Where's the check-in counter for Emirates?

順：Emirates' counter, please?

2-03 ▶ 要在哪裡做安檢？

完：Which way is the security check?

順：Security checks, please?

2-04 ▶ 8號登機門在哪裡？

完：Where is Gate 8?

順：Gate 8, please?

2-05 ▶ 10號登機門在哪裡？

完：Where is Gate 10?

順：Gate 10, please?

2-06 ▶ 請問免稅商店在哪裡？

完：Excuse me. Where're the duty-free shops?

順：Duty-free shops, please?

2-07 ▶ 請問航班告示牌在哪裡？

完：Excuse me. Where's the flight-information board?

順：Flight-information board, please?

2-08 ▶ 請問洗手間在哪裡？

完：Excuse me. Where's the bathroom?

順：Bathroom, please?

2-09 ▶ 請問吸菸室在哪裡？

完：Excuse me. Where's the smoking room?

順：Smoking room, please?

2-10 ▶ 請問這附近有育嬰室嗎？

完：Excuse me. Is there any nursing room around here?

順：Nursing room, please?

2-11 ▶ 請問這附近有沒有餐廳？

完：Excuse me. Is there any restaurant around here?

順：Restaurant, please?

2-12 ▶ 請問華航的貴賓室在哪裡？

完：Excuse me. Where's the VIP lounge for China Airlines?

順：VIP lounge for China Airlines, please?

2-13 ▶ 請問退稅櫃檯在哪裡？

完：Excuse me. Where's the tax-refund counter?

順 : Tax-refund counters, please?

2-14 ▶ 請問醫務室在哪裡？
完 : Excuse me. Where's the infirmary?
順 : Infirmary, please?

2-15 ▶ 請問兌幣機在哪裡？
完 : Excuse me. Where's the exchanging machine?
順 : Exchanging machine, please?

單字片語維他命 Useful Vocabulary

🔻 **entrance** [`ɛntrəns] ⓝ 入口

🔻 **carousel** [,kærυ`zɛl] ⓝ 行李轉盤

🔻 **infirmary** [ɪn`fɜmərɪ] ⓝ 醫務室

🔻 **restroom** [`rɛst,rum] ⓝ 廁所；洗手間

🔻 **check-in counter** 登機櫃檯

🔻 **service counter** 服務櫃檯

🔻 **taxi stand** 計程車招呼站

🔻 **leasing counter** 租車櫃檯

🔻 **post office** 郵局

🔻 **exchanging machine** 兌幣機

🔊》 MP3 007

救急情境演練 Situation

A : I want the seat which is close to the lavatory.
我要距離廁所近的位子。

B : Yes, please wait a second.
好的,請稍候。

A : Please give me a seat by the window.
請給我靠窗的位子。

B : I'm sorry. We only have the middle seat.
很抱歉,我們只剩中間的位子。

A : Please give me a seat by the right aisle.
請給我靠走道右邊的位子。

B : There are only seats by the left aisle.
只剩靠走道左邊的位子了。

A : We'll sit together.
我們要坐在一起。

B : It's the holiday season now, I'm afraid that there is no option.
現在是假日,恐怕沒辦法。

A : Please check my luggage all the way through to Hong Kong.
我的行李麻煩直掛香港。

B : How much luggage do you want to check in?
您要託運幾件行李?

A : 5, please.

五件，麻煩你。

B : Your luggage is over-weight. You have to pay extra charges.
您的行李超重了，需要付額外的費用。

KEY SENTENCES
關鍵句　(完 →完整句・順 →順口句)

2-16 ▶ 請給我一個靠窗的位子。
完 : Please give me a window seat.
順 : Window seat, please.

2-17 ▶ 請給我一個靠走道的位子。
完 : Please give me an aisle seat.
順 : Aisle seat, please.

2-18 ▶ 我想要一個放腳空間比較大的位置。
完 : I'd like a seat with some legroom.
順 : Seat with legroom, please.

2-19 ▶ 您要託運幾件行李？
完 : How much luggage do you want to check in?
順 : How much luggage?

2-20 ▶ 我的行李麻煩直掛馬德里。
完 : Please check my luggage all the way through to Madrid.
順 : All the way through to Madrid, please.

2-21 ▶ 我的行李麻煩直掛吉隆坡。

完：Please check my luggage all the way through to Kuala Lumpur.

順：All the way through to Kuala Lumpur, please.

2-22 ▶ 我的行李麻煩直掛首爾。

完：Please check my luggage all the way through to Seoul.

順：All the way through to Seoul, please.

2-23 ▶ 我的行李麻煩直掛東京。

完：Please check my luggage all the way through to Tokyo.

順：All the way through to Tokyo, please.

2-24 ▶ 你的行李超重了。

完：Your luggage is over-weight.

順：It's over-weight.

2-25 ▶ 抱歉，因為機位超賣，所以我們需要有人自願放棄。

完：Sorry, due to over-booking, so we need volunteers.

順：It's over-booked, so, any volunteers?

2-26 ▶ 我們將免費提供住宿地點，並每天提供一百美元的零用金。

完：We'll offer free accommodation and US$ 100 per day.

順：Free accommodation and US$ 100.

2-27 ▶ 我們將安排明天的早班飛機飛往目的地。

完：We'll arrange an early flight to the destination tomorrow morning.

順：Early flight for tomorrow morning.

2-28 ▶ 我們將安排稍晚的班機飛往目的地。

完：We'll arrange a later flight to the destination.

順：There's a later flight to the destination.

2-29 ▶ 有興趣者，請與我們的櫃檯同仁聯絡。

完：If you are interested, please contact with our staff at the counter.

順：Please contact us.

單字片語維他命 Useful Vocabulary

➤ **path** [pæθ] **n** 通道

➤ **aisle** [aɪl] **n** 座席間的走道

➤ **extra** [`ɛkstrə] **a** 額外的

➤ **lavatory** [`lævə,torɪ] **n** 廁所

➤ **legroom** [`lɛg,rum] **n** 放腳空間

➤ **volunteer** [,vɑlən`tɪr] **n** 自願者

➤ **accommodation** [ə,kɑmə`deʃən] **n** 住處

➤ **over-booking** [`ovə,bukɪŋ] **n** 機位超賣

➤ **over-weight** [`ovə,wet] **a** 超重的

➤ **due to** 由於；因為

041

🔊 MP3 008

救急情境演練 Situation

A: Is flight KN-304 delayed?
中國聯合航空的304號班機誤點了嗎？

B: Sorry, it is delayed.
很抱歉，這班飛機誤點了。

A: Why is the flight delayed?
班機為何誤點？

B: There's a typhoon over the Pacific Ocean.
太平洋上有颱風盤旋。

A: What's the new take-off time?
新的起飛時刻是？

B: 10:10 p.m..
晚上十點十分。

A: When's the boarding time?
登機時間是？

B: 7:10 p.m..
晚上七點十分。

A: Where's the boarding gate?
登機門在哪裡？

B: At C54. Please go upstairs and turn right.
C54號門，請上樓右轉。

A: I can't wait so long. May I change the flight?
我等不了那麼久，我可以換班機嗎？

B: Hmm, follow me, please.
嗯，請跟我來。

KEY SENTENCES
關鍵句 🔑 （完→完整句‧順→順口句）

2-30 ▶ 請在16號登機門登機。
完：Please board at Gate 16.
順：Gate 16, please.

2-31 ▶ 五號登機門請上二樓後左轉。
完：For Gate 5, please go upstairs and turn left.
順：Gate 5, go upstairs and turn left.

2-32 ▶ 七號登機門請上三樓後右轉。
完：For Gate 7, please go to the 3rd floor and turn right.
順：Gate 7, go to 3rd floor and turn right, please.

2-33 ▶ 請向前走右轉至十號登機門。
完：For Gate 10, please go straight and turn right.
順：Gate 10, go straight and turn right, please.

2-34 ▶ 請向前走左轉至26號登機門。
完：For Gate 26, please go straight and turn left.
順：Gate 26, go straight and turn left, please.

2-35 ▶ 登機時間是幾點？
完：What is the boarding time?
順：When is the boarding?

2-36 ▶ 飛機準時嗎？

完：Is the plane on time?

順：Plane on time?

2-37 ▶ 誤點的原因是什麼？

完：What's the reason for the delay?

順：Why did it delay?

2-38 ▶ 飛機會誤點多久？

完：How long will the flight be delayed?

順：Delayed for how long?

2-39 ▶ 新的起飛時間是什麼時候？

完：When is the new take-off time?

順：New take-off time, please?

2-40 ▶ 我要轉國泰航空的**601**號班機。

完：I'm connecting with CX-601.

順：Connecting CX-601.

2-41 ▶ 我要轉日航的**425**號班機。

完：I'm connecting with JL-425.

順：Connecting JL-425.

2-42 ▶ 我要轉港龍航空的**908**號班機。

完：I'm connecting with KA-908.

順：Connecting KA-908.

單字片語維他命 Useful Vocabulary

✈ **strait** [stret] n 海峽

✈ **typhoon** [taɪˋfun] n 颱風

✈ **hurricane** [ˋhɝɪˌken] n 颶風

✈ **boarding time** 登機時間

✈ **boarding gate** 登機門

✈ **metal detector** 金屬探測器

✈ **the Pacific Ocean** 太平洋

✈ **the Atlantic Ocean** 大西洋

✈ **the Indian Ocean** 印度洋

✈ **the Mediterranean Sea** 地中海

Bon Voyage!

🔊 MP3 009

救急情境演練 Situation

A: How many cartons of cigarette can a person bring?
請問一個人可以帶幾條菸？

B: One.
一條。

A: How many bottles of wine can a person bring?
請問一個人可帶多少瓶酒？

B: One.
一瓶。

A: If I want to bring more?
若想多帶一些呢？

B: Need to declare.
需要申報。

A: Do you have Chanel No. 5?
你有香奈兒五號香水嗎？

B: I'm sorry. It's running out of stock now. Would you like to see any substitutes?
很抱歉，目前這款香水缺貨中，您要看其他款嗎？

A: Forget it. Please recommend me some nice brands of white wine.
算了，請幫我推薦品牌不錯的白酒。

B: I recommend this one, many of our

customers like it.
我推薦這款白酒，我們有很多顧客都很喜歡。

A : Well, please get me a carton of cigarette and a bottle of white wine.
好，請給我一條菸跟一瓶白酒。

B : OK, boarding card and passport, please.
好的，請給我您的登機證跟護照。

KEY SENTENCES
關鍵句 （完→完整句‧順→順口句）

2-43 ▶ 這瓶酒多少錢？
完 : How much is this bottle of wine?
順 : How much is it?

2-44 ▶ 換成臺幣是多少錢？
完 : How much is that in NTD?
順 : In NTD, how much?

2-45 ▶ 我要買一條七星淡菸。
完 : I'd like to buy a carton of Mild Seven.
順 : Mild Seven, please.

2-46 ▶ 我要這瓶香水。
完 : I'd like to take this bottle of perfume.
順 : This one, please.

2-47 ▶ 請問你有香奈兒五號香水嗎？
完 : Do you have Chanel No. 5?
順 : Chanel No. 5, please?

2-48 ▶ 請問這裡有賣古馳的皮包嗎?

完 : Do you have a Gucci bag?

順 : A Gucci bag, please?

2-49 ▶ 我需要男用皮夾。

完 : I need a wallet.

順 : A wallet, please.

2-50 ▶ 我需要女用錢包。

完 : I need a purse.

順 : A purse, please.

2-51 ▶ 我要買些巧克力,可以幫我介紹嗎?

完 : I need some chocolate. Could you recommend me some brands?

順 : Some brands for chocolate, please?

2-52 ▶ 這裡著名的烈酒品牌有哪些?

完 : What are the famous brands for liquor in this area?

順 : Famous brands for liquor, please?

2-53 ▶ 請幫我介紹當地品牌的紅酒。

完 : Please recommend me local brands for red wine.

順 : Local brands for red wine, please.

2-54 ▶ 請幫我介紹牌子不錯的白酒。

完 : Please recommend me some nice brands of white wine.

順 : Nice brands of white wine, please.

2-55 ▶ 請幫我介紹當地的名產。

完：Please recommend me some local specialty.

順：Some local specialty, please.

2-56 ▶ 你知道可以帶多少瓶酒進臺灣嗎？

完：Do you know how many bottles I can bring into Taiwan?

順：How many bottles can I bring into Taiwan?

單字片語維他命 Useful Vocabulary

🔖 **carton** [`kɑrtṇ] **n** 一紙箱的量

🔖 **cigarette** [ˌsɪgə`rɛt] **n** 紙菸

🔖 **cigar** [sɪ`gɑr] **n** 雪茄菸

🔖 **declare** [dɪ`klɛr] **v** 申報(納稅品等)

🔖 **perfume** [`pɝfjum] **n** 香水

🔖 **Eau de cologne** [ˌodəkə`lon] **n** 古龍水

🔖 **substitute** [`sʌbstəˌtjut] **n** 代替品

🔖 **makeup** [`mekˌʌp] **n** 化妝品

🔖 **liquor** [`lɪkə] **n** 烈酒

🔖 **run out of stock** 缺貨

🔊 MP3 010

救急情境演練 Situation

Ⓐ : We'll invite passengers with orange card to board now.
現在我們請持有橘色登機證的旅客先登機。

Ⓐ : Economy class will have to wait.
經濟艙必須再等一下。

Ⓐ : Now, passengers with orange card after the row 40 to board first, please.
現在，請40排以後持有橘色登機證的旅客先排隊登機。

Ⓐ : You can board now.
您們現在可以登機了。

Ⓑ : Could you help me find my seat?
可以幫我找座位嗎？

Ⓐ : Yes, this is row 47 of the window.
可以，這是 47排靠窗的位子。

Ⓑ : Could you tell me how to fasten my seat belt?
你可以教我繫安全帶的方法嗎？

Ⓐ : Yes, I can.
好，可以。

Ⓑ : I can't find my seat.
我找不到我的位子。

Ⓐ : May I see your boarding pass?
可以看一下您的登機證嗎？

B：Sure.
當然可以。

A：Your seat is 40B, this way, please.
您的座位是40B，這邊請。

KEY SENTENCES
關鍵句 （完→完整句・順→順口句）

2-57 ▶ 我們即將登機。
完：We're now ready for boarding.
順：Boarding now.

2-58 ▶ 請持有頭等艙機票的旅客先登機。
完：We'll invite passengers with first class tickets to board first.
順：Passengers with first class tickets first.

2-59 ▶ 請有小孩的旅客先登機。
完：We'll invite passengers with children to board first.
順：Passengers with children first.

2-60 ▶ 請年長的旅客先登機。
完：We'll invite elderly passengers to board first.
順：Elderly passengers first.

2-61 ▶ 請持有商務艙機票的旅客先登機。
完：We'll invite passengers in business class to board first.

順：Passengers in business class board first.

2-62 ▶ 現在請持有經濟艙機票的旅客登機。

完：We'll invite passengers in economy class to board now.

順：Passengers in economy class please board now.

2-63 ▶ 現在請持有橘色登機證的人先登機。

完：We'll now invite passengers with orange card to board first.

順：Passengers with orange card board first now.

單字片語維他命 Useful Vocabulary

🔖 **board** [bord] **v** 登上(交通工具)

🔖 **row** [ro] **n** 橫排

🔖 **column** [`kɑləm] **n** 直排

🔖 **fasten** [`fæsn] **v** 繫緊

🔖 **buckle** [`bʌkl] **v** 扣上

🔖 **seat belt** 安全帶

🔖 **life jacket** 救生衣

🔖 **oxygen mask** 氧氣罩

🔖 **exit sign** 逃生標示

🔖 **safety demonstration** 飛安設備演示

現在自助旅行者的年齡已逐漸下降，記得我第一次自助旅行是在高中畢業的時候，那時經濟狀況較拮据，出發前有位愛旅行的學姊送我一本自助旅行的英文書，我從書中發現「國際學生證」(ISIC，International Student Identity Card)的資訊，眼睛頓時雪亮。當時電腦還未發達，只能靠書信與電話來聯繫，但為了能夠控制預算並玩得盡興，我還是設法申請了一張國際學生證，有了它，我一路流浪，直到無法再使用它為止。國際學生證一向都是自助旅遊者的好幫手，可享有多種優惠，但僅限學生才能申請使用；而國際青年優惠卡(ISE Youth Card)則由「International Student Exchange」授權開立，此機構於一九八七年在美國成立，主要宗旨是要建立一個屬於年輕族群的聯盟，以取得旅行時的各項優惠。該機構共發行三種不同身份的優惠卡，包含學生卡、青年卡及教師卡。

只要是二十六歲以下的青年，都可申請國際青年卡並享有優惠。與青年旅館證(IYHF Card，International Youth Hotel Federation Card，參看Part 7【背包客旅遊筆記】)不同的是，在旅遊時持有國際青年卡，可享百分之五到五十的優惠。如景點入場券、旅遊行程，另外，還有醫療緊急救助及二十四小時緊急服務專線等保障，幫

助青年朋友在海外旅行時處理緊急需求。此外還有五十多國的優惠,例如巴黎的艾菲爾鐵塔門票優惠;二十五歲以下的旅人可享二折優惠、歐洲租車(Auto Europe)則享有九折優惠、瑞士鐵力士山套票可享八折優惠、澳洲國鐵長途旅程可享五折優惠、倫敦塔門票可享三英鎊優惠、在紐西蘭購物最多可享八五折優惠及住宿最多享八折的優惠、去澳洲旅遊則享有約九折的優惠、埃及各大景點參觀券可享約五折等優惠。

要如何擁有以上這些豐富的優惠呢?假如想要辦理ISIC國際學生證的話,可以準備:申請表格(可先從後述的網頁列印、填妥)、一張二吋照片與國內學生證或國外入學許可影本,到財團法人康文文教基金會辦理,該會網址為:http://www.travel934.org.tw/。

假如想要辦理ISE國際青年優惠卡的話,可以準備:一張二吋照片、護照影本(以參看英文姓名)、出生年月日以及新臺幣七百元的卡費,至有青年旅遊服務的旅行社辦理;亦可上:http://www.isecard.com/world/index.php網頁查詢最新的優惠細節。

Part. 3

機上篇

Unit 3-1 座位

Unit 3-2 行李

Unit 3-3 飲料

Unit 3-4 機內用餐

Unit 3-5 詢問其他服務

Unit 3-6 機內購物

Unit 3-7 不舒服時

Unit 3-8 與鄰座應對

Unit 3-9 飛機抵達前

＊ 健康筆記

🔊 MP3 011

救急情境演練 Situation

A : Where do I put my luggage?
我的行李要放哪？

B : I'll help you put the luggage.
我來幫您放置行李。

A : Are there any window seats left? If it's possible, I'd like to change my seat.
有剩下任何靠窗的座位嗎？可以的話，我想換座位。

B : Sorry, this is fully occupied.
不好意思，本班機客滿了。

A : Could you please help me put this briefcase up?
你可以幫我把那個公事包放上去嗎？

B : Please be careful of your head.
請小心您的頭。

A : I'd like to have a blanket and a pillow.
我要一條毛毯和一個枕頭。

B : Here you are.
這是您要的毛毯跟枕頭。

A : May I change my earphone? Mine is dead.
我可以更換耳機嗎？我的壞了。

B : OK. Here you are.
好的，這是耳機。

A : May I use my iPad now?

我現在可以使用iPad了嗎？

B : No, you can not use electronic devices until the seat belt sign has been turned off.
不行，在安全帶燈號熄滅前，您都不能使用電子設備。

KEY SENTENCES
關鍵句 🔑 (完 →完整句 · 順 →順口句)

3-01 ▶ **56D**的座位在哪裡？
完 : Where's seat 56D?
順 : Seat 56D, please?

3-02 ▶ **20E**的座位在哪裡？
完 : Where's seat 20E?
順 : Seat 20E, please?

3-03 ▶ **17B**的座位在哪裡？
完 : Where's seat 17B?
順 : Seat 17B, please?

3-04 ▶ 可否告訴我座位位置？
完 : Would you show me my seat, please?
順 : My seat, please?

3-05 ▶ 有人坐在我的位子上。
完 : Someone is sitting in my seat.
順 : Someone is in my seat.

3-06 ▶ 我先生和我的座位分開了，我們想坐在一

起。

完：My husband and I are separated; we'd like to sit together.

順：My husband and I want to be together.

3-07 ▶ 您介意跟我換位子嗎？

完：Would you mind changing the seat with me?

順：Change the seats, OK?

3-08 ▶ 我可以把座位往後傾斜嗎？

完：May I recline my seat?

順：Recline seat, OK?

3-09 ▶ 請繫上安全帶。

完：Please fasten your seat belts.

順：Fasten your seat belts.

3-10 ▶ 請把椅背豎直。

完：Please straighten up your seat.

順：Straighten up, please.

3-11 ▶ 請關掉您的手機。

完：Please switch off your mobile phone.

順：No mobile phone.

3-12 ▶ 請您關掉電子用品。

完：Please switch off your electrical devices.

順：No electrical devices.

單字片語維他命 Useful Vocabulary

- **occupied** [`ɑkjʊpaɪd] **a** 滿的;有人佔據的
- **briefcase** [`brif,kes] **n** 公事包
- **armrest** [`ɑrm,rɛst] **n** 扶手
- **aisle seat** 靠走道的座位
- **window seat** 靠窗戶的座位
- **center seat** 中間的座位
- **seat pocket** 前座椅背附袋
- **seat belt sign** 安全帶燈號
- **switch off** 關閉
- **electronic device** 電子設備

He travels the fastest who travels alone.

★　★　★　★　★

單獨旅行的人走得最快。

救急情境演練 Situation

A: There's no space here.
這裡沒有空位了。

B: I'll make some space for you.
我幫您移出空位來。

A: There's no space to put my carry-on bag.
我的隨身袋無處可放。

B: You can put it in the compartment above the seat.
您可以放在座位上方的置物箱。

A: I think it's very inconvenient.
我覺得很不方便。

B: For security, you can't put it on your feet.
為了安全，您不可以把它放在腳上。

A: Could I put it below the front seat?
我可以把它放在前座下方嗎？

B: Yes, you can.
好，您可以放在那裡。

A: Could you help me to put my bag up?
可以幫我把包包放上去嗎？

B: Let me give you a hand.
讓我助您一臂之力。

A: Could you move your luggage a little?
你可以把行李挪過去一點嗎？

🅱 : Excuse me, I'll move it.
不好意思，我把它挪開。

KEY SENTENCES
關鍵句 🔑

（完 → 完整句・順 → 順口句）

3-13 ▶ 我可以把行李放在這裡嗎？
完 : May I put my baggage here?
順 : Baggage here, OK?

3-14 ▶ 可以幫我把包包放上去嗎？
完 : Could you help me to put my bag up?
順 : Help me with it, OK?(用手示意)

3-15 ▶ 這裡沒有空位了，我的行李該放在哪裡呢？
完 : There's no space here. Where should I put my baggage?
順 : No space. Where to put my baggage?

3-16 ▶ 我的隨身行李無處可放。
完 : There's no space to put my carry-on luggage.
順 : No space for this.

3-17 ▶ 可否移一下你的行李？
完 : Could you move your luggage a little?
順 : Move it a little, OK?(用手示意)

3-18 ▶ 可否幫我把西裝袋掛在衣櫃裡？

完：Could you hang this suit bag in the closet for me, please?

順：Hang this in the closet, OK? (用手示意)

3-19 ▶ 我可以把傘放在這裡嗎？

完：May I put my umbrella here?

順：Umbrella here, OK?

3-20 ▶ 我可以把手杖放在這裡嗎？

完：May I put my cane here?

順：Cane here, OK?

3-21 ▶ 這裡沒有空位了，我的吉他該放在哪裡呢？

完：There's no space here. Where should I put my guitar?

順：No space. Where to put my guitar?

3-22 ▶ 這裡沒有空位了，我的助步器該放在哪裡呢？

完：There's no space here. Where should I put my walker?

順：No space. Where to put my walker?

3-23 ▶ 可否移一下你的手提箱？

完：Could you move your suitcase a little?

順：Move it a little, OK?(用手示意)

3-24 ▶ 可否移一下你的袋子？

完：Could you move your bag a little?

順：Move it a little, OK?(用手示意)

單字片語維他命 Useful Vocabulary

🔖 **baggage** [`bægɪdʒ] **n** 行李

🔖 **valise** [vəˋlis] **n** 手提旅行袋

🔖 **compartment** [kəmˋpɑrtmənt] **n** 置物箱；行李箱

🔖 **space** [spes] **n** 空間

🔖 **room** [rum] **n** 空間

🔖 **security** [sɪˋkjʊrətɪ] **n** 安全

🔖 **notebook** [ˋnotˌbʊk] **n** 筆記型電腦

🔖 **inconvenient** [ˌɪnkənˋvinjənt] **a** 不便的

🔖 **carry-on luggage** 隨身行李

🔖 **give sb. a hand** 助⋯一臂之力

Do in Rome as the Romans do.

★ ★ ★ ★ ★

入境隨俗。

🔊 MP3 013

救急情境演練 Situation

A : Would you like some drinks?
你想喝點飲料嗎？

B : What kind of drinks do you have?
有什麼樣的飲料呢？

A : There're black tea and coffee.
有紅茶跟咖啡。

B : Are there any alcoholic drinks?
有含酒精的飲料嗎？

A : Yes, we have red wine and beer, too.
是的，我們也有紅酒和啤酒。

B : I'd like to have a cup of coffee.
我想要一杯咖啡。

A : Would you like some wine or beer, too?
您還需要紅酒或啤酒嗎？

B : Hmm, red wine, please.
嗯，請給我紅酒。

A : Need some ice?
需要冰塊嗎？

B : Ok, thank you.
好，謝謝你。

A : Does your coffee need sugar or cream?
您的咖啡要加糖還是奶精？

A : Sugar, please.
請加糖。

KEY SENTENCES
關鍵句 🔑

(完 → 完整句 · 順 → 順口句)

3-25 ▶ 您要飲料嗎？
完：Do you need anything to drink?
順：Drinks?

3-26 ▶ 不用，謝謝。
完：No, thanks.
順：No.

3-27 ▶ 我想要一杯水。
完：I'd like to have a glass of water.
順：Water, please.

3-28 ▶ 請再給我一杯好嗎？
完：May I have one more glass?
順：One more glass, please?

3-29 ▶ 請給我們兩杯咖啡好嗎？
完：May we have two cups of coffee, please?
順：Two cups of coffee, please?

3-30 ▶ 可以給我糖和奶精嗎？
完：May I have some sugar and cream?
順：Sugar and cream, please?

3-31 ▶ 請給我一杯啤酒。
完：Please get me a glass of beer.
順：A glass of beer, please.

3-32 ▶ 您要果汁嗎？

完：Do you want some juice?

順：Any juice?

3-33 ▶ 我想要一杯紅酒。

完：I'd like to have a glass of red wine.

順：A glass of red wine, please.

3-34 ▶ 我想要一杯蘋果汁。

完：I'd like to have a glass of apple juice.

順：A glass of apple juice, please.

3-35 ▶ 我想要一杯熱牛奶。

完：I'd like to have a glass of hot milk.

順：A glass of hot milk, please.

3-36 ▶ 請給我一杯綠茶。

完：Get me a cup of green tea, please.

順：A cup of green tea, please.

3-37 ▶ 請給我一杯香檳。

完：Get me a glass of champagne, please.

順：A glass of champagne, please.

單字片語維他命 Useful Vocabulary

- **drink** [drɪŋk] **n** 飲料
- **beverage** [`bɛvərɪdʒ] **n** 飲料
- **coffee** [`kɔfɪ] **n** 咖啡
- **cocoa** [`koko] **n** 可可
- **milk** [mɪlk] **n** 牛奶
- **juice** [dʒus] **n** 果汁
- **lemonade** [ˌlɛmən`ed] **n** 檸檬水
- **black tea** 紅茶
- **mineral water** 礦泉水
- **soft drink** 不含酒精的飲料

救急情境演練 Situation

A: Excuse me. Is there a menu?
請問有菜單嗎?

B: It's in the back of the front seat pocket.
在前座椅背附袋裡。

A: Only these two kinds of food?
只提供這兩種食物嗎?

B: Yes, only these two kinds of food.
是的,只有這兩款。

A: I need a vegetarian package.
我需要一份素食套餐。

B: Did you made a prior reservation?
您有事先預訂嗎?

A: No, I didn't.
沒有。

B: I'll check for you if we have an extra vegetarian package.
我為您查看是否有多的素食餐點。

A: That's OK. Could you bring me some more peanuts and bread?
不要緊。可以多給我一些花生和麵包嗎?

B: Of course. Please wait a moment.
當然可以,請稍候。

B: Here you are.
這是您要的花生和麵包。

Ⓐ：Thanks a lot!
　多謝！

（完 →完整句 · 順 →順口句）

3-38 ▶ 您要吃牛排還是雞肉呢？
完：Do you want steak or chicken?
順：Steak or chicken?

3-39 ▶ 您的晚餐要吃牛肉還是魚？
完：Would you like beef or fish for dinner?
順：Beef or fish?

3-40 ▶ 我要牛排。
完：I want steak.
順：Steak, please.

3-41 ▶ 請給我雞肉。
完：I'll have the chicken, please.
順：Chicken, please.

3-42 ▶ 我想要喝點白酒搭配魚肉。
完：I'd like some white wine to go with the fish.
順：White wine and fish, please.

3-43 ▶ 你們有泡麵嗎？
完：Do you have any instant noodles?
順：Any instant noodles?

3-44 ▶ 您要蛋還是麵？

完：Do you want eggs or noodles?
順：Eggs or noodles?

3-45 ▶ 您要再多一點麵包嗎？

完：Do you want more bread?
順：More bread?

3-46 ▶ 可否再多給我一些堅果？

完：Could you bring me some more nuts?
順：More nuts, please?

3-47 ▶ 您用完餐點了嗎？

完：Have you finished?
順：Finished?

3-48 ▶ 是的，謝謝。

完：Yes, thanks.
順：Yes.

3-49 ▶ 不，我還沒用完。

完：No, I haven't finished yet.
順：No, not yet.

3-50 ▶ 我用完餐了，請幫我把它收走。

完：I've finished it. Please take it away.
順：Finished. Please take it away.

單字片語維他命 Useful Vocabulary

- **nut** [nʌt] **n** 堅果
- **pudding** [`pʊdɪŋ] **n** 布丁
- **jelly** [`dʒɛlɪ] **n** 果凍
- **refreshment** [rɪ`frɛʃmənt] **n** 茶點
- **curry** [`kɝɪ] **n** 咖哩餐
- **soup** [sup] **n** 湯
- **seafood** [`si͵fud] **n** 海鮮
- **allergic** [ə`lɝdʒɪk] **a** 過敏的
- **macaroni** [͵mækə`ronɪ] **n** 通心粉
- **instant noodles** 速食麵；泡麵

Travel NEWS ✈

準備工作越早越好，這樣對節省費用大有好處，至少在行前一個月要作好旅行的準備，包括簽證申請、路線規劃、機票與車票預訂、酒店預訂、疫苗注射、行李打包等。

救急情境演練 Situation

A : Pardon me. Could you say that again?
不好意思，你可以再說一遍嗎？

B : Did you order a vegetarian meal?
請問您是點素食餐點嗎？

A : Can you speak slower?
你可以說慢一點嗎？

B : A...ve...ge...ta...rian mea...l.
素…食…餐…點。

A : Oh, yes. It's mine!
喔，對，素食餐點是我的！

A : Please get me a pillow.
請給我一個枕頭。

B : Here you are.
枕頭給您。

A : Thank you.
謝謝你。

B : It's my pleasure.
這是我的榮幸。

A : Excuse me. I can't hear anything on this headset.
不好意思，這副耳機聽不到聲音。

B : You have to plug it into the headset jack.
你得插上耳機插孔。

Ⓐ : Thanks. Now, I can hear the music.
　　謝啦，我現在可以聽到音樂了。

KEY SENTENCES
關鍵句 🔑
（完 →完整句・順 →順口句）

3-51 ▶ 你可以再說一遍嗎？

完：Would you repeat that?

順：Pardon me?

3-52 ▶ 抱歉，你剛才說什麼？

完：Pardon me. What did you say?

順：Pardon?

3-53 ▶ 請說慢一點。

完：Please speak slowly.

順：Slowly, please.

3-54 ▶ 請給我一條毯子。

完：Please get me a blanket.

順：A blanket, please.

3-55 ▶ 要怎麼打開閱讀燈啊？

完：How do I turn this overhead light on?

順：How to turn on the light?

3-56 ▶ 有會說中文的服務人員嗎？

完：Does there any staff speaks Chinese?

順：Any Chinese-speaking staff?

3-57 ▶ 您有中文報紙嗎？

完：Do you have Chinese newspapers?

順：Any Chinese newspapers?

3-58 ▶ 請問有中文雜誌嗎？

完：Are there any Chinese magazines?

順：Any Chinese magazine?

3-59 ▶ 請給我兩張明信片。

完：Please get me two postcards.

順：Two postcards, please.

3-60 ▶ 請給我撲克牌好嗎？

完：May I have some playing cards?

順：Playing cards, please?

3-61 ▶ 這副耳機聽不到聲音。

完：I can't hear anything on this headset.

順：This headset doesn't work.

3-62 ▶ 我看不到電影，可以換位子嗎？

完：I can't see the movie. Could I move to another seat?

順：Can't see movie. Move to another seat, OK?

3-63 ▶ 請將耳機交還給空服人員。

完：Please return the earphone to flight attendants.

順：Earphones, please.

單字片語維他命 Useful Vocabulary

➤ **jigsaw** [`dʒɪg͵sɔ] **n** 拼圖
➤ **manual** [`mænjʊəl] **n** 手冊
➤ **instruction** [ɪn`strʌkʃən] **n** 操作指南
➤ **hierarchical menu** 階層式選單
➤ **overhead light** 頭部上方的閱讀小燈
➤ **model toy** 模型玩具
➤ **key chain** 鑰匙圈
➤ **Rubik's Cube** 魔術方塊
➤ **Pardon me.** 不好意思。(請人再次說明時使用。)
➤ **My pleasure.** 這是我的榮幸。

Who lives sees much.
Who travels sees more.

★ ★ ★ ★ ★

長壽者見識多;旅遊者見識廣。

MP3 016

救急情境演練 Situation

A：I want to buy some duty-free items.
我想買點免稅商品。

B：What would you like?
請問您需要什麼？

A：Do you have any souvenirs?
你們有賣紀念品嗎？

B：This is our newest catalogue.
這是我們最新的目錄。

A：Please give me this set of skin care products.
請給我這組肌膚保養品。

B：Do you have to pay cash or charge?
您要付現還是刷卡？

A：Can I pay with my MasterCard?
我可以用萬事達卡付帳嗎？

B：Yes, you can.
是的，可以的。

A：May I have a catalogue of duty-free goods?
可以給我一份免稅商品目錄嗎？

B：Yes, here you are.
可以，這給您。

A：I'll take this diamond brooch, please.
我要這個鑽石胸針，麻煩你。

B：By credit card, or by cash?
是要刷卡、還是付現？

KEY SENTENCES

關鍵句 🔑

（**完**→完整句・**順**→順口句）

3-64 ▶ 給我一份免稅商品目錄好嗎？

完：May I have a catalogue of duty-free goods?

順：A Duty-free catalogue, please?

3-65 ▶ 有賣免稅商品嗎？

完：Do you sell any duty-free items?

順：Any Duty-free items?

3-66 ▶ 有什麼牌子的菸呢？

完：What brands of cigarette do you have?

順：What brands?

3-67 ▶ 我要買酒，請幫我推薦。

完：I'd like to buy wine, please recommend me some.

順：Recommend some wine for me, please.

3-68 ▶ 麻煩你，我要買這個。

完：I'll take this one, please.

順：This one, please.

3-69 ▶ 麻煩你，我要買巧克力

完：I'd like to buy some chocolate, please.

順：Chocolate, please.

3-70 ▶ 麻煩你，我要買這個胸針。

完：I'd like to buy the brooch, please.
順：The brooch, please.

3-71 ▶ 這個手鐲多少錢？

完：How much is this bracelet?
順：This bracelet, how much?

3-72 ▶ 這瓶香水多少錢？

完：How much is this bottle of perfume?
順：This perfume, how much?

3-73 ▶ 可以用新臺幣付款嗎？

完：May I pay in NT dollars?
順：NT dollars, OK?

3-74 ▶ 這裡收旅行支票嗎？

完：Do you accept traveler's checks here?
順：Traveler's checks, OK?

3-75 ▶ 我可以刷卡支付嗎？

完：May I pay by credit card?
順：By credit card, OK?

單字片語維他命 Useful Vocabulary

➤ **duty-free** [`djutɪ`fri] **a** 免稅的

➤ **souvenir** [`suvə,nɪr] **n** 紀念品

➤ **brooch** [brotʃ] **n** 女用胸針

➤ **skin care product** 肌膚保養品

➤ **traveler's check** 旅行支票

➤ **MasterCard** 萬事達卡

➤ **Visa card** 威士卡

➤ **American Express card** 美國運通卡

➤ **JCB card** 日財卡

➤ **Diner card** 大來卡

🔊 MP3 017

救急情境演練 Situation

Ⓐ：Do you have medicine for airsickness?
請問有暈機藥嗎？

Ⓑ：Yes, please wait.
有的，請您稍等。

Ⓐ：I'm not feeling well after the turbulence.
亂流之後我覺得不太舒服。

Ⓑ：What services do you need?
您還需要什麼服務呢？

Ⓐ：Would you please bring me an airsickness bag?
你可以給我一個嘔吐袋嗎？

Ⓑ：This is an airsickness bag.
這是您要的嘔吐袋。

Ⓐ：I feel a little cold.
我有點冷。

Ⓑ：I'll help you to add one blanket.
我幫您加條毯子。

Ⓐ：I also need a pillow.
我還要一個枕頭。

Ⓑ：Anything else?
還需要別的嗎？

Ⓐ：No, that's all.
不用，這樣就好了。

B：I'll bring them soon.
我很快就拿過來。

（完 →完整句・順 →順口句）

3-76 ▶ 您不舒服嗎？
完：Are you feeling sick?
順：Are you OK?

3-77 ▶ 我暈機了。
完：I'm airsick.
順：Airsick.

3-78 ▶ 我想嘔吐。
完：I feel nauseous.
順：Nauseous.

3-79 ▶ 可以給我一個嘔吐袋嗎？
完：Could I have an airsickness bag?
順：Airsickness bag, please?

3-80 ▶ 你有治胃痛的藥嗎？
完：Do you have medicine for an upset stomach?
順：Any medicine for stomachache?

3-81 ▶ 可以給我一些暈機藥嗎？
完：May I have some medicine for airsickness?
順：Any medicine for airsickness, please?

3-82 ▶ 我不太舒服，請問有地方讓我躺一下嗎？

完：I don't feel very good. Is there a place where I could lie down?

順：I am sick. Is there any place to lie down?

3-83 ▶ 你要我叫空服員嗎？

完：Would you like me to call a flight attendant?

順：Need a flight attendant?

3-84 ▶ 如果您需要幫忙的話，請告訴我。

完：Please let me know if I can help you somehow.

順：Ask me for help, OK?

3-85 ▶ 你要用我的枕頭嗎？

完：Would you like to use my pillow?

順：Use my pillow?

3-86 ▶ 你要不要再多蓋一條毯子？

完：Do you want one more blanket?

順：One more blanket?

單字片語雜他命 Useful Vocabulary

🔻 **turbulence** [`tɜbjələns] **n** 亂流

🔻 **airsick** [`ɛr͵sɪk] **a** 暈機的

🔻 **nauseous** [`nɔʃɪəs] **a** 想吐的

🔻 **uncomfortable** [ʌn`kʌmfətəbḷ] **a** 不舒服的

🔻 **tinnitus** [tɪ`naɪtəs] **n** 耳鳴

🔻 **aspirin** [`æspərɪn] **n** 阿斯匹靈；解熱鎮痛劑

🔻 **Band-Aid** [`bænd͵ed] **n** 護創膠布；OK繃

🔻 **first aid kit** 急救箱

🔻 **airsickness bag** 嘔吐袋

🔻 **medicine for airsickness** 暈機藥

Travel NEWS ✈

英文精通當然最好，只要能講一般的生活用語就可邁出第一步，遇到英文不通時，就用肢體語言及畫圖來表示。

MP3 018

救急情境演練 Situation

A: Excuse me. May I lean the back of the seat backward?
不好意思，我可以把椅背向後傾斜嗎？

B: Yes, you can.
好，可以。

A: Would you mind pulling down the shade? I'd like to take a nap.
你介意拉下遮陽板嗎？我想小睡一下。

B: No, I don't mind.
不，我不會介意。

A: Excuse me. Could you show me how to operate the personal TV?
不好意思，你可以教我操作這具個人電視嗎？

B: Here are the instructions.
這是說明書。

A: Thank you.
謝謝你。

B: Don't mention it.
不客氣。

A: My ears are popping.
我的耳朵塞住了。

B: Try chewing gum.
嚼口香糖試試。

A: I still feel sick. Do you have an airsick bag?

　　我還是覺得不舒服，你有嘔吐袋嗎？

B：Oh, wait! Here you are, are you OK?
　　喔，等等！嘔吐袋拿去，你還好吧？

KEY SENTENCES
關鍵句 （完→完整句・順→順口句）

3-87 ▶ 不好意思，我想去上廁所。

完：Excuse me. I'd like to go to the lavatory.

順：Excuse me.(示意要起身離座)

3-88 ▶ 如果你要起來的話，請告訴我。

完：Please tell me when you want to stand up.

順：When you want to go, tell me, please.

3-89 ▶ 如果你要起來的話，我不介意你把我叫醒。

完：I don't mind if you wake me up when you want to stand up.

順：You can wake me anytime.

3-90 ▶ 你過不去，因為有手推車堵在走道上。

完：I don't think you can go through the aisle because a cart is blocking it.

順：You can't pass. A cart is there.

3-91 ▶ 廁所有很多人在排隊。

完：There're many people waiting for the lavatory.

順：Many people are waiting for the lavatory.

3-92 ▶ 請問要如何操作這些按鈕？

完：Excuse me. How do I operate these buttons?

順：How to use these?(用手示意)

單字片語維他命 Useful Vocabulary

❧ **lean** [lin] **V** 倚；靠

❧ **backward** [`bækwəd] **a** 向後的

❧ **shade** [ʃed] **n** 遮光板；遮陽板

❧ **operate** [`apə,ret] **V** 操作

❧ **chew** [tʃu] **n** 嚼

❧ **gum** [gʌm] **n** 口香糖

❧ **poker** [`pokə] **n** 撲克牌遊戲

❧ **channel** [`tʃænl̩] **n** 頻道

❧ **subtitle** [`sʌb,taɪtl̩] **n** 字幕

❧ **take a nap** 小睡片刻

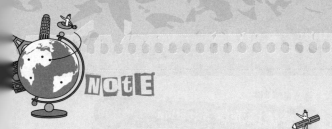

MP3 019

救急情境演練 Situation

A：Could you bring me one immigration card?
可以給我一張入境卡嗎?

B：Yes, please.
好的,請等一下。

A：Could you help me with this immigration card?
你可以教我填入境卡嗎?

B：Please fill the flight information in here.
請在這裡填寫班機資料。

A：What does this mean?
這是什麼意思?

B：Write down your airline and the flight.
寫下您的航空公司與航班。

A：Could you give me one more Customs declaration card?
你可以再給我一張海關申報單嗎?

B：Yes, please wait a minute.
好的,請等一下。

A：What is "contraband"?
什麼是「contraband」?

B：Some items may endanger the flight, such as firearms, knives, etc.
是指一些會危及飛行的物品,像是火藥、刀械等物。

Ⓐ : What are "duty-free items"?
　　什麼是「duty-free items」？

Ⓑ : Such as your purchases on the plane or in the duty-free shops.
　　凡是您在飛機上、或在免稅商店中購買的物品都算。

KEY SENTENCES
關鍵句 　（完→完整句・順→順口句）

3-93 ▶ 請注意，我們現正經過亂流。

完 : Attention, please. We're now flying through turbulence.

順 : Attention, please. There is some turbulence.

3-94 ▶ 請回到您的座位坐好，並繫緊安全帶。

完 : Please go back to your own seat and fasten your seat belt.

順 : Go back and fasten your seat belt, please.

3-95 ▶ 請給我一張入境登記表好嗎？

完 : May I have a disembarkation form?

順 : A disembarkation form, please.

3-96 ▶ 能告訴我怎麼填這張表格嗎？

完 : Could you tell me how to fill in this form?

順 : How to fill it in?

3-97 ▶ 需要海關申報單嗎？

完 : Do you need a Customs declaration form?

順：Need a Customs declaration form?

3-98 ▶ 現在當地時間是上午九點鐘。

完：The local time now is 9:00 a.m..

順：It's 9:00 a.m..

3-99 ▶ 和出發地的時差有九小時。

完：There is 9 hours difference from the time of departure place.

順：It's 9 hours difference from departure place.

單字片語維他命 Useful Vocabulary

◥ **land** [lænd] **V** 著陸

◥ **destination** [ˌdɛstə`neʃən] **n** 目的地

◥ **latitude** [`lætəˌtjud] **n** 緯度

◥ **longitude** [`landʒəˌtjud] **n** 經度

◥ **temperature** [`tɛmprətʃə] **n** 溫度；氣溫

◥ **contraband** [`kantrəˌbænd] **n** 違禁品；禁運品

◥ **immergration card** 入境卡

◥ **disembarkation form** 入境登記表

◥ **Customs declaration form** 海關申報單

◥ **security check** 安檢

背包客旅遊筆記 BON VOYAGE!

　　我們在搭機前，應先考量自己的健康狀況是否適合投入這趟旅程。若得了輕微感冒，有鼻塞、咳嗽、流鼻水等症狀，建議在行前先詢問醫生、或乾脆延後行程；如果行程無法延後，請記住一定要戴上口罩、多喝水，在起飛及降落前可按照醫囑使用藥品減緩不適。但若是發現罹患流感，為避免掃了遊興並顧及公民道德，還是等病好了再出發吧！

　　此外，高危險群旅客，像是有心臟病、糖尿病、氣喘等疾病的患者，要在行前請教醫師是否適合搭機旅行；有長期病史的乘客，例如慢性肺病患者或精神失調者，在出發前要請醫生做徹底檢查，並告知航空公司任何在飛航中可能需要使用的醫療設備，並提供醫療證明給航空公司。

　　另一方面，懷孕滿三十六週的孕婦通常不得搭機；懷孕三十二至三十六週者，務必請產檢醫生填寫航空公司的專用診斷書，並經航空公司同意才能搭機。各國移民局對懷孕後期都有不同限制，別忘了在出國前要查清楚相關規定，以免到時無法入境。

　　有些人聽說過「經濟艙症候群」，其實只要搭乘長途客機，任何旅客都有可能發生血栓塞、呼吸困難，甚至是中風等症狀。以下提供幾個方法，以避免「經濟艙症候群」的發生：

1. 可以的話，儘量選擇前面的座位，如此可以避免發生暈機的狀況。因為機艙內有壓力變化，會發生耳咽管阻塞、失衡或耳朵疼痛等問題。建議：若發生這種狀況，可多打幾個哈欠、吞吞口水，或嚼食口香糖，來減緩不適。

2. 旅客在搭機前，盡量選擇穿著輕便寬鬆的服裝，讓身體在搭機時擁有舒適感。

3. 每隔一到二小時，就要站起來走動一下，上個廁所也好，找機會伸展四肢，保持血液暢通；有些航空公司會教導乘客作些簡易的伸展操，不妨試試。

4. 由於機艙內很乾燥，容易口乾舌燥，所以要多補充水份，不過要避免飲用酒類、咖啡等刺激性的飲料。

5. 如同先前提過的，因為機上相當乾糙，有些人會出現皮膚搔癢的情形，可抹些乳液減緩不適、在臉上噴水或敷上保濕面膜。在機上不應該戴隱形眼鏡，因為眼睛會太乾燥，建議改戴眼鏡。

搭乘飛機雖然快捷便利，但由於客艙內低壓造成的氣體壓力效應、低氧、低濕度以及長時間處於客艙狹窄的空間等情形，仍對身體不適的旅客造成影響。不過，只要在行前做好醫療諮詢及必要的醫護安排，了解客艙的特性，還是可以享受愉快的旅程，快快樂樂地出門、平平安安地回家！

Part. 4

入 境 篇

Unit 4-1 入境審查：說明目的

Unit 4-2 入境審查：說明住宿

Unit 4-3 入境審查：機票和攜帶的錢財

Unit 4-4 行李提領

Unit 4-5 行李遺失

Unit 4-6 海關

* 行李筆記

🔊 MP3 020

救急情境演練 Situation

🅐 : Here are my passport, disembarkation card, and flight ticket.
這是我的護照、入境登記表與機票。

🅑 : What's the purpose of your visit?
請問您來這裡的目的是？

🅐 : I'm planning to visit my relatives.
我要去拜訪親戚。

🅑 : How long will you stay here?
預計停留多久時間？

🅐 : 2 weeks.
兩週。

🅑 : Are you going to other places?
你會到其他地方去嗎？

🅐 : No, I don't.
不，我不會。

🅑 : Welcome to New York.
歡迎你到紐約。

🅑 : Please open your bag. Do you have any plants or meat products?
請打開袋子，你有帶植物或肉製品嗎？

🅐 : No.
沒有。

🅑 : Any fruit or vegetables?
有帶水果或蔬菜嗎？

A : No.
沒有。

關鍵句 （完→完整句．順→順口句）

4-01 ▶ 請給我看你的護照好嗎？
完 : May I see your passport, please?
順 : Passport, please?

4-02 ▶ 你此行的目的為何？
完 : What's your purpose of your visit?
順 : Purpose?

4-03 ▶ 來觀光。
完 : I'm a tourist.
順 : Tourist.

4-04 ▶ 我是跟旅行團來的。
完 : I'm with a tour.
順 : With a tour.

4-05 ▶ 我來參加商展。
完 : I have come to attend a trade fair.
順 : For a trade fair.

4-06 ▶ 我來出差。
完 : I'm here on business.
順 : For business.

4-07 ▶ 我被調來紐約的分公司。

完：I've been assigned to our company's New York branch.

順：To work in our New York branch.

4-08 ▶ 我在貿易公司工作。

完：I work for a trading company.

順：I work at a trading company.

4-09 ▶ 我是來學習英文的。

完：I'm here to study English.

順：Study English.

4-10 ▶ 我來參加我朋友的婚禮。

完：I have come to attend my friend's wedding.

順：For my friend's wedding.

4-11 ▶ 我來拜訪親戚。

完：I'm visiting relatives.

順：To visit relatives.

4-12 ▶ 我是來參加一場科學會議的。

完：I'm here for a science conference.

順：For a science conference.

4-13 ▶ 我是來演講的。

完：I'm giving a speech.

順：For a lecture.

4-14 ▶ 我是來度假的。

完：I'm enjoying a vacation.
順：For a vacation.

4-15 ▶ 可否告知搭乘的班機號碼？
完：May I know your flight number?
順：Your flight number, please?

4-16 ▶ 我搭乘的是聯合航空**904**號班機。
完：My flight was UA-904.
順：UA-904.

4-17 ▶ 會在東京停留多久？
完：How long will you stay in Tokyo?
順：How long in Tokyo?

4-18 ▶ 會在華盛頓停留多久？
完：How long will you stay in Washington?
順：How long in Washington?

4-19 ▶ 會在溫哥華停留多久？
完：How long will you stay in Vancouver?
順：How long in Vancouver?

4-20 ▶ 會在這裡停留一週。
完：I'll stay here for one week.
順：One week.

4-21 ▶ 預計停留五天。
完：I plan to stay five days.
順：About five days.

4-22 ▶ 我將停留到十號星期一。

完：I will be here until Monday, the tenth.
順：Until Monday, the tenth.

4-23 ▶ 我會先在尼斯停留兩天，然後前往托利多。

完：I will be staying in Nice for two days and then I am going to Toledo.
順：Two days in Nice and then to Toledo.

4-24 ▶ 我會先在柏林停留一天，然後前往阿姆斯特丹。

完：I'll be staying in Berlin for one day and then I'm going to Amsterdam.
順：One day in Berlin and then to Amsterdam.

4-25 ▶ 你來之前有去其他國家嗎？

完：Have you been to other countries before you come here?
順：Other countries before coming here?

4-26 ▶ 你會去其他國家嗎？

完：Are you visiting other countries?
順：Visiting other countries?

4-27 ▶ 現在還不太確定。

完：I'm not quite sure yet.
順：Not sure yet.

單字片語維他命 Useful Vocabulary

- **purpose** [`pɝpəs] **n** 目的
- **relative** [`rɛlətɪv] **n** 親戚
- **wedding** [`wɛdɪŋ] **n** 婚禮
- **tourist** [`tʊrɪst] **n** 觀光客
- **tour** [tʊr] **n** 旅遊；旅行團
- **study** [`stʌdɪ] **v** 學習
- **conference** [`kɑnfərəns] **n** 研討會
- **trade fair** 商展
- **be on business** 出差
- **give a speech** 演講

Wherever you are, it's
the entry point.

★　★　★　★　★

無論你在哪裡，都是新的開始。

◀)) MP3 021

救急情境演練 Situation

A：Where are you staying?
請問你的住宿地點是？

B：Hotel.
我住飯店。

A：Which hotel, please?
請問是哪間飯店？

B：I'll stay at Hilton Hotel.
我會入住希爾頓飯店。

A：Please fill the hotel address in here.
請在這裡填寫飯店住址。

B：Here you are.
這是飯店住址。

A：How long will you stay here?
會在這裡停留多久？

B：I'll stay here for a week.
我會待在這裡一個星期。

A：What's the purpose of your visit?
你來此的目的為何？

B：For a workshop.
參加專題研討會。

A：What line of business are you in?
你從事哪一行？

B：I'm a teacher in college.
我是大學老師。

KEY SENTENCES
關鍵句 🔑

(完 →完整句・順 →順口句)

4-28 ▶ 你會住在哪裡？

完：Where're you staying?

順：Where do you stay?

4-29 ▶ 我會住在飯店，但我並未預約。

完：I'll be staying at hotel, but I don't have a reservation yet.

順：At a hotel, but no reservation yet.

4-30 ▶ 我會住在朋友家。

完：I'm going to stay at a friend's house.

順：A friend's house.

4-31 ▶ 我會住在親戚家。

完：I'm going to stay at my relative's place.

順：My relative's place.

4-32 ▶ 我會住在假日旅社。

完：I'll stay at Holiday Inn.

順：Holiday Inn.

4-33 ▶ 我會住在表哥家。

完：I'm going to stay at my cousin's place.

順：My cousin's place.

4-34 ▶ 我會住在同學家。

完：I'm going to stay at my classmate's place.

101

順：My classmate's place.

4-35 ▶ 我會住在青年旅館。

完：I'm going to stay at the hostel.
順：At the hostel.

4-36 ▶ 我會住在希爾頓飯店。

完：I'll stay at Hilton Hotel.
順：Hilton Hotel.

4-37 ▶ 我會住在麗池酒店。

完：I'll stay at Ritz Hotel.
順：Ritz Hotel.

4-38 ▶ 這是旅館的電話。

完：This is the hotel telephone number.
順：Here you are.(遞出名片)

4-39 ▶ 這是旅館的住址。

完：This is the hotel address.
順：Here you are.(遞出名片)

單字片語維他命 Useful Vocabulary

- **stay** [ste] **V** 暫住；停留
- **inn** [ɪn] **n** 小旅館；客棧
- **hotel** [ho`tɛl] **n** 旅館；飯店
- **motel** [mo`tɛl] **n** 汽車旅館
- **tavern** [`tævən] **n** 小客棧
- **roadhouse** [`rod͵haus] **n** 旅館；酒店
- **workshop** [`wɜk͵ʃɑp] **n** 工作坊；專題研討會
- **name card** 名片
- **have a reservation** 預約
- **visiting professor** 客座教授

PASS

🔊 MP3 022

救急情境演練 Situation

A：How much cash do you have?
你帶了多少現金？

B：1,000 USD.
一千元美金。

A：Do you have other currency?
還有其他貨幣嗎？

B：10,000 NT dollars.
一萬元新臺幣。

A：Do you have other currency?
還有其他貨幣嗎？

B：Traveler's checks.
旅行支票。

A：How much money in traveler's checks?
面額是多少？

B：1,000 USD.
一千元美金。

A：Do you have a return ticket for Taiwan?
你有回臺灣的機票嗎？

B：I have a return ticket, but I haven't made a reservation yet.
我有回程機票，但還沒有訂位。

A：Please show me your return ticket.
請出示你的回程機票。

B : Here you are.
在這裡。

KEY SENTENCES

關鍵句　（完 →完整句・順 →順口句）

4-40 ▶ 你有多少現金？
完 : How much cash do you have?
順 : How much cash?

4-41 ▶ 還有其他貨幣嗎？
完 : Do you have other currency?
順 : Other currency?

4-42 ▶ 我有面額一千元美元的旅行支票。
完 : I have US$ 1,000 in traveler's checks.
順 : Traveler's checks for US$ 1,000.

4-43 ▶ 我有面額五百元美元的旅行支票。
完 : I have US$ 500 in traveler's checks.
順 : Traveler's checks for US$ 500.

4-44 ▶ 我身上有三千元日幣。
完 : I have 3,000 Yens with me.
順 : 3,000 Yens.

4-45 ▶ 我身上有五千元歐元。
完 : I have 5,000 Euros with me.
順 : 5,000 Euros.

4-46 ▶ 我有兩千元新台幣和七千元美金。

完：I have NT$ 2,000 and US$ 7,000.

順：NT$ 2,000 and US$ 7,000.

4-47 ▶ 我有四千元英鎊。

完：I have 4,000 Pounds.

順：4,000 Pounds.

4-48 ▶ 我有三千元披索。

完：I have 3,000 Pesos.

順：3,000 Pesos.

4-49 ▶ 你有回臺灣的機票嗎？

完：Do you have a return ticket for Taiwan?

順：A return ticket for Taiwan?

4-50 ▶ 請出示你的回程機票。

完：Please show me your return ticket.

順：Your return ticket, please.

4-51 ▶ 我有回程的機票，可是還沒有訂位。

完：I have a return ticket but I haven't made a reservation yet.

順：A return ticket, but no reservation yet.

單字片語維他命 Useful Vocabulary

- **currency** [`kɜənsɪ] n 貨幣
- **NTD** 新臺幣
- **USD** 美金
- **Yen** 日幣
- **Won** 韓圜
- **Pound** 英鎊
- **Euro** 歐元
- **Rupee** 盧比
- **Peso** 披索
- **return ticket** 回程票

Travel NEWS

目前歐盟及其二十七個會員國，評估我國皆符合歐盟相關規定後，同意修改歐盟相關法規(regulation)，將我國自需要申根簽證方能入境申根公約地區之國家改列為免申根簽證國。

🔊 MP3 023

救急情境演練 Situation

A: Could you show me where the baggage claim area is?
你可以告訴我行李提領處在哪裡嗎？

B: The next layer of floor.
在下一層樓。

A: Where's the baggage carousel?
行李輸送帶在哪？

B: In front of the Customs checkpoint.
在海關檢查哨前面。

A: How do I know my baggage has arrived?
我要怎麼知道行李已經到了？

B: Marquee displays.
跑馬燈的字幕會顯示。

A: Where do I get a cart?
哪裡有手推車？

B: In the right hand side.
在右手邊。

A: Does the luggage come out here?
行李會從這裡出來嗎？

B: Yes.
會的。

A: Where is it?
在哪裡？

B：Just follow the "Baggage Claim" sign.
沿著「領取行李」的標示走就可以看到了。

KEY SENTENCES

關鍵句 （完 →完整句 · 順 →順口句）

4-52 ▶ 我要到哪裡提領行李呢？

完：Where can I pick up my luggage?

順：Luggage area, please?

4-53 ▶ 請告訴我行李提領區在哪裡？

完：Could you tell me where the baggage claim area is?

順：Baggage claim area, please?

4-54 ▶ 華航613號班機的行李在哪裡？

完：Where are the bags from CI-613?

順：CI-613's bags, please?

4-55 ▶ 聯合航空752號班機的行李在哪裡？

完：Where is the luggage from UA-752?

順：UA-752's luggage, please?

4-56 ▶ 土耳其航空849號班機的行李在哪裡？

完：Where is the luggage from TK-849?

順：TK-849's luggage, please?

4-57 ▶ 大溪地航空290號班機的行李在哪裡？

完：Where is the luggage from TN-290?

順：TN-290's luggage, please?

4-58 ▶ 我需要幫忙搬行李，麻煩了。

完：I need a hand with my bags, please.

順：Help me with the bags, OK?

4-59 ▶ 讓我來，哪些是您的行李？

完：Let me help you with that. Show me which bags are yours.

順：Allow me. Which bags are yours?

4-60 ▶ 麻煩你，褐色提袋都是我的。

完：All of my bags are brown, please.

順：The brown ones, please.

4-61 ▶ 這是我的行李提領標籤。

完：Here's my claim tag.

順：Here you are.(用手示意)

4-62 ▶ 這些是我的行李。

完：These are my baggage.

順：They are mine.(用手示意)

4-63 ▶ 我可以使用這臺行李推車嗎？

完：May I use this baggage cart?

順：May I?(用手示意)

4-64 ▶ 我有件行李受損了，請問哪裡可以申訴？

完：One of my bags was damaged. Where do I go to make a claim?

順：My bag was damaged. Where to make a claim?

單字片語維他命 Useful Vocabulary

🔖 **layer** [`leə] **n** 層

🔖 **marquee** [mar`ki] **n** 跑馬燈字幕

🔖 **follow** [`falo] **v** 沿著…行進

🔖 **damage** [`dæmɪdʒ] **n** 損害

🔖 **line up** 排隊

🔖 **make a claim** 申訴

🔖 **baggage claim area** 行李提領處

🔖 **claim tag** 提領標籤

🔖 **baggage cart** 行李推車

🔖 **Customs checkpoint** 海關檢查哨

*He who strays discovers
new paths.*

★ ★ ★ ★ ★

迷路的人會發現新的道路。

🔊 MP3 024

救急情境演練 Situation

A: Excuse me. I can't find my luggage.
不好意思，我找不到我的行李。

B: Which flight?
您搭乘的班機是？

A: I took CA-128. Has all the luggage arrived?
我搭中國國際航空128號班機，行李都到了嗎？

B: Yes. Have all come out.
已經全都出來了。

A: One of my suitcases is missing.
我有個行李箱不見了。

B: Oh. Don't worry.
喔，別擔心。

A: What can I do? Where's the lost-and-found counter?
我該怎麼辦？失物招領的櫃檯在哪？

B: You can go to the desk for assistance.
您可以向服務臺尋求協助。

A: I'd like to report a lost suitcase.
我想申報行李遺失。

B: Please show me your baggage claim ticket.
請給我看您的行李條。

A: I think my suitcase has been lost.
我想我的行李箱丟了。

B：We'll try to find it for you.
我們會試圖幫您找到它的。

KEY SENTENCES
關鍵句 （完→完整句．順→順口句）

4-65 ▶ 請問中國國際航空613號班機的行李全都出來了嗎？

完：Excuse me. Has all the baggage from CA-613 come out?

順：All baggage from CA-613 arrives?

4-66 ▶ 行李遺失中心在哪裡呢？

完：Where's the lost luggage office?

順：Lost luggage office, please?

4-67 ▶ 我的行李遺失了。

完：My baggage is missing.

順：Missing baggage.

4-68 ▶ 你能幫我查查看嗎？

完：Could you please check it for me?

順：Check it for me, OK?

4-69 ▶ 您掉了幾件行李？

完：How many pieces of baggage have you lost?

順：How many pieces lost?

4-70 ▶ 您搭乘的班機是？

完：Which flight did you take?

順：Which flight?

4-71 ▶ 請描述您的行李。

完：Please describe your luggage.

順：Describe your luggage.

4-72 ▶ 我的行李是棕色的、塑膠製、有輪子。

完：My baggage is a brown plastic one with wheels.

順：It's brown, plastic and with wheels.

4-73 ▶ 是中型的黑色行李箱。

完：It's a middle size black suitcase.

順：A middle, black suitcase.

4-74 ▶ 你行李箱裡面有什麼？

完：What's in your suitcase?

順：What's inside?

4-75 ▶ 請填寫這張表格。

完：Please fill in this form.

順：Fill in it, please.

4-76 ▶ 我們將提供您每天五十元美金購買日常用品。

完：We'll offer you US$ 50 per day for you to purchase daily items.

順：US$ 50 per day for daily items.

4-77 ▶ 我必須買一些今晚會用到的東西。

完：I have to buy what I need for tonight.
順：Buy things for tonight.

4-78 ▶ 我們找到行李後會通知您。

完：We'll keep you informed when we find your luggage.
順：We will inform you.

4-79 ▶ 我們找到行李後，會直接送到您的旅館。

完：After we find your luggage, we'll send it to your hotel directly.
順：We will send your luggage to your hotel.

單字片語維他命 Useful Vocabulary

▼ **assistance** [ə`sɪstəns] **n** 援助；幫助

▼ **miss** [mɪs] **v** 遺失

▼ **describe** [dɪ`skraɪb] **v** 描述

▼ **wheel** [hwil] **n** 輪子

▼ **sticker** [`stɪkə] **n** 貼紙

▼ **zipper** [`zɪpə] **n** 拉鍊

▼ **come out** 出來；出現

▼ **baggage claim ticket** 行李條

▼ **lost luggage office** 行李遺失中心

▼ **lost-and-found counter** 失物招領櫃檯

🔊 MP3 025

救急情境演練 Situation

A：Please open your luggage.
麻煩請打開行李。

B：OK!
好的！

A：What's this?
這是什麼東西？

B：This is my personal prescription.
這是我的私人處方藥品。

A：Do you have raw food or contraband?
有帶生食或違禁品嗎？

B：No. Only individual supplies.
沒有，只有個人用品。

A：OK, you may go.
好，您可以通關了。

B：Thanks.
謝謝。

A：Please open your suitcase.
請打開您的行李箱。

B：Why?
為什麼？

A：It's the regulation.
這是規定。

B：Hey! Don't mess up my dress!
嘿！別弄亂我的洋裝！

KEY SENTENCES
關鍵句 (完 →完整句 · 順 →順口句)

4-80 ▶ 海關在哪裡？
完：Where's the Customs?
順：The Customs, please?

4-81 ▶ 請給我你的海關申報單。
完：Please show me your Customs declaration card.
順：Customs declaration card, please.

4-82 ▶ 我們必須要檢驗一下你的行李。
完：We'll have to get your luggage examined.
順：Examine luggage, please.

4-83 ▶ 你有攜帶任何蔬果、肉類或植物入境嗎？
完：Do you bring any fruits, vegetables, fresh meats or plants into this country?
順：Any fruit, vegetable, meat or plants?

4-84 ▶ 你有攜帶任何武器或毒品嗎？
完：Do you bring any weapons or drugs with you?
順：Any weapons or drugs?

4-85 ▶ 禁止攜帶水果。
完：It's prohibited to bring fruits.
順：No fruits.

4-86 ▶ 你有任何東西需要申報嗎？

完：Do you have anything to declare?

順：Anything to declare?

4-87 ▶ 我沒有要申報的。

完：I have nothing to declare.

順：Nothing.

4-88 ▶ 你有帶任何違禁品嗎？

完：Do you have any contraband?

順：Any contraband?

4-89 ▶ 你有攜帶酒或菸嗎？

完：Do you have any alcohol or tobacco?

順：Any alcohol or tobacco?

4-90 ▶ 這個箱子裡面有什麼？

完：What's there in the box?

順：What's in it?

4-91 ▶ 這箱子裡的東西是要做什麼用的？

完：What are the things in the box for?

順：What it for?(用手示意)

4-92 ▶ 請出示這箱子的發票和包裝明細。

完：Please show me the invoice and packing list of this box.

順：Invoice and packing list, please.

4-93 ▶ 這是我攜帶的物品。

完：These are my belongings.
順：My belongings.

4-94▶ 這是我要帶回臺灣的土產。

完：This is the souvenir that I am taking back to Taiwan.

順：The souvenir.

4-95▶ 這些是要送朋友的禮物。

完：These're gifts for my friends.

順：Gifts.

4-96▶ 這是胃藥。

完：This medicine is for the stomach.

順：For the stomach.

4-97▶ 我有四條菸。

完：I have four cartons of cigarettes.

順：Four cartons of cigarettes.

4-98▶ 這個我需要付稅嗎？

完：Do I have to pay any duty on this?

順：Any duty?

4-99▶ 驗完護照及安檢後，往前直走。

完：Get through the passport control and security check, then go straight on.

順：After passport control and security check, go straight.

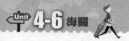

Unit 4-6 海關

單字片語維他命 Useful Vocabulary

- **personal** [`pɜsn̩] **a** 個人的；私人的
- **pass** [pæs] **v** 通過
- **regulation** [ˌrɛgjə`leʃən] **n** 規定；規則
- **tariff** [`tærɪf] **n** 關稅
- **Customs** [`kʌstəmz] **n** 海關
- **seed** [sid] **n** 種子
- **weapon** [`wɛpən] **n** 武器
- **drug** [drʌg] **n** 毒品
- **tobacco** [tə`bæko] **n** 菸草
- **raw food** 生食

背包客旅遊筆記 BON VOYAGE!

　　根據現行的飛航安全規定，除旅客證件外，一般隨身行李都要經過航空公司的許可才能帶上飛機；但託運行李的限制較少，乘客應儘量將物品放入託運行李內。

　　在美國發生九一一事件後，對於隨身行李的規定趨嚴，每位旅客隨身攜帶的液體、膠狀或噴霧類物品的個別體積不得超過一百毫升，所有液體、膠狀或噴霧類物品均應分裝在不超過一公升、且可重複密封的透明塑膠袋內。但嬰兒食品、藥物或是其他醫療物品，若事先向安檢人員申報並獲得同意，則不在此規範內。

　　經過多日的旅遊及購物後，旅客的行李一定會增量不少，因此行李的整理功夫就是門學問了。如有特殊或大件的物品，導遊或領隊應該在旅客購物時，商請店家幫忙宅配；可裝入行李箱的也應儘量摺疊，縮小面積、體積；尤其因為國際能源價格持續飆漲的關係，各家航空公司都陸續減少載重量，藉以減少用油量，因此，旅客行李超重的收費金額會大幅增加，旅客託運行李件數的重量限制也比之前來得更嚴格了。

　　以搭機赴美為例，每位旅客限帶兩件免費託運行李，每件限重三十二公斤；隨身的手提行李，以一件可放在飛機座椅下者為限。旅客所攜帶的隨身行李尺寸為：長五十六公分、寬三十六

公分、高二十三公分;可攜帶放在膝上的物品,包括照相機、女用皮包、外套、大衣、小型樂器、圖書、美術品等。

如果想帶心愛的寵物一起去旅行呢?這就得先做好前置作業了。所有的寵物都要用行李託運或者是貨運的方式來載運,有些國家對寵物的進出口與檢疫有特殊規定,在出發至該國前務必要打聽清楚。

寵物的種類也要加以注意,只有貓、狗、兔子、烏龜、青蛙、昆蟲類可以接受託運服務,假如是「鼠」、「魚」、「蛇」類,航空公司是不接受乘載的。

即使寵物主人多麼疼愛自家的寵物,牠們仍要遵照航空公司的規範。牠們必須被裝載於寵物專用的籠子裡,籠身要牢固而且底部不漏。長度不得少於寵物身長加半高之總和;寬度是寵物肩膀寬度的兩倍;高度是寵物站立時,頭部不會觸碰到籠子的頂端。

至於寵物託運的收費,則是以超重行李來收費,寵物會連同附屬的籠子一起過磅,未滿十公斤者,以十公斤來計算;超過十公斤者,就按照寵物的實際重量來收費。

Part. 5

旅客服務篇

Unit 5-1 詢問銀行服務

Unit 5-2 詢問匯率與貨幣

Unit 5-3 旅客服務中心

＊ 網站筆記

◄)) MP3 026

救急情境演練 Situation

A: Where's the bank in the airport?
請問機場內的銀行在哪裡？

B: In the lobby of the 1st floor.
在一樓大廳。

A: I want to change Australian dollars.
我要換澳幣。

B: Please fill in this form first.
請先填寫這張表格。

A: How should I fill it out? Fill the number in here?
我該如何填寫？在這裡填寫數字嗎？

B: Yes, it's OK to fill out the number only.
是的，只要填寫數字即可。

A: Please exchange these US dollars to Australian dollars.
請將這些美元兌換成澳幣。

B: How much?
要兌換多少錢？

A: 500 Australian dollars.
五百元澳幣。

A: By the way, I'd like to cash some travler's checks, too.
對了，我也想兌換旅行支票。

B: How much do you want to cash?

你想兌換多少金額？

A：1,000 Australian dollars.
一千元澳幣。

（完 →完整句．順 →順口句）

5-01 ▶ 這附近有銀行嗎？

完：Is there any bank around here?
順：Any bank here?

5-02 ▶ 這車站附近有銀行嗎？

完：Are there any banks around the station?
順：Any banks here?

5-03 ▶ 請問匯兌窗口在哪裡？

完：Excuse me. Where's the exchange window?
順：Exchange window, please?

5-04 ▶ 你們有賣旅行支票嗎？

完：Do you sell traveler's checks?
順：Traveler's checks?

5-05 ▶ 這裡可以買加幣嗎？

完：Can I buy Canadian dollars here?
順：Canadian dollars?

5-06 ▶ 我可以電匯到芝加哥嗎？

完：Can I wire some money to Chicago?
順：Wire money to Chicago, OK?

5-07 ▶ 我可以電匯到維也納嗎？

完：Can I wire some money to Vienna?

順：Wire money to Vienna, OK?

5-08 ▶ 我可以電匯到坎培拉嗎？

完：Can I wire some money to Canberra?

順：Wire money to Canberra, OK?

5-09 ▶ 我想兌換旅行支票。

完：I'd like to cash some traveler's checks.

順：Cash these, please.

5-10 ▶ 我要兌換三百塊美金。

完：I'd like to exchange US$ 300.

順：Exchange US$ 300.

5-11 ▶ 我要兌換五百塊歐元。

完：I'd like to exchange 500 Euros.

順：Exchange 500 Euros.

5-12 ▶ 我要兌換兩千塊日幣。

完：I'd like to exchange 2,000 Yens.

順：Exchange 2,000 Yens.

5-13 ▶ 請將這些美金換成澳幣。

完：Please exchange these US dollars to Australian dollars.

順：All to Australian dollars, please.

5-14 ▶ 我想把二十美元找開。

完：I'd like to have change for a twenty.
順：Change for a twenty, please.

5-15 ▶ 你可以告訴我匯款要填哪種單子嗎？

完：Could you tell me which form is for remittance, please?
順：Which form is for remittance?

5-16 ▶ 我需要匯款給我丈夫／太太。

完：I need to remit to my husband.
順：Remit to my wife, please.

單字片語維他命 Useful Vocabulary

🔖 **bank** [bæŋk] **n** 銀行

🔖 **account** [əˋkaʊnt] **n** 帳戶；戶頭

🔖 **deposit** [dɪˋpɑzɪt] **V** 存款

🔖 **withdraw** [wɪðˋdrɔ] **V** 提款

🔖 **transfer** [ˋtrænsfɝ] **V** 轉帳

🔖 **remit** [rɪˋmɪt] **V** 匯款

🔖 **wire** [waɪr] **V** 電匯

🔖 **remittance** [rɪˋmɪtŋs] **n** 匯款；匯款額

🔖 **exchange window** 匯兌窗口

🔖 **foreign exchange rate difference** 外幣匯差

🔊 MP3 027

救急情境演練 Situation

A：I want to change US dollars.
我要換美金。

B：How many US dollars do you want to change?
你要換多少美金？

A：1,200 USD.
一千兩百元美金。

B：What's the denomination?
面額各是多少？

A：Ten 100-dollar bills, twenty 10-dollar bills.
一百元十張，十元二十張。

B：Please fill the number in here.
請在這裡填寫數字。

A：Any commission?
需要手續費嗎？

B：No.
不需要。

A：I want to change Yens.
我要換日圓。

B：How many Yens do you want to change?
你想換多少日圓？

A：5,000 Yens.
五千日圓。

B：Here you are.
這是您的兌款。

KEY SENTENCES
關鍵句 （完 →完整句・順 →順口句）

5-17 ▶ 請告知今天的匯率。
完：Please tell me the exchange rate of today.
順：Exchange rate, please.

5-18 ▶ 請問英鎊的匯率是多少？
完：What's the exchange rate for Pounds?
順：Exchange rate for Pounds, please?

5-19 ▶ 請問美元的匯率是多少？
完：What's the exchange rate for US dollars?
順：Exchange rate for US dollars, please?

5-20 ▶ 請問一百元美金可以換多少澳幣？
完：How many Australian dollars for US$ 100?
順：US$ 100 for Australian dollars, please?

5-21 ▶ 您要換什麼貨幣？
完：What currency do you want?
順：What currency?

5-22 ▶ 我要各種面額的硬幣。
完：I'd like to have coins of all sizes.
順：Coins for all sizes, please.

5-23 ▶ 我要換二十美元面額和一些小鈔。

完：I'd like to change twenties and some small bills.

順：Twenties and small bills, please.

5-24 ▶ 我要四張十元和十張壹元。

完：I'd like to have four ten dollars and ten one dollar.

順：Four ten and ten one, please.

5-25 ▶ 可否請你把這一百元的鈔票換成五張二十元的鈔票呢？

完：Would you break this 100-dollar bill into five 20-dollar bills?

順：Five 20-dollar bills, please?

5-26 ▶ 可否請你把這五百元的鈔票換成五張一百元的鈔票呢？

完：Would you break this 500-dollar bill into five 100-dollar bills?

順：Five 100-dollar bills, please?

5-27 ▶ 可否請你把這一千元的鈔票換成二十個五十元的硬幣呢？

完：Would you break this 1000-dollar bill into twenty 50-dollar coins?

順：Twenty 50-dollar coins, please?

5-28 ▶ 手續費是多少錢呢？

完：How much is the commission?

順：Any commission?

單字片語維他命 Useful Vocabulary

- **bill** [bɪl] **n** 鈔票
- **leaf** [lif] **n** (鈔票或書籍)張；頁
- **balance** [`bæləns] **n** 餘額；結餘
- **denomination** [dɪˏnɑmə`neʃən] **n** 面額
- **commission** [kə`mɪʃən] **n** 手續費；佣金
- **exchange rate** 匯率
- **crtificate of deposit** 定存單
- **on-line banking** 網路銀行
- **club savings deposits** 零存整付
- **non-drawing time savings deposits** 整存整付

Travel NEWS

掌握容易拿到簽證的三個原則：有正當的
理由、有承擔旅費的經濟實力、將按時回國。

🔊 MP3 028

救急情境演練 Situation

A: Is there tourism-related information?
有旅遊相關的資料嗎？

B: I'll show it to you.
我拿給您。

A: Is this free?
這是免費的嗎？

B: Sorry, you have to purchase it.
抱歉，這需要購買。

A: How much is it?
多少錢？

B: One is 10 Canadian dollars.
一本是十元加幣。

A: It's so expensive.
好貴喔。

B: This is the official pricing.
這是公定價格。

A: What's the fastest way to go to downtown?
到市區最快的方式為何？

B: You may take the underground.
您可以搭乘地鐵。

A: Where's the nearest station around here?
離這邊最近的車站在哪裡？

B: About 2 blocks.
大概隔兩個街區。

KEY SENTENCES

關鍵句 （完→完整句・順→順口句）

5-29 ▶ 請問旅遊服務中心在哪裡？

完：Excuse me. Where can I find the tourist information center?

順：Tourist information center, please?

5-30 ▶ 請問哪裡有旅遊情報？

完：Excuse me. Where can I get some tourist information?

順：Tourist information, please?

5-31 ▶ 旅遊簡介是免費的。

完：Those tourist brochures are free.

順：They are free.(用手示意)

5-32 ▶ 不好意思，哪裡可以拿到市區地圖呢？

完：Excuse me. Where can I get a map of the city?

順：The city map, please?

5-33 ▶ 請給我一張地圖。

完：Please give me a map.

順：A map, please.

5-34 ▶ 請問有附價格和詳細說明的簡介嗎？

完：May I get a brochure with prices and details?

順：A brochure with prices and details, please?

133

5-35 ▶ 請給我一些旅館的情報好嗎？

完：May I get some information about hotels, please?

順：Hotel information, please?

5-36 ▶ 這間旅館離機場有多遠？

完：How far is this hotel from the airport?

順：How far from the airport?(用手指地圖)

5-37 ▶ 請幫我介紹火車站附近的旅館。

完：Please recommend me some hotels near the train station.

順：Hotels near train station, please?

5-38 ▶ 機場附近有旅館嗎？

完：Are there any hotels near the airport?

順：Any hotels near airport, please?

5-39 ▶ 請幫我打電話預約一間客房。

完：Please make a call and reserve a room for me.

順：Reserve a room for me, please.

5-40 ▶ 請問要怎麼去市區？

完：How do I get to the city?

順：How to go to city?

5-41 ▶ 到市區最快的方式是什麼？

完：What's the fastest way to go to downtown?

順：The fastest way to downtown, please?

5-42 ▶ 去市區最好的方式是什麼？

完：What's the best way to get downtown?

順：The best way to downtown, please? (用手指地圖)

5-43 ▶ 請問有開往城裡的巴士或地鐵嗎？

完：Is there a bus or subway into town?

順：Any bus or subway into town?

5-44 ▶ 請問到市區的公車多久來一班？

完：How often is the bus to the downtown?

順：How often?

5-45 ▶ 到市區的公車每十分鐘一班。

完：There is a bus to the downtown every 10 minutes.

順：Every 10 minutes.

5-46 ▶ 請告訴我去青年旅館的方式。

完：Please tell me how to get to the hostel.

順：How to get to the hostel, please?

5-47 ▶ 到主題樂園要搭哪一線地鐵？

完：Which subway should I take to the theme park?

順：Which subway to the theme park?

5-48 ▶ 到凱悅飯店要搭哪一路公車？

完：Which bus should I take to Hyatt Hotel?

順：Which bus to Hyatt Hotel?

5-49 ▶ 哪一路公車開往市區？

完：Which bus goes downtown?

順：Downtown bus, please?

5-50 ▶ 計程車招呼站在哪裡？

完：Where is the taxi stand?

順：Taxi stand, please?

5-51 ▶ 公車站牌在哪裡？

完：Where is the bus stop?

順：Bus stop, please?

5-52 ▶ 請問我要搭哪條線的地鐵到市中心啊？

完：Excuse me. Could you tell me which line I should take to go to the downtown?

順：Which line to downtown, please?

5-53 ▶ 下一班公車什麼時候會來？

完：When will the next bus come?

順：When is the next bus?

5-54 ▶ 搭計程車到市區要多少錢？

完：How much does it cost to go downtown by taxi?

順：How much by taxi to downtown?

5-55 ▶ 搭機場專車要多少錢？

完：How much does the airport bus cost?

順：Airport bus, how much?

5-56 ▶ 請問有沒有去希爾頓飯店的接駁車？

完：Is there any shuttle bus to Hilton Hotel?

順：Any shuttle bus to Hilton?

5-57 ▶ 我可以在這裡報名參加市區觀光嗎？

完：Can I book a city tour here?

順：Book a city tour here, OK?

5-58 ▶ 我可以在這裡給手機充電嗎？

完：May I charge my mobile phone here?

順：Charge mobile phone here, OK?

單字片語雜他命 Useful Vocabulary

❧ **map** [mæp] **n** 地圖

❧ **backpacker** [`bæk, pækɚ] **n** 背包客

❧ **tram** [træm] **n** 有軌電車

❧ **monorail** [`manə, rel] **n** 單軌電車

❧ **downtown** [, daun`taun] **n** 城市的商業區

❧ **one-day pass** 一日券

❧ **bus station** 客運車站

❧ **official pricing** 公定價格

❧ **tourist information** 旅遊情報

❧ **tourist information center** 旅遊服務中心

蒐集行前資料是背包客該做的首要功課。在此要推薦一個實用的旅遊資訊網頁，「背包客棧旅遊網」：http://www.backpackers.com.tw/forum/(臉書專頁連結：https://www.facebook.com/#!/backpackers.com.tw)。這是匯集各地背包客旅遊資訊的交流空間與論壇，你可以在此遇到許多「前輩」背包客，並能上傳旅遊心情文章與相片；如果想「揪團」自助旅行，也可貼文徵求同好，例如該站的「志工旅行」專區，非常歡迎滿腔熱血的旅人起義來歸；旅人們也會在這個空間張貼提醒公告，要全球各地的背包客注意自身安全。

「背包客棧旅遊網」除了提供方便的「網路訂房」功能外，還有「國際訂房比價」系統，以供預算斟酌。通常，背包客可以利用網路訂房功能選擇住房的地點、時間與人數，並上國際訂房比價系統進行比價，找到最優惠的落腳處。

你可以在「背包客棧旅遊網」找到網路訂房網站的連結，像是：http://zh.hotels.com/http://zh.hotels.com/，該網站提供中文化服務；若想去歐洲旅遊，則可上：http://www.venere.com/?ref=873159，該站則為英文網站。

Part. 6

住宿篇

Unit 6-1 預約訂房

Unit 6-2 登記住宿：有預約

Unit 6-3 登記住宿：未預約

Unit 6-4 詢問住宿費用

Unit 6-5 詢問房間設備

Unit 6-6 預定住宿天數

Unit 6-7 詢問飯店設施

Unit 6-8 詢問飯店設施的營業時間

Unit 6-9 寄放行李

* 「方便」筆記

MP3 029

救急情境演練 Situation

A : I want to book a room.
我要訂房。

B : What kind of room do you want to book?
請問您要什麼房型？

A : I'd like to reserve a family room for two nights.
我要預約一間家庭房，住兩晚。

B : Sorry, we only have a single room.
很抱歉，我們只剩一間單人套房了。

A : Then, we need an extra bed for our kid.
那我們要加一張床給小孩。

B : We can add a bed for you.
我們會為您加床。

A : How much to add a bed?
請問加床需要多少錢？

B : 30 USD.
加一床要美金三十元。

A : Is the breakfast included?
有附早餐嗎？

B : Yes, it is.
有的，我們有附早餐。

A : What's the earliest shuttle bus?
最早的一班接駁車是幾點？

B: At 9 a.m..
早上九點鐘。

KEY SENTENCES
關鍵句 （完 →完整句．順 →順口句）

6-01 ▶ 我想預訂兩間單人房。

完：I'd like to reserve two single rooms.

順：Two single rooms, please.

6-02 ▶ 我要預訂一月十日到十三日，一間雙人房。

完：I'd like to reserve one double room from January 10 to 13.

順：One double room from January 10 to 13, please.

6-03 ▶ 我想要一間有陽臺的房間。

完：I'd like to have a room with a balcony.

順：Room with a balcony, OK?

6-04 ▶ 我想加一張床。

完：I'd like to have one extra bed in the room.

順：One extra bed, OK?

6-05 ▶ 今晚有空房嗎？

完：Is there any room available for tonight?

順：Any room available for tonight?

6-06 ▶ 真抱歉，都客滿了。

完：I'm sorry. It's full.
順：Sorry, full.

6-07 ▶ 可以幫我介紹附近的旅館嗎？

完：Could you recommend me a hotel nearby?
順：Any hotel nearby, please?

6-08 ▶ 住一個晚上要多少錢呢？

完：How much does it cost for one night?
順：One night, how much?

6-09 ▶ 一間雙人房每晚多少錢？

完：How much is a double room for one night?
順：A double room, how much?

6-10 ▶ 有含早餐嗎？

完：Is the breakfast included?
順：With breakfast?

6-11 ▶ 你們有接駁車服務嗎？

完：Do you have a shuttle bus service?
順：Any shuttle bus service?

6-12 ▶ 我們每三十分鐘有一班接駁車開往機場。

完：The shuttle bus goes to the airport every 30 minutes.
順：Every 30 minutes.

6-13 ▶ 您大約幾點會抵達飯店？

完：When will you arrive at the hotel?

順：When to arrive?

6-14 ▶ 我大約會在晚上十一點抵達。

完：I'll arrive on / about 11:00 p.m..

順：Arrive around 11:00 p.m..

6-15 ▶ 還有什麼需要協助的嗎？

完：Is there anything else I can assist you?

順：Any other things I can do for you?

單字片語維他命 Useful Vocabulary

reserve [rɪˋzɝv] **v** 預約；預訂

cancellation [͵kænsḷˋeʃən] **n** 取消

king-size [ˋkɪŋ͵saɪz] **n** 特大的

available [əˋveləbḷ] **a** 有空的

view [vju] **n** 景觀；景色

suite [swit] **n** 套房

shuttle bus 接駁車

single room 單人房

double room 雙人房

reservation center 訂房中心

🔊)) MP3 030

救急情境演練 Situation

A : I have a reservation.
我有訂房。

B : Can you tell me the booking name?
可以告訴我訂房者的大名嗎？

A : Sam Huang.
黃山姆。

B : Sorry, we can't find this name in our booking information.
抱歉，我們的訂房資料裡找不到這個名字。

A : Rick Chen, please.
麻煩改查陳瑞克。

B : Yes, a single business room.
有的，是間單人商務客房。

A : Is this a non-smoking room? I'd like to have a non-smoking room.
請問這間是禁菸客房嗎？我想住禁煙客房。

B : I'll change it to the non-smoking room for you.
我幫您換到禁菸客房去。

A : Do you have a shuttle bus service?
你們有接駁車服務嗎？

B : Yes, we do.
有的，我們有接駁車。

B : When will you arrive at the hotel?

您幾點會抵達飯店？

A : Around 8:30 p.m..
　　大約晚上八點半。

KEY SENTENCES
關鍵句🔑 　（完 →完整句・順 →順口句）

6-16 ▸ 請問您有預約嗎？

完 : Do you have any reservation?

順 : Any reservation?

6-17 ▸ 我從臺灣預約了一間雙人房。

完 : I made a reservation for one double room from Taiwan.

順 : I reserved one double room from Taiwan.

6-18 ▸ 我在臺北預約的。

完 : I made a reservation in Taipei.

順 : Reserved in Taipei.

6-19 ▸ 我在巴黎預約的。

完 : I made a reservation in Paris.

順 : Reserved in Paris.

6-20 ▸ 我在里斯本預約的。

完 : I made a reservation in Lisbon.

順 : Reserved in Lisbon.

6-21 ▸ 我透過電話預約的。

完 : I made a reservation through telephone.

順：Through the phone.

6-22 ▶ 我透過網路預約的。

完：I made a reservation through the Internet.

順：Through the Internet.

6-23 ▶ 你們預約的名字是？

完：The reservation is under the name of?

順：What name?

6-24 ▶ 我用「Dan Dale」的名字訂了一間單人房。

完：I should have a reservation for a single room under the name "Dan Dale."

順：Reserved a single room under "Dan Dale."

6-25 ▶ 我朋友瑞塔‧泰勒幫我訂了一間附有客廳的客房。

完：My friend Rita Tailor booked a suite for me.

順：Rita Tailor booked a suite room for me.

6-26 ▶ 我用「Fanny Kim」的名字訂了一間家庭房。

完：I should have a reservation for a family room under the name "Fanny Kim."

順：Reserved a family room under "Fanny Kim."

單字片語維他命 Useful Vocabulary

- **queen-size** [`kwin ˌsaɪz] **a** 大號的
- **full-size** [`ful`saɪz] **a** 全尺寸的(比大號小)
- **rollaway** [`roləˌwe] **n** 有滾輪可收式躺椅
- **penthouse** [`pɛntˌhaus] **n** 位於頂樓的豪華客房
- **luxury room** 豪華客房
- **standard room** 標準客房
- **business room** 商務客房
- **presidential suite** 總統套房
- **suite room** 附有客廳的客房
- **non-smoking room** 禁菸客房

Paths are made by walking.

★ ★ ★ ★ ★

路是人走出來的。

MP3 031

救急情境演練 Situation

A : I'd like to have a room for two nights for today and tomorrow.
我今、明兩晚想要一個房間。

B : What kind of the room?
您需要什麼樣的房型？

A : I'd like to have a double room with twin beds.
我想要一間有兩張床的雙人房。

B : Sorry, we only have single rooms now.
很抱歉，目前只剩下單人房了。

A : Are there other rooms?
有其他房型嗎？

B : I'm sorry, there're no other rooms.
抱歉，已經沒有了。

A : Will you be fully booked next week?
你們下週會全部被訂滿嗎？

B : You can start booking now.
您現在可以預訂。

A : Well. May we change to a double room with twin beds, next weekends?
那我們可以改成下週末、一間有兩張床的雙人房嗎？

B : Sure. Please give me your passport.
可以，請給我您的護照。

A：Here you are.
給你。

B：Please fill in this form.
請填表格。

KEY SENTENCES
關鍵句 🔑 （完 →完整句 · 順 →順口句）

6-27 ▶ 我沒有預約。
完：I don't have a reservation.
順：No reservation.

6-28 ▶ 你們有空房嗎？
完：Do you have any vacant room?
順：Any vacant room?

6-29 ▶ 請問有幾位要入住？
完：How many persons will be staying in the room?
順：How many persons, please?

6-30 ▶ 我們總共三個人。
完：We are a party of three.
順：Three.

6-31 ▶ 我們總共五個人。
完：We are a party of five.
順：Five.

6-32 ▶ 如果不介意，請帶我去看房間。

完：Please show me the room, if you don't mind.

順：Can I see the room?

6-33 ▶ 請問您比較喜歡什麼樣的房間？

完：What kind of room would you prefer?

順：What room do you like?

6-34 ▶ 你有沒有大一點的房間？

完：Do you have any bigger rooms?

順：Any bigger rooms?

6-35 ▶ 我要這一間房間。

完：I'll take this room.

順：This is OK.

6-36 ▶ 我要有一對單人床的房間。

完：I'd like to have a twin-bedded room.

順：A twin-bedded room, please.

6-37 ▶ 我現在可以登記住宿了嗎？

完：Can I check in now?

順：Check in, OK?

6-38 ▶ 請填一下這份表格。

完：Please fill in this form.

順：Fill in it, please.

單字片語維他命 Useful Vocabulary

➤ **full** [ful] a 滿的

➤ **maid** [med] n 女侍

➤ **vacant** [`vekənt] a 未被佔用的

➤ **passport** [`pæs‚port] n 護照

➤ **housephone** [`haus‚fon] n 內線電話

➤ **mini-bar** [`mɪnɪ‚bar] n 迷你吧檯

➤ **family room** 家庭房

➤ **twin-bedded room** 有一對單人床的房間

➤ **Do not disturb.** 請勿打擾(告示牌)

➤ **Cleaning.** 清掃中(告示牌)

Bon Voyage!

151

🔊 MP3 032

救急情境演練 Situation

A : How much does it cost for one night?
一晚要多少錢？

B : 150 USD.
美金一百五十元。

A : My budget is 100 dollars. What would you recommend?
我的預算是一百元，你的建議是？

B : A single room is 120 USD.
一般單人房是美金一百二十元。

A : Do you have any other cheaper ones?
你有別間比較便宜的嗎？

B : This is the cheapest one.
這是最便宜的房型了。

A : Since it's not a holiday, can you give me a discount?
既然不是假日，可以給我個折扣嗎？

B : Members have a discount!
會員有優惠！

A : Then, I want to become a member.
那麼，我想成為你們的會員。

B : Please give me your ID.
請給我您的證件。

A : Here you are.
給你。

B：Please fill in this form.
請填表格。

KEY SENTENCES
關鍵句 🔑 （完 →完整句 · 順 →順口句）

6-39 ▶ 單人房的價格是多少錢？
完：How much is the rate for a single room?
順：A single room, how much?

6-40 ▶ 一間雙人房多少錢？
完：How much is a double room?
順：A double room, how much?

6-41 ▶ 一間豪華客房要多少錢？
完：How much is a luxury room?
順：A luxury room, how much?

6-42 ▶ 一晚要價美金三百七十元。
完：It costs 370 USD for one night.
順：370 USD for a night.

6-43 ▶ 一晚要價歐元90元。
完：It costs 90 Euros for one night.
順：90 Euros for a night.

6-44 ▶ 含稅和服務費嗎？
完：Does that include tax and scrvice charge?
順：Including tax and service charge?

6-45 ▶ 價錢包括稅和服務費。

完：The tax and service charge are included.

順：Including tax and service charge.

6-46 ▶ 住三晚以上房價打七五折。

完：We offer a 25% discount if you stay for more than three nights.

順：There's a 25% discount if you stay more than three nights.

6-47 ▶ 請問你要如何付費？

完：How are you going to pay?

順：How to pay?

6-48 ▶ 我要用信用卡。

完：I'd like to pay by credit card.

順：By credit card.

6-49 ▶ 我要付現金。

完：I'd like to pay in cash.

順：In cash, please.

6-50 ▶ 我可以用旅行支票支付嗎？

完：May I pay for it by traveler's check?

順：By traveler's check, OK?

單字片語維他命 Useful Vocabulary

- **budget** [`bʌdʒɪt] **n** 預算
- **provide** [prə`vaɪd] **v** 提供
- **discount** [`dɪskaʊnt] **n** 折扣
- **pay** [pe] **v** 付；支付
- **bill** [bɪl] **n** 帳單
- **sign** [saɪn] **v** 簽名
- **deposit** [dɪ`pɑzɪt] **n** 押金；訂金
- **recommend** [ˌrɛkə`mɛnd] **v** 推薦
- **dotted line** 虛線
- **service charge** 服務費

Travel NEWS

　　大幅度地蒐集旅遊資訊，再根據地圖規劃出自己想走的行程，為特別喜歡的地點預留較長時間，做好初步計劃後，可請教有經驗的旅人。

155

MP3 033

救急情境演練 Situation

A: What kind of breakfast do you offer?
你們提供什麼樣的早餐？

B: Western-style buffet.
西式自助餐。

A: What time is breakfast served?
早餐幾點供應？

B: From 7 to 10 in the morning.
從早上七點供應到十點。

A: Are these facilities free to roomers?
這些設施對房客都是免費的嗎？

B: Yes. They are free.
是的，都是免費的。

A: Could you introduce some good sightseeing spots near your hotel?
你可以介紹貴旅館附近不錯的觀光景點嗎？

B: This is the travel guide.
這是旅遊指南。

A: Is there any cable to connect the Internet in the room?
你們的房間有連接網路電纜嗎？

B: Yes, it is.
有，房裡有連接網路。

A: Is there any hair dryer in the room?
房裡有吹風機嗎？

🅱: Yes. One is in the bathroom, and another one is near the dressing table.
有，一把在浴室，一把在梳妝檯旁邊。

關鍵句 （完 →完整句・順 →順口句）

6-51 ▶ 所有房間都有空調嗎？

完: Are all the rooms air-conditioned?

順: All with air conditioner?

6-52 ▶ 房間有暖氣嗎？

完: Is there any heater in the room?

順: With heater?

6-53 ▶ 房裡有電視嗎？

完: Does the room have a TV?

順: With TV?

6-54 ▶ 房裡有吹風機嗎？

完: Is there any hair dryer in the room?

順: With hair dryer?

6-55 ▶ 可以教我使用衣櫃裡的保險箱嗎？

完: Could you tell me how to use the safe in the closet?

順: How to use the safe in the closet?

6-56 ▶ 可以教我使用床頭音響嗎？

完: Could you tell me how to use the bedside

stereo?

順：How to use the bedside stereo?

6-57 ▶ 我們可以要有海景的房間嗎？

完：Could we get a room with a view of the ocean?

順：A room with view of ocean, OK?

6-58 ▶ 我要一間有花園的房間。

完：I'd like to have a room with a garden.

順：A room with a garden, please.

6-59 ▶ 我要一間有淋浴設備的雙人房。

完：I'd like to have a double room with shower.

順：Double room with shower, please.

6-60 ▶ 我要一間有陽臺的家庭房。

完：I'd like to have a family room with a balcony.

順：A family room with a balcony, please.

6-61 ▶ 我要一間有按摩浴缸的房間。

完：I'd like to have a room with a Jacuzzi.

順：A room with a Jacuzzi, please.

6-62 ▶ 房裡有網路纜線嗎？

完：Is there any cable to connect the Internet in the room?

順：With the Internet in the room?

單字片語維他命 *Useful Vocabulary*

- **buffet** [bu`fe] **n** 自助餐
- **facility** [fə`sɪlətɪ] **n** 設施；設備
- **cable** [`kebl] **n** 電纜
- **balcony** [`bælkənɪ] **n** 陽臺
- **bathroom** [`bæθ,rum] **n** 浴室；化妝室
- **sightseeing spot** 觀光景點
- **travel guide** 旅遊導覽
- **hair dryer** 吹風機
- **dressing table** 梳妝檯
- **air conditioner** 空調

The only way out is through.

★ ★ ★ ★ ★

解決的唯一途徑是經歷。

🔊 MP3 034

救急情境演練 Situation

Ⓐ : I want to stay for a week.
我要住一週。

Ⓑ : What time to check out?
請問退房時間是？

Ⓐ : Next Friday.
下週五。

Ⓑ : We're fully booked at this weekend.
我們這個週末客滿。

Ⓐ : You mean this weekend is full?
你是說這個週末都沒有客房囉？

Ⓑ : I'm so sorry. We have no any room.
很抱歉，已經沒有了。

Ⓐ : Oh, what a pity!
喔，真可惜！

Ⓑ : If we have any room available, we will notify you.
如果我們有任何空房，會通知您。

Ⓑ : How many days are you going to stay?
請問您要住幾天？

Ⓐ : Well, I'll be staying just for two nights.
那我住兩個晚上就好了。

Ⓑ : By credit card, or in cash?
要刷卡、還是付現？

160

A : By credit card, thanks.
要刷卡，謝謝。

KEY SENTENCES
關鍵句 (完→完整句・順→順口句)

6-63 ▶ 請問您要住幾天？
完 : How many days are you going to stay?
順 : How many days?

6-64 ▶ 我會在星期日上午離開。
完 : I'm leaving on Sunday morning.
順 : Leave on Sunday morning.

6-65 ▶ 我會住兩晚。
完 : I'll be staying for two nights.
順 : Two nights.

6-66 ▶ 我打算週二一大早離開。
完 : I plan to check out early Tuesday morning.
順 : Leave on early Tuesday morning.

6-67 ▶ 我要續住兩天。
完 : I'd like to continue to stay 2 days.
順 : Stay 2 more days.

6-68 ▶ 我會住兩個星期。
完 : I'll be staying for two weeks.
順 : Two weeks.

6-69 ▶ 我會住十五天。

完：I'm going to stay for fifteen days.

順：Fifteen days.

6-70 ▶ 我會在週四下午離開。

完：I'm leaving on Thursday afternoon.

順：Leave on Thursday afternoon.

6-71 ▶ 我打算下週六傍晚離開。

完：I plan to check out next Saturday evening.

順：Leave next Saturday evening.

6-72 ▶ 我要續住到下週三。

完：I'd like to continue to next Wednesday.

順：Continue to next Wednesday.

6-73 ▶ 我要續住一週。

完：I'd like to continue to stay for a week.

順：Stay for one more week.

單字片語雜他命 Useful Vocabulary

- **weekend** [`wik`ɛnd] **n** 週末
- **notify** [`notə,faɪ] **v** 通知
- **in cash** 付現
- **by credit card** 刷卡
- **take care of** 留意
- **be fully booked** 被訂滿了
- **registration card** 住宿登記卡
- **wake-up call** 晨起通知服務
- **housekeeping section** 房務部
- **48 hour notice** 四十八小時前的訂退房通知

Travel NEWS

如果想要省下旅費，建議避開旅遊旺季出遊，最好向同一家航空公司訂機票，以便協調行程。

MP3 035

救急情境演練 Situation

A : What recreational facilities can I use?
我可以使用什麼娛樂設施呢？

B : All the facilities in the club.
俱樂部裡的所有設施。

A : Do you have a Chinese restaurant?
你們有中餐廳嗎？

B : On the 45th floor.
在45樓。

A : Are there other restaurants on the 45th floor?
45樓還有什麼餐廳？

B : There're a buffet restaurant and a steak restaurant.
還有自助餐廳和牛排館。

A : Which floor has the famous music restaurant?
那間出名的音樂餐廳在幾樓？

B : On the 22nd floor.
在22樓。

A : Where's the Japanese restaurant?
日本料亭在哪裡？

B : It's on your left side.
在您的左手邊。

A : Where's the pay phone?

公用電話在哪裡？

B：It's just around the corner.
就在轉角處。

KEY SENTENCES
關鍵句 （完→完整句・順→順口句）

6-74 ▶ 餐廳在哪裡？

完：Where's the dinning room?
順：Dinning Room, please?

6-75 ▶ 餐廳在您的右手邊。

完：The restaurant is on your right side.
順：Your right side.(用手示意)

6-76 ▶ 內線電話在哪裡？

完：Where's a housephone?
順：Housephone, please?

6-77 ▶ 緊急出口在哪裡？

完：Where's the emergency exit?
順：Emergency exit, please?

6-78 ▶ 俱樂部在幾樓？

完：Which floor is the club in this building?
順：What floor is the club?

6-79 ▶ 這裡附設的日本料亭在幾樓？

完：Which floor is the Japanese restaurant this building?

順：Where's the Japanese restaurant this building?

6-80 ▸ 健身房在哪層樓？

完：Which floor is the gym in this building?

順：What floor is the gym?

6-81 ▸ 圖書室在哪裡？

完：Where's the reading room?

順：Reading room, please?

6-82 ▸ 溫泉浴場在哪裡？

完：Where's the spa?

順：Spa, please?

6-83 ▸ 商務中心在哪裡？

完：Where's the business center?

順：Business center, please?

Take a trip down memory lane.

★ ★ ★ ★ ★

回想你所有的美好回憶。

單字片語維他命 Useful Vocabulary

- **corner** [`kɔrnɚ] **n** 角落
- **gym** [dʒɪm] **n** 健身房
- **club** [klʌb] **n** 俱樂部
- **spa** [spɑ] **n** 溫泉浴場
- **sauna** [`saʊnə] **n** 三溫暖
- **reading room** 圖書室
- **recreational facility** 娛樂設施
- **steak restaurant** 牛排館
- **pay phone** 公用電話
- **emergency exit** 逃生出口

Bon voyage!

🔊 MP3 036

救急情境演練 Situation

Ⓐ : What are the pool's opening hours?
請問游泳池的開放時間是？

Ⓑ : From 6 a.m. to 10 p.m..
從早上六點到晚上十點。

Ⓐ : Should I pay an extra charge?
需要額外費用嗎？

Ⓑ : VIP roomers don't have to pay.
貴賓級房客不用。

Ⓐ : How about other public facilities' opening hours?
其他公共設施營業時間呢？

Ⓑ : The same.
一樣。

Ⓐ : The spa is closed now?
溫泉浴場現在沒有開放嗎？

Ⓑ : Sorry, it's in maintenance now.
不好意思，目前維修中。

Ⓐ : What time do you serve breakfast?
早餐的供應時間是？

Ⓑ : The breakfast is served from 6 a.m. to 10 a.m..
從上午六點到十點供應早餐。

Ⓐ : What time does the shopping center close?
購物中心幾點打烊？

B : 12:00 a.m..
午夜十二點。

KEY SENTENCES
關鍵句 （完 →完整句 · 順 →順口句）

6-84 ▶ 什麼時候退房？
完 : When's the checkout?
順 : Checkout time, please?

6-85 ▶ 我幾點可以吃早餐？
完 : What time can I have my breakfast?
順 : Breakfast time, please?

6-86 ▶ 早餐幾點開始供應？
完 : What time do you serve breakfast?
順 : Breakfast time, please?

6-87 ▶ 早餐從上午六點到十點。
完 : The breakfast is served from 6 a.m. to 10 a.m..
順 : Breakfast time is from 6 a.m. to 10 a.m..

6-88 ▶ 咖啡廳幾點開？
完 : What time does the coffee shop open?
順 : Coffee shop hours, please?

6-89 ▶ 購物中心幾點關？
完 : What time does the shopping center close?

順：The shopping center, when does it close?

6-90 ▶ 酒吧的營業時間是晚上六點到凌晨三點。

完：The bar is served from 6 p.m. to 3 a.m..

順：The bar opens from 6 p.m. to 3 a.m..

6-91 ▶ 下午茶從下午兩點供應到五點。

完：The afternoon tea is served from 2 p.m. to 5 p.m..

順：Afternoon tea time is from 2 p.m. to 5 p.m..

6-92 ▶ 健身房目前維修中。

完：The gym is in maintenance now.

順：It's in maintenance now.

6-93 ▶ 三溫暖幾點營業？

完：What time does the sauna open?

順：The sauna's opening hours, please?

Travel NEWS

　　若想搭乘火車遊歐，可備好行程計劃，向歐鐵票務人員接洽，選擇最適合自己的票種。大多數路線可選坐夜車；搭夜車除可省去住宿費，還節省出白天的遊覽時間。

單字片語維他命 Useful Vocabulary

- **bar** [bɑr] **n** 酒吧
- **serve** [sɜv] **v** 供應
- **breakfast** [`brɛkfəst] **n** 早餐
- **lunch** [lʌntʃ] **n** 午餐
- **supper** [`sʌpə] **n** 晚餐
- **maintenance** [`mentənəns] **n** 維修;保養
- **opening hour** 開放、營業時間
- **afternoon tea** 下午茶
- **coffee shop** 咖啡店
- **shopping center** 購物中心

Travel like Ghandi, with simple clothes, open eyes and an uncluttered mind.

★　★　★　★　★

如同甘地穿著儉樸的衣著、帶著開闊的眼界以及一絲不苟的心去旅行。

171

MP3 037

救急情境演練 Situation

A：I'd like to check in luggage.
我想寄放行李。

B：How many pieces?
有多少件？

A：Three.
三件。

B：Please fill in the form.
請填表。

A：I'll come to take them about in the morning after tomorrow.
我大概後天早上回來拿。

B：Yes, I know.
好的，我知道了。

A：Is there anything else I should note?
還有其他要注意的嗎？

B：No. This is your retrieving card.
沒有了，這是您的領物牌。

A：May I park my luggage in here?
我可以把行李寄放在這裡嗎？

B：Yes, you may park it here.
可以，你可以寄放在這裡。

A：I'll come back and take it at this evening.
我大概今天傍晚回來拿。

B：OK, here is your retrieving card.
　　好的，這是您的領物牌。

關鍵句 （完 →完整句 · 順 →順口句）

6-94 ▶ 請幫我把行李送到我的房間。

完：Please take my luggage to my room.

順：Porter, please.(用手示意)

6-95 ▶ 我可以自己拿行李。

完：I can take my luggage by myself.

順：I'll take it.

6-96 ▶ 我不需要人幫忙拿行李。

完：I don't need a porter.

順：No porter.

6-97 ▶ 我可以寄放行李嗎？

完：May I park my luggage in here?

順：May I park it?

6-98 ▶ 我今晚會來拿。

完：I'll come back and take it at tonight.

順：I will take it at tonight.

6-99 ▶ 還有其他要注意的嗎？

完：Is there anything else I should note?

順：Anything else?

單字片語雜他命 Useful Vocabulary

- **porter** [`pɔrtɚ] **n** 腳夫
- **park** [pɑrk] **v** 寄放
- **locker** [`lɑkɚ] **n** 寄物櫃
- **code** [kod] **n** 密碼
- **key** [ki] **n** 鑰匙
- **token** [`tokən] **n** 代幣
- **by oneself** 獨自
- **come back** 回來
- **retrieving card** 領物牌
- **surveillance camera** 監視器

　　出門在外，總有三急，但在回應「nature call」(想上廁所的生理反應)時，可別貽笑大方囉！以下分享關於出國「方便」的心得。

　　有次參加半自助旅行團(就是既可享受跟團的方便，又可擁有個人自由時間的那種旅行團)的行程，到了英國，一路上都住青年旅館(hostel)，住起來既經濟又舒適。不過，這回同行的團員，可闖了個大禍。

　　一早，我們一行人正要集合上路，但是左等右等，就是不見導遊與某家人(由媽媽、女兒與兒子組成)，正當大家還在議論紛紛之際，導遊滿臉不高興地出現了，在大家的詢問之下，導遊說他們一家三口在忙著刷洗房間廁所的「馬桶」，並向館方道歉。

　　原來在歐洲，許多青年旅館的房間浴室內都會設置一個長形、像是馬桶的裝置，但它的實際用途並不是馬桶，而是專門讓人便後洗屁屁、或讓女性在生理期間清洗下體用的，它的排水口設計跟浴室洗手盆是一樣的，要是房客以為是馬桶而誤用的話，「歹誌就大條了」！這也難怪導遊的臉色會不好看，想必是因為沒有好好教育團員，而被館方臭罵了一頓，而這家人則要忙著刷洗、道歉了。

　　另一方面，早年我國由於下水道設備不佳，

為了防止馬桶阻塞，養成了在廁所放置垃圾筒丟棄如廁後衛生紙的習慣。但國人前往歐、美、日等地旅行時，常會發現，如廁後要將衛生紙沖入馬桶、而非丟入垃圾筒；至於廁所內設置的垃圾筒，則是用來裝無法分解的女性衛生用品等垃圾。國外的衛生紙可溶於水，沖入馬桶後容易分解。不過，紙質纖維較長的「面紙」，就不適合這麼做了。

在國內旅行，很容易找到「方便」的地方。一旦出門在外，就不一定會那麼「方便」囉！

假如在歐洲旅行，上廁所是要收費的，有些著名的觀光景點，想要「方個便」，甚至要索價一歐元！因此，建議帶些零錢在身上，以免發生想上廁所時，身上只有大鈔、找不開的窘境。在國內旅行時，偶爾還可以到速食店的廁所應應急，但國外有很多速食店的廁所是不對外開放的。因此，建議：如果有找到免費廁所，就盡量利用，像是博物館、美術館的廁所，大可放心地使用。

Part. 7

飯 店 篇

Unit 7-1 客房服務：餐飲
Unit 7-2 客房服務：送洗
Unit 7-3 客房服務：其他
Unit 7-4 飯店內的商店
Unit 7-5 住宿抱怨
Unit 7-6 留言
Unit 7-7 飯店附屬設施
Unit 7-8 使用飯店設施
Unit 7-9 改變行程
Unit 7-10 退房
＊ 青年之家筆記

🔊 MP3 038

救急情境演練 Situation

A : This is room 216. I need room service.
這裡是216號房，我需要客房服務。

B : What service do you need?
您需要什麼服務？

A : Do you have midnight snacks?
請問有提供宵夜嗎？

B : Yes, the menu is in the service manual.
有的，菜單就在服務手冊裡。

A : I want a sandwich.
我要一份三明治。

B : Do you need other food?
您還需要什麼嗎？

A : Give me a pot of apple juice, too.
我還要一壺蘋果汁。

B : We'll send them to your room after 10 minutes.
十分鐘後為您送到客房。

A : This is room 205.
這裡是205號房。

B : May I help you?
我可以為您服務嗎？

A : Please bring my breakfast at 9:00 a.m. tomorrow.
明早九點鐘請送早餐過來。

B: 9:00 a.m., OK.
　　好的，九點鐘。

關鍵句　（完 →完整句・順 →順口句）

7-01 ▶ 請問您住幾號房？
完：May I know your room number, please?
順：Room number, please?

7-02 ▶ 這裡是301號房。
完：This is room 301.
順：Room 301.

7-03 ▶ 我的房號是602。
完：My room number is 602.
順：Room 602.

7-04 ▶ 請幫我送兩杯紅茶來房間。
完：Plcasc bring me two cups of black tea to my room.
順：Two cups of black tea, please.

7-05 ▶ 要幾點送早餐到您的房間？
完：When should we bring your breakfast to your room?
順：When to bring the breakfast?

7-06 ▶ 八點請幫我送早餐來。
完：Please bring my breakfast at 8:00.

順：8:00, breakfast, please.

7-07 ▶ 我的果汁還沒送來。

完：The juice hasn't come yet.

順：The juice is late.

7-08 ▶ 我想要歐式早餐。

完：I'd like to have the continental breakfast.

順：The continental breakfast, please.

7-09 ▶ 我想要美式早餐。

完：I'd like to have the American breakfast.

順：The American breakfast, please.

7-10 ▶ 我想喝粥。

完：I'd like to have rice porridge.

順：Rice porridge, please.

Travel NEWS

　　歐洲火車站一般為開放式，有人工售票口和自動售票機，有的火車站還有淋浴間，對於背包客來說非常方便。

單字片語雜他命 Useful Vocabulary

- **pot** [pat] **n** 壺
- **sandwich** [`sændwɪtʃ] **n** 三明治
- **hamburger** [`hæmbɝgɚ] **n** 漢堡
- **rice porridge** 粥;稀飯
- **oatmeal** [`ot,mil] **n** 燕麥粥
- **cereal** [`sɪrɪəl] **n** 穀片
- **yoghurt** [`jogɚt] **n** 優格;酸乳酪
- **room number** 房號
- **midnight snack** 宵夜
- **room service** 客房服務

Bon Voyage!

🔊 MP3 039

救急情境演練 Situation

A：I have clothes to wash.
我有衣服要送洗。

B：You just put them into the laundry bag, and the room service staff will deal with it.
您只要放進洗衣袋，客房服務人員會去處理。

A：When will my laundry be OK?
我送洗的衣服什麼時候會好？

B：After 3 hours.
三個小時後。

A：I want my suits ironed.
我的西裝要燙。

B：You can also put them into the laundry bag.
您一樣放進洗衣袋即可。

A：Please handle them carefully.
麻煩小心處理。

B：OK, we'll be particularly careful.
是的，我們會特別小心。

B：May I help you?
我可以為您服務嗎？

A：When can I have the laundry done?
我的衣服何時能洗好？

B：By tonight.
今晚前可以洗好。

182

A：Thank you very much.
十分感謝你。

KEY SENTENCES
關鍵句 （完→完整句·順→順口句）

7-11▶我要送洗衣物。

完：I'd like to have laundry service.
順：Laundry service, please.

7-12▶我的西裝今晚以前可否洗好？

完：Can I get my suit cleaned by tonight?
順：Is tonight, OK?(用手示意)

7-13▶請幫我燙這件外套。

完：I'd like to get this coat pressed.
順：Press this, please. (用手示意)

7-14▶請幫我洗襯衫。

完：I'd like to get these shirts laundered.
順：Launder this, please. (用手示意)

7-15▶請問衣服什麼時候可以洗好？

完：When can I have the laundry done?
順：When will the laundry finish?

7-16▶衣服晚上八點前可以洗好嗎？

完：The laundry will be done before 8:00
p.m.?
順：Before 8:00 p.m., OK?

7-17 ▶ 我今天傍晚可以取回嗎？

完：Can I get this back this evening?
順：Is this evening, OK?

7-18 ▶ 我明天可以取回嗎？

完：Can I get this back tomorrow?
順：Tomorrow, OK?

7-19 ▶ 我希望越快越好。

完：I need this as soon as possible.
順：A.S.A.P.

7-20 ▶ 我送洗的衣服還沒送到。

完：My laundry hasn't come yet.
順：My laundry is late.

7-21 ▶ 我送洗的大衣還沒送到。

完：My overcoat hasn't come yet.
順：My overcoat is late.

單字片語維他命 Useful Vocabulary

🔖 **iron** [`aɪən] **v** 熨；燙平

🔖 **bleach** [blitʃ] **n** 漂白劑

🔖 **suits** [suts] **n** 西裝

🔖 **dress** [drɛs] **n** 洋裝；連身裙

🔖 **laundry** [`lɔndrɪ] **n** 送洗的衣服

🔖 **A.S.A.P.** 越快越好(= As Soon As Possible)

🔖 **tumble dry** 烘乾

🔖 **laundry bag** 洗衣袋

🔖 **washing liquid** 洗衣精

🔖 **washing softner** 衣物柔軟精

*A ship in a harbor is safe, but
that's not what ships are built for.*

★　★　★　★　★

船隻停泊在港灣是安全的，
但那並非建造船隻的目的。

🔊 MP3 040

救急情境演練 Situation

A：The TV is out of order.
電視壞掉了。

B：We'll send someone to repair.
我們會派人去維修。

A：Excuse me. I can't find the TV remote control.
不好意思，我找不到電視遙控器。

B：It's just on the dressing table.
就放在梳妝檯上。

A：Could you send someone to fix the faucet now? It's leaking.
可以馬上派人來修水龍頭嗎？它在漏水。

B：They're going to your room now.
他們正前往您的客房中。

A：May I postpone my checkout?
我可以延後離開時間嗎？

B：How long will you postpone?
您要延後多久時間？

A：I'd like to continue to stay 3 days.
我想續住三天。

B：But you may change the room. Is that OK for you?
不過您可能會換房間，那樣方便嗎？

A：It's all right. Which room will I change to?

不要緊，我要被換去哪一房呢？

B：To Room 562.
換到562號房。

KEY SENTENCES
關鍵句　（完→完整句・順→順口句）

7-22 ▶ 請幫我送牙刷和牙膏來。

完：Please bring me toothbrush and toothpaste.

順：Toothbrush and toothpaste, please.

7-23 ▶ 請借我一把吹風機。

完：Please borrow me a hair dryer.

順：A hair dryer, please.

7-24 ▶ 可以幫我多送條毯子來嗎？

完：Could you bring me one more blanket?

順：One more blanket, please?

7-25 ▶ 我想要一壺熱開水。

完：I would like to have a kettle of running hot water.

順：A kettle of hot water, please.

7-26 ▶ 我需要一些冰塊。

完：I need some ice.

順：Some ice, please.

7-27 ▶ 請問製冰機在哪裡？

完 : Where's the ice machine?
順 : Ice machine, please?

7-28 ▸ 明天早上請叫我起床。

完 : Please wake me up tomorrow morning.
順 : A wake-up call, please.

7-29 ▸ 請明天早上五點半叫醒我。

完 : Please wake me up at 5:30 a.m. tomorrow.
順 : A wake-up call at 5:30 a.m., please.

7-30 ▸ 請幫我設定明早七點起床。

完 : Please set up a wake-up call for me tomorrow morning at 7:00.
順 : Wake-up call at 7:00 a.m., please.

7-31 ▸ 我需要本市的地圖。

完 : I need a map for this city.
順 : A city map, please.

7-32 ▸ 請問你有當地的旅遊情報嗎？

完 : Do you have any local tourist information?
順 : Any tourist information, please?

單字片語維他命 Useful Vocabulary

- **leak** [lik] **V** 漏；滲
- **repair** [rɪˋpɛr] **V** 修理
- **faucet** [ˋfɔsɪt] **n** 水龍頭
- **heater** [ˋhitɚ] **n** 暖氣機
- **refrigerator** [rɪˋfrɪdʒəˌretɚ] **n** 冰箱
- **set up** 設定
- **remote control** 遙控器
- **air conditioner** 空調
- **ice machine** 製冰機
- **toilet articles** 盥洗用具

Travel NEWS

　　想要預訂住處，可在網路訂房系統尋找城市，選定一家旅館，輸入居住日期，網站系統會告知是否訂滿。以信用卡訂房，系統會自動扣下所訂房價的百分之十，當做床位保留訂金。

🔊 MP3 041

救急情境演練 Situation

Ⓐ: I want to change US dollars.
我要換美金。

Ⓑ: You can go to the lobby and ask the Information Desk.
您可以到大廳的服務臺詢問。

Ⓐ: May I exchange money here?
請問這裡可以兌換貨幣嗎？

Ⓑ: You can go to the next counter.
請到下一個櫃檯。

Ⓐ: What's the exchange rate today?
請問今天的匯率是？

Ⓑ: This is all the information for today.
這是今天所有的資訊。

Ⓐ: I want to change 500 US dollars, please.
麻煩你，我要換五百元美金。

Ⓑ: Please fill this form out.
請填表。

Ⓐ: I need a massage. Do you have a beauty salon?
我需要按摩，你們有美容沙龍嗎？

Ⓑ: Yes, it's on the fifth floor.
有的，在五樓。

Ⓐ: Have the duty-free shops in your hotel？
你們飯店裡有免稅商店嗎？

B：Yes, they're all on the third floor.
　　有的，都在三樓。

KEY SENTENCES
關鍵句 （完→完整句‧順→順口句）

7-33 ▶ 這裡有賣電池嗎？
完：Can I buy batteries here?
順：Batteries, please?

7-34 ▶ 有賣明信片嗎？
完：Do you have any postcards?
順：Postcards, please?

7-35 ▶ 有賣這一帶的導覽手冊嗎？
完：Do you have a guidebook for the area?
順：Guidebook, please?

7-36 ▶ 有賣本市地圖嗎？
完：Do you have a map of the city?
順：Map of the city, please?

7-37 ▶ 有賣泳衣嗎？
完：Do you have swimming suits?
順：Swimming suits, please?

7-38 ▶ 這間飯店裡有免稅商店嗎？
完：Do you have the duty-free shops in this hotel?
順：Have the duty-free shops?

7-39 ▶ 這間飯店有禮品店嗎？
完： Do you have the gift shops in this hotel?
順： Have the gift shops?

7-40 ▶ 這間飯店有珠寶店嗎？
完： Do you have the jewelry shop in this hotel?
順： Have the jewelry shop?

7-41 ▶ 這間飯店有藥局嗎？
完： Do you have the pharmacy in this hotel?
順： Have the pharmacy?

7-42 ▶ 你們有男士理髮店嗎？
完： Do you have a barbershop?
順： Any barbershops here?

7-43 ▶ 你們有鞋店嗎？
完： Do you have a shoe store?
順： Any shoe stores here?

7-44 ▶ 你們有眼鏡行嗎？
完： Do you have a glasses store?
順： Any glasses stores here?

單字片語維他命 Useful Vocabulary

- **lobby** [ˋlɑbɪ] **n** 大廳
- **film** [fɪlm] **n** 底片；膠卷
- **battery** [ˋbætərɪ] **n** 電池
- **transformer** [træns`fɔrmə] **n** 變壓器
- **charger** [ˋtʃɑrdʒə] **n** 充電器
- **massage** [mə`sɑʒ] **n** 按摩
- **masseuse** [mæ`sɜz] **n** 女按摩師
- **masseur** [mæ`sɜ] **n** 男按摩師
- **beauty salon** 美容沙龍
- **rechargeable battery** 充電式電池

MP3 042

救急情境演練 Situation

A : Do you have a time limit for hot water? The water isn't hot enough.
你們的熱水是限時供應的嗎？水不夠熱耶。

B : No, we have no time limit for hot water. We'll check it for you.
不，我們沒有限定熱水時間。我們會為您查看狀況。

A : The towels aren't clean. Could you please bring me some clean ones?
這些毛巾不乾淨，你可以再送幾條乾淨的過來嗎？

B : We'll replace your new towels.
我們馬上為您更換新毛巾。

A : People next to my door are very noisy. Could you do something to stop that?
我隔壁的房客很吵，你可以阻止他們嗎？

B : We'll handle it for you.
我們馬上為您處理。

A : I want to change the room.
我要換房間。

B : I'm sorry. Today is holiday and we're full.
不好意思，今天是假日，客滿了。

A : My key card does not work.
我的房卡壞了。

B：We'll send a technician to check it for you.
我們派一名技師去幫您查看。

A：Did anyone find my mobile phone in my room？
有人在我房裡撿到手機嗎？

B：Our cleaning ladies got one. Is this yours?
我們的清潔婦撿到一支，這是您的嗎？

KEY SENTENCES
關鍵句 （**完**→完整句・**順**→順口句）

7-45 ▶ 鎖壞了。
完：The door lock is broken.
順：The lock doesn't work.

7-46 ▶ 我被鎖在門外。
完：I'm locked out of my room.
順：I'm locked out.

7-47 ▶ 沒有熱水。
完：There's no hot water.
順：No hot water.

7-48 ▶ 我房間的檯燈壞掉了。
完：The lamp in my room is out of order.
順：The lamp doesn't work.

7-49 ▶ 我隔壁房間太吵了。
完：The room next to mine is too noisy.
順：It's too noisy.

7-50 ▶ 我房間的空調壞了。

完：The air conditioner in my room is out of function.

順：The air conditioner doesn't work.

7-51 ▶ 電視壞掉了。

完：The television does not work.

順：The television is broken.

7-52 ▶ 我的房間沒有打掃。

完：My room hasn't been cleaned.

順：Not cleaned.

7-53 ▶ 馬桶不通。

完：The toilet doesn't flush.

順：Toilet's jammed.

7-54 ▶ 有人闖入我的房間。

完：Someone broke into my room.

順：Someone intruded into my room.

7-55 ▶ 請問有沒有人在房裡拾獲我的手機？

完：Is there anyone find my mobile phone in my room?

順：Anybody got my mobile phone?

單字片語維他命 Useful Vocabulary

- **lock** [lɑk] **n** 鎖
- **towel** [`tauəl] **n** 毛巾
- **noisy** [`nɔɪzɪ] **a** 喧鬧的
- **handle** [`hændḷ] **v** 處理
- **replace** [rɪ`ples] **v** 替換；取代
- **technician** [tɛk`nɪʃən] **n** 技術人員
- **time limit** 時限
- **key card** 房卡
- **be out of function** 故障
- **cleaning lady** 清潔婦

> *Travel makes one modest. You see what a tiny place you occupy in the world.*
>
> ★ ★ ★ ★ ★
>
> 旅行使人謙恭，你會發現自己在世上所佔據的是多麼小的一塊地方。

MP3 043

救急情境演練 Situation

A : I want to leave a message.
我要留言。

B : Please tell me the message.
請留言。

A : To Room 211: Jack will be back at 10 o'clock at night.
給211號房的房客：傑克晚上十點才會回來。

B : Yes, I've noted it for you.
好的，我已為您註明。

A : I have a message for the visitor, Mr. Huang.
我有個訊息要給訪客黃先生。

B : Please give me the full name of Mr. Huang.
請給我黃先生的全名。

A : Sam Huang.
黃山姆。

B : Yes, please.
好的，請說。

A : To Sam in Room 143: Sandy will wait for him in the lobby at 11:00 a.m..
給143號房的山姆：珊迪上午十一點會在大廳等他。

B : I'll tell him for you.
我會轉告他的。

A : Is there any fax for Room 253?

有253號房的傳真嗎？

B : No.
　　沒有。

（完→完整句・順→順口句）

7-56 ▶ 有任何給我的留言嗎？

完 : Are there any messages for me?

順 : Any messages for me?

7-57 ▶ 請留言。

完 : Please tell me the messages.

順 : Message, please.

7-58 ▶ 請問112號房有沒有任何留言？

完 : Is there any message for Room 112?

順 : Any message for Room 112?

7-59 ▶ 請幫我留言給506號房的張先生。

完 : Please take a message for Mr. Chang in Room 506 for me.

順 : A message to Mr. Chang in Room 506, please.

7-60 ▶ 有沒有225號房的傳真？

完 : Is there any fax for Room 225?

順 : Any fax for Room 225?

7-61 ▶ 有沒有205號房的包裹？

完：Is there any parcel for Room 205?
順：Any parcel for Room 205?

7-62 ▶ 有沒有364號房的便條？
完：Is there any message for Room 364?
順：Any note for Room 364?

7-63 ▶ 有沒有719號房的信？
完：Is there any letter for Room 719?
順：Any letter for Room 719?

7-64 ▶ 有沒有給傑克‧林恩的留言？
完：Is there any message for Jack Lynn?
順：Any message for Jack Lynn?

單字片語維他命 Useful Vocabulary

➤ **message** [`mɛsɪdʒ] **n** 訊息；口信

➤ **fax** [fæks] **n** 傳真

➤ **note** [not] **n** 便條

➤ **telegram** [`tɛlə,græm] **n** 電報

➤ **visitor** [`vɪzɪtə] **n** 訪客

➤ **bouquet** [bu`ke] **n** 花束

➤ **notice** [`notɪs] **v** 注意

➤ **manager** [`mænɪdʒə] **n** 經理

➤ **concierge** [,kɑnsɪ`ɛrʒ] **n** 門房；旅館服務臺職員

➤ **front desk** 櫃檯

MP3 044

救急情境演練 Situation

A : Where's the business center?
商務中心在哪裡？

B : In the seventh floor, the living room.
在七樓的交誼廳。

A : Does it have computers and network?
有電腦與網路嗎？

B : Yes, you can go there and surf the Internet.
有的，您可以到那裡上網。

A : May I receive a fax there?
那裡可以接收傳真嗎？

B : Yes, there will be staffs to serve you.
可以的，那裡會有服務人員為您服務。

A : Do I need to pay for it?
需要費用嗎？

B : Business center receptionists will give you instructions.
商務中心櫃檯的服務人員會為您說明。

A : I want to receive a fax.
我要接收傳真。

B : Give me your key card, please.
請給我您的房卡。

A : How much is it?
多少錢？

B：We'll include it on your bill.
我們會記在您的帳上。

KEY SENTENCES
關鍵句 （完→完整句．順→順口句）

7-65▶ 我要發傳真。

完：I want to send a fax.
順：Fax, please.

7-66▶ 請問我要如何打國際電話到臺灣？

完：Please tell me how to make an international phone call to Taiwan?
順：How do I call back to Taiwan?

7-67▶ 請問這裡可以換外幣嗎？

完：May I exchange foreign currency here?
順：Exchange here, OK?

7-68▶ 請幫我寄這封信。

完：Please mail this letter for me.
順：Mail this, please. (用手示意)

7-69▶ 請問在哪裡可以寄包裹？

完：Where can I mail a package?
順：Where to mail?

7-70▶ 這份報告請幫我影印兩份。

完：Please make two photocopies of this report.

順：Two copies of this, please.

7-71 ▶ 請幫我把包包放到行李寄放室。

完：Please put my bags in the checkroom.

順：In the checkroom, please.(用手示意)

7-72 ▶ 請問貴重物品要放在哪裡？

完：Where can I leave my valuables?

順：Where to put my valuables?

7-73 ▶ 請問房間內有沒有保險箱？

完：Is there any safe deposit box in the room?

順：Any safe deposit box in the room?

7-74 ▶ 交誼廳在哪裡？

完：Where's the living room?

順：Living room, please?

7-75 ▶ 室內泳池在哪裡？

完：Where's the indoor swimming pool?

順：Indoor swimming pool, please?

7-76 ▶ 健康中心在哪裡？

完：Where's the health center?

順：Health center, please?

單字片語維他命 Useful Vocabulary

- **network** [ˋnɛt͵wɝk] **n** 網路
- **staff** [stæf] **n** 職員；工作人員
- **photocopy** [ˋfotə͵kɑpɪ] **n** 影本
- **checkroom** [ˋtʃɛk͵rum] **n** 行李寄放室
- **business center** 商務中心
- **living room** 交誼廳
- **foreign currency** 外幣
- **safe deposit box** 保險箱
- **surf the Internet** 上網；瀏覽網路
- **make an international phone call** 打國際電話

To travel hopefully is better than to arrive.

★ ★ ★ ★

滿懷希望地旅行比到達目的地更美好。

🔊 MP3 045

救急情境演練 Situation

Ⓐ : I want to use the sauna.
我要使用三溫暖。

Ⓑ : Please give me the key card.
請給我房卡。

Ⓐ : Here you are.
這是我的房卡。

Ⓑ : Let me register it.
我登記一下。

Ⓐ : Are there towels inside there?
請問裡面有浴巾嗎？

Ⓑ : For environmental protection, we don't provide towels.
為了環保，我們並未提供浴巾。

Ⓐ : You mean that I have to get back to my room to take the towel?
你的意思是我必須回客房拿嗎？

Ⓑ : Yes, please.
是的，麻煩您使用客房的。

Ⓐ : Excuse me. Is there a spa here?
請問這裡有溫泉浴場嗎？

Ⓑ : Yes, it's in the C building.
有的，在C館。

Ⓐ : For free?
是免費的嗎？

B : No, but we have a discount for our roomers.
不，但我們的房客有優惠。

KEY SENTENCES
關鍵句 (完→完整句・順→順口句)

7-77 ▶ 請問健身房在哪裡？

完 : Excuse me. Where's the gym?.
順 : The gym, please?

7-78 ▶ 請問韻律室在哪裡？

完 : Excuse me. Where's the aerobic room?
順 : Aerobic room, please?

7-79 ▶ 請問有三溫暖嗎？

完 : Excuse me. Is there a sauna here?
順 : Any sauna here?

7-80 ▶ 請問有溫泉浴場嗎？

完 : Excuse mc. Is there a spa here?
順 : Any spa here?

7-81 ▶ 這裡有游泳池嗎？

完 : Is there a swimming pool here?
順 : Any swimming pool here?

7-82 ▶ 飯店有男性理髮廳嗎？

完 : Does the hotel have a barbershop?
順 : Barbershop, please?

7-83 ▶ 房客可以免費使用游泳池嗎？

完：Is the pool free for the roomers?

順：Free?(用手示意)

7-84 ▶ 請問會議室在哪裡？

完：Excuse me. Where's the conference room?

順：Conference room, please?

7-85 ▶ 請問拍賣會的會議室在哪裡？

完：Excuse me. Where's the conference room for the auction?

順：Conference room for the auction, please?

單字片語維他命 Useful Vocabulary

🔻 **roomer** [ˋrumɚ] **n** 房客

🔻 **register** [ˋrɛdʒɪstɚ] **v** 登記

🔻 **auction** [ˋɔkʃən] **n** 拍賣會

🔻 **secretary** [ˋsɛkrəˌtɛrɪ] **n** 秘書

🔻 **receptionist** [rɪˋsɛpʃənɪst] **n** 接待員

🔻 **barbershop** [ˋbɑrbɚˌʃɑp] **n** 理髮店(男)

🔻 **health center** 健康中心

🔻 **swimming pool** 游泳池

🔻 **aerobic room** 韻律室

🔻 **conference room** 會議室

NotE

🔊 **MP3 046**

救急情境演練 Situation

A : I want to extend my stay.
我想要延長住宿時間。

B : How long do you want to extend?
請問要延長多久呢？

A : How much does it cost to continue staying for one day?
續住一天需要多少錢？

B : US$80 a day.
一天是八十元美金。

A : I'd like to continue to stay for 3 days.
我要續住三天。

B : I'll help you extend it for 3 days.
我來為您延期三天。

A : Please remind me to check out.
請提醒我退房時間。

B : Please rest assured that I'll remind you.
請您放心，我會提醒您的。

A : Do you have any half-day tours?
有半日遊的行程嗎？

B : What do you prefer, city tour or country tour?
你喜歡市區還是郊區的行程？

A : I'd like the city tour.
市區。

B：This is the brochure.
這是行程手冊。

KEY SENTENCES
關鍵句 （完→完整句・順→順口句）

7-86▶ 我要再多住一晚。

完：I want to stay here for one more night.

順：One more night, please.

7-87▶ 我想要提前一天離開。

完：I'd like to leave one day ahead.

順：To leave one day earlier, please.

7-88▶ 如果有人找我，請告訴他我人在咖啡廳。

完：If anyone asks for me, please tell him I'll be in the coffee shop.

順：I'll be in the coffee shop.

7-89▶ 請給我303號房的鑰匙。

完：Please give me the key for Room 303.

順：Key for Room 303, please.

7-90▶ 我把房間的鑰匙弄丟了。

完：I've lost the key of my room.

順：I have lost my kcy.

7-91▶ 請再給我一把新的房間鑰匙。

完：Please give me a new room key.

順：New room key, please.

單字片語維他命 Useful Vocabulary

- **extend** [ɪk`stɛnd] **v** 延長
- **remind** [rɪ`maɪnd] **v** 提醒
- **ahead** [ə`hɛd] **ad** 提前；事先
- **brochure** [bro`ʃur] **n** 小冊子
- **vinery** [`vaɪnərɪ] **n** 葡萄園；葡萄溫室
- **scuba-diving** [`skubə‚daɪvɪŋ] n. 水肺潛水
- **rock climbing** 攀岩
- **half-day tour** 半日遊
- **city tour** 城市遊覽
- **country tour** 郊外遊覽

Travel NEWS

「招手」在希臘意味著「下地獄」；希臘人表示告別時，是把手背朝向對方招手。

MP3 047

救急情境演練 Situation

A : This is my key, I want to check out.
這是我的鑰匙，我要退房。

B : Did you eat any food in the refrigerator?
請問您有食用冰箱的食物嗎？

A : I drank some mineral water.
我喝了礦泉水。

B : It's free.
那是免費的。

A : I made some local calls.
我打了幾通市內電話。

B : This is your phone bill.
這是您的電話費帳單。

B : In cash, or by credit card?
您要付現還是刷卡？

A : By credit card.
刷卡。

B : The credit amount of this card is full.
這張信用卡的額度已經滿了。

A : Then, I'll pay in cash.
那我要付現。

B : These are your accommodation details and receipts.
這些是您的住宿明細與收據。

A : Thank you.
承蒙您。

（完→完整句・順→順口句）

7-92 ▶ 我要退房。

完 : I'd like to check out.
順 : Check out, please.

7-93 ▶ 有拿冰箱裡的東西嗎？

完 : Have you taken anything in the fridge?
順 : Taking anything from the fridge?

7-94 ▶ 有，我喝了一瓶水。

完 : Yes, I've drunk a bottle of water.
順 : Yes, a bottle of water.

7-95 ▶ 我吃了一條巧克力棒。

完 : I've eaten a chocolate bar.
順 : A chocolate bar.

7-96 ▶ 我吃了一包洋芋片。

完 : I've eaten a package of potato chip.
順 : One package of potato chip.

7-97 ▶ 我可以寄放行李到五點嗎？

完 : May I leave my luggage here until five o'clock?
順 : Put my baggage here until five, OK?

7-98 ▶ 這是您的帳單。
完：Here's your bill.
順：It's your bill.

7-99 ▶ 這是您的收據。
完：Here's your receipt.
順：It's your receipt.

單字片語維他命 Useful Vocabulary

- receipt [rɪ`sit] n 收據
- expire [ɪk`spaɪr] v 過期
- chocolate bar 巧克力棒
- mineral water 礦泉水
- local call 市內電話
- long distance call 長途電話
- phone bill 電話費帳單
- get through 接、打通電話
- credit amount 信用額度
- accommodation details 住宿明細

　　想必享受過自助旅行的人，對前面提到的青年旅館「hostel」都不會陌生。全球已有六十六個國家成為「國際青年旅館聯盟」的會員(我國於二零零六年，在瑞士舉辦的Davos-IYHF第四十六屆年會上，成功申請成為正式會員)。青年旅館的住宿費用較為低廉，如果有辦國際青年旅館聯盟會員卡(IYHF Membership Card，International Youth Hotel Federation Membership Card)的話，更可以享有折扣優待。

　　要幾歲才能辦國際青年旅館聯盟的會員卡呢？其實是沒有年齡限制的。持有此卡的旅人，不僅可入住六千多家位於全球一百零八個國家的青年旅館，更可在旅行時「一卡在手，優惠享透透」：會員可享購買機票、搭乘巴士、纜車、渡輪或租車等交通優惠；參觀博物館和美術館等門票優惠；大啖各異國美食的餐廳優惠；參加各國當地行程的優惠；參觀名勝景點、購買紀念品的折扣等優惠。甚至盡享兌換外幣；購買旅遊保險、旅遊用品、國際電話卡；參加滑雪、登山、攀岩、溯溪等活動優惠。

　　一提到國際青年旅館，給大眾的印象就是「簡陋」。其實並非各地的青年旅館都是那樣，有些館舍設施還滿不錯的，重點在於青年旅館提供了更多與各地旅人交流的機會。

　　大多數的青年旅館一定會提供通舖，有些則以上下舖來規劃床位，一間從四人到八人不等。因此，當你需要一個床位時，就是a single bed(單人床)。如果你不習慣跟一群陌生人同住，也可以選擇a private room(單人房)、或double room(雙人房)。

　　另外，有些青年旅館還會提供家庭房(family room)，供全家出遊者投宿；有些館舍甚至提供網路連結(Internet access)、免費的炊煮設備(guest kitchen / kitchen facilities)、租車服務(car rental)、酒吧(bar)、洗衣設備(laundry facilities)；有的館舍還提供有線電視(cable TV)、冰箱(fridge)、車站或機場的接駁車(shuttle bus)服務。這樣看來，青年旅館可一點都不陽春呢！想知道更多關於青年旅館的訊息，可上財團法人中華民國國際青年之家協會的網頁：http://www.yh.org.tw/index.asp查詢。

Part. 8

異地用餐篇

Unit 8-1 詢問餐廳
Unit 8-2 預約餐廳
Unit 8-3 進入餐廳
Unit 8-4 點菜
Unit 8-5 點酒
Unit 8-6 用餐
Unit 8-7 談論菜色
Unit 8-8 餐後
Unit 8-9 速食店
＊ 飲食筆記

🔊 MP3 048

救急情境演練 Situation

A : Is there any famous restaurant here?
這裡有什麼著名的餐廳呢？

B : There's one with good Chinese food.
有間中餐館的菜還不錯。

A : Is it expensive?
貴嗎？

B : No, it's not expensive.
不會，並不貴。

A : What's the name of that restaurant?
那間餐館叫什麼名字？

B : Hong Kong Dim Sum House.
「香港茶樓」。

A : Can you take me there?
可以帶我去嗎？

B : I'm just going to bring you there.
我正想帶你去呢。

A : What kind of food do they serve?
它們有什麼菜？

B : Their "Yum Cha" is famous.
它們的「飲茶」很出名。

A : "Yum Cha" means?
「飲茶」是指？

B : You can have tea and dim sum there.

你可以在那邊享用茶和點心。

KEY SENTENCES
關鍵句🔑 （完 →完整句・順 →順口句）

8-01 ▶ 你能否推薦這附近不錯的餐廳呢？

完：Could you recommend a nice restaurant near here?

順：A nice restaurant nearby, please?

8-02 ▶ 最近的義大利餐廳在哪裡？

完：Where's the nearest Italian Restaurant?

順：The nearest Italian restaurant, please?

8-03 ▶ 這附近有好吃的墨西哥餐廳嗎？

完：Is there a good Mexican restaurant nearby?

順：A good Mexican restaurant nearby, please?

8-04 ▶ 你知道哪裡有好吃的印度餐廳嗎？

完：Do you know a good Indian restaurant?

順：A good Indian restaurant, please?

8-05 ▶ 這附近有法國餐廳嗎？

完：Is there a French restaurant nearby?

順：Any French restaurant nearby?

8-06 ▶ 這附近有中國餐廳嗎？

完：Is there a Chinese restaurant nearby?

順：Any Chinese restaurant nearby?

8-07 ▸ 這附近有咖啡廳嗎？

完：Is there a coffee shop nearby?

順：Any coffee shop nearby?

8-08 ▸ 這附近有碳烤餐廳嗎？

完：Is there a grill house nearby?

順：Any grill house nearby?

8-09 ▸ 這附近有海鮮餐廳嗎？

完：Is there a seafood restaurant nearby?

順：Any seafood restaurant nearby?

8-10 ▸ 哪裡可以吃到一些當地風味的食物？

完：Where can I have some local food?

順：Local food, please?

8-11 ▸ 你知道哪裡有比較特別的餐廳嗎？

完：Do you know where a special restaurant is?

順：Special restaurant, please?

8-12 ▸ 它們有什麼菜？

完：What kind of food do they serve?

順：What food?

單字片語維他命 Useful Vocabulary

🍃 **expensive** [ɪk`spɛnsɪv] **a** 高價的；昂貴的

🍃 **cheap** [tʃip] **a** 便宜的

🍃 **yummy** [`jʌmɪ] **n** 美味的東西

🍃 **prefer** [prɪ`fɜ] **v** 偏好…

🍃 **dim sum** 點心(粵語譯音)

🍃 **yum cha** 飲茶(粵語譯音)

🍃 **local food** 在地食物

🍃 **Italian food** 義大利菜

🍃 **Japanese food** 日本料理

🍃 **French cuisine** 法國菜

A rolling stone gathers no moss.

★　★　★　★　★

滾石不生苔。

MP3 049

救急情境演練 Situation

A : I want to book.
我要訂位。

B : How many people?
請問有幾位？

A : 4.
四個人。

B : What time?
什麼時候？

A : At 6 o'clock this evening.
今天傍晚六點。

B : Please tell me your name and phone number.
請問您的大名與電話。

A : Maggie Chen, 0938-123123.
陳瑪姬，0938-123123。

B : The booking is OK. It will be reserved for 10 minutes.
已經訂位成功，會為您保留十分鐘。

A : Do we have to wear formal dresses?
我們要穿著正式服裝嗎？

B : Yes, please.
是的，請著正式服裝。

A : Can I just order drink for kids?
小孩可以只點飲料嗎？

B : Our minimum charge is 80 dollars.
我們的最低消費額是八十元。

KEY SENTENCES
關鍵句 🔑

（完 →完整句・順 →順口句）

8-13 ▶ 請問你們幾點開始供應晚餐？

完 : When do you start to serve dinner?
順 : When is dinner?

8-14 ▶ 我們晚上五點半開始供應晚餐。

完 : We start to serve dinner at 5:30 p.m..
順 : From 5:30 p.m..

8-15 ▶ 我要訂位，傍晚六點，六個人。

完 : I'd like to book a table for six people at 6:00 in the evening.
順 : A table for six at 6:00 p.m., please.

8-16 ▶ 我要訂位，晚上八點，四個人。

完 : I'd like to book a table for four people at 8:00 in the evening.
順 : A table for four at 8:00 p.m., please.

8-17 ▶ 我要預約靠窗的桌位。

完 : I'd like to reserve a table by the window.
順 : A table by the window, please.

8-18 ▶ 抱歉，靠窗的桌位都滿了。

完 : I'm sorry. Tables by the window are all

occupied.

順：Sorry, they're occupied.

8-19 ▶ 我要預約包廂的位子。

完：I'd like to reserve a table in the room.

順：A table in the room, please.

8-20 ▶ 還有包廂的位子嗎？

完：Do you have any table in the room available?

順：Any table in the room available?

8-21 ▶ 請著正式服裝。

完：You have to wear a formal dress.

順：Formal dresses, please.

8-22 ▶ 這裡可以只點飲料嗎？

完：Can I just order a drink here?

順：Only drink, OK?

Travel is fatal to prejudice,
bigotry, and narrow-mindedness.

★ ★ ★ ★ ★

旅行可以摧毀偏見、盲從與心胸狹窄。

單字片語維他命 Useful Vocabulary

- **order** [`ɔrdə] **V** 點菜
- **book** [buk] **V** 訂位
- **booth** [buθ] **n** 包廂
- **accept** [ək`sɛpt] **V** 接受
- **vacancy** [`vekənsɪ] **n** 空位
- **dress code** 著裝標準
- **formal dress** 正式服裝
- **minimum charge** 最低消費
- **be reserved** 被訂位了
- **reservation on the phone** 電話訂位

Travel NEWS ✈

記下旅行支票的號碼，一份放在住處，一份隨身攜帶。每兌換一張，就記錄下兌換地點及金額。若支票遺失或被竊時，可及時向當地的支票兌換處報失，重新補領。

MP3 050

救急情境演練 Situation

A：I need the menu.
我需要菜單。

B：Here you are.
這是菜單。

A：Could you introduce it for me?
可以為我介紹嗎？

B：Do you want à la carte or set meal?
您要單點還是套餐？

A：What's the difference?
有何差別？

B：Set meal includes drink and dessert.
套餐有附飲料跟甜點。

A：How about the price?
價錢呢？

B：The difference of US$ 5.
相差五元美金。

A：Do you have any vegetarian food?
你們有素食餐點嗎？

B：Yes, it's on the back of the menu.
有的，在菜單背面。

A：I'd like to order a set meal of vegetarian food.
我要點一份素食套餐。

🅑 : All right.
　　好的。

KEY SENTENCES
關鍵句 🔑

（完 →完整句・順 →順口句）

8-23 ▶ 你們營業了嗎？
完 : Are you open now?
順 : Open?

8-24 ▶ 你們還有供應午餐嗎？
完 : Are you still serving lunch now?
順 : Lunch, OK?

8-25 ▶ 我們一共九個人。
完 : We are a party of nine.
順 : Nine.

8-26 ▶ 請問有五個人的位子嗎？
完 : Do you have a table for five people?
順 : A table for five?

8-27 ▶ 請問有一個人的位子嗎？
完 : Do you have a table for one person?
順 : A table for one?

8-28 ▶ 可否給我非吸菸區的位子？
完 : Could I have a table in non-smoking area?
順 : Non-smoking area, please?

8-29 ▶ 可否給我露台上的位子？

完：Could I have a table on the terrace?

順：Terrace area, please?

8-30 ▶ 請稍候，我將為您帶位。

完：Please wait. I'll guide you to your seats.

順：I'll guide you.

8-31 ▶ 我要一份商業套餐。

完：I'd like to have a business set.

順：A business set, please.

8-32 ▶ 我要一份當日午餐。

完：I'd like to have a lunch of the day.

順：A lunch of the day, please.

8-33 ▶ 我要加點一份甜點。

完：I'd like to have one more dessert.

順：One more dessert, please.

Good company in a journey makes the way to seem the shorter.

★ ★ ★ ★ ★

好旅伴似乎能使旅程縮短。

單字片語維他命 Useful Vocabulary

- **menu** [`mɛnju] **n** 菜單
- **à la carte** [ˌɑləˋkɑrt] **n** 單點
- **dessert** [dɪˋzɝt] **n** 甜點
- **price** [praɪs] **n** 價格
- **party** [`pɑrtɪ] **n** 一夥人
- **terrace** [`tɛrəs] **n** 平臺屋頂；露臺
- **share** [ʃɛr] **v** 共同享用
- **set meal** 套餐
- **business set** 商業套餐
- **lunch of the day** 當日午餐

Travel NEWS

如果旅行支票沒有用完，可到銀行換回同種貨幣的現金，但得支付手續費。

231

MP3 051

救急情境演練 Situation

A : I need the menu.
我需要菜單。

B : This is our menu.
這是本餐廳的菜單。

A : Do you have menu in French?
你們有法文菜單嗎?

B : Sorry, we only have menus in Chinese, English and Japanese.
抱歉,我們只有中、英、日文版的菜單。

A : Well, I need the menu in English.
那我要英文版的菜單。

B : Here you are.
在這裡。

A : Do you have minimum charge here?
這裡有最低消費額嗎?

B : Our minimum charge is 100 dollars.
我們的最低消費額為一百元。

A : Include the service charge?
有包含服務費嗎?

B : Yes.
有的。

A : Do you have vegetarian food?
你們有素食餐點嗎?

B : Yes, turn over the menu, please.
有的，請翻過菜單來看。

KEY SENTENCES
關鍵句 🔑 （完 →完整句・順 →順口句）

8-34 ▸ 請給我菜單好嗎？
完 : May I have a menu, please?
順 : Menu, please?

8-35 ▸ 有英文的菜單嗎？
完 : Do you have a menu in English?
順 : English menu, please?

8-36 ▸ 有中文的菜單嗎？
完 : Do you have a menu in Chinese?
順 : Chinese menu, please?

8-37 ▸ 我能點菜了嗎？
完 : Could I take the order?
順 : Order, OK?

8-38 ▸ 再多給我一枝湯匙。
完 : I'd like to have one more spoon.
順 : One more spoon, please.

8-39 ▸ 再多給我一個碗。
完 : I'd like to have one more bowl.
順 : One more bowl, please.

8-40 ▶ 我還沒決定要點什麼。

完：I haven't decided on anything yet.

順：Not ready.

8-41 ▶ 麻煩您再等一下。

完：Please wait for one more moment.

順：Please wait.

8-42 ▶ 我們要兩份主廚特餐。

完：We'd like to have two Chef's specials.

順：Two Chef's specials, please.

8-43 ▶ 我要一份今日特餐。

完：I'd like to have one of today's specials.

順：One today's specials, please.

8-44 ▶ 我的附餐要一份水牛城雞翅。

完：I'd like to have one Buffalo wings for my side order.

順：One Buffalo wings for side orders, please.

8-45 ▶ 我的附餐要一份馬鈴薯泥。

完：I'd like to have one mashed potatoes for my side order.

順：One mashed potatoes for side orders, please.

單字片語維他命 Useful Vocabulary

- **spoon** [spun] **n** 湯匙
- **napkin** [`næpkɪn] **n** 餐巾
- **include** [ɪn`klud] **v** 包括
- **ready** [`rɛdɪ] **a** 準備好的
- **valet parking** 代客泊車
- **table service** 點菜服務
- **service charge** 服務費
- **side orders** 附餐
- **today's specials** 今日特餐
- **Chef's specials** 主廚特餐

Bon voyage!

MP3 052

救急情境演練 Situation

A : What wine do you recommend?
你推薦什麼酒呢？

B : You are eating red meat. I suggest the red wine.
您吃的是紅肉，我建議配紅酒。

A : How about seafood?
那海鮮呢？

B : Then, I suggest the white wine.
那我會建議配白酒。

A : Is it X.O.?
是X.O.級(酒齡六年以上)的白蘭地嗎？

B : I'm sorry. It's V.S.O.P..
很抱歉，是V.S.O.P.級(酒齡四年以上)的。

A : Well, give me a bottle of La Rioja red wine, 1982.
那麼，給我一瓶1982年份的La Rioja紅酒好了。

B : OK. How about dessert?
好的，要點什麼甜點呢？

A : Tiramisu, please.
提拉米蘇，麻煩你。

B : Certainly.
好的。

B : Anything else?
還要來點別的嗎？

A：No, thanks. That's all.
　　不，謝了，這樣就好。

KEY SENTENCES
關鍵句 🔑

（完 →完整句・順 →順口句）

8-46 ▶ 給我酒單好嗎？
完：May I have the wine list?
順：Wine list, please?

8-47 ▶ 你們有不含酒精的飲料嗎？
完：Do you have non-alcoholic drinks?
順：Any soft drinks?

8-48 ▶ 你們有什麼餐前酒？
完：What kind of aperitif do you have?
順：What aperitif?

8-49 ▶ 有沒有當地的酒？
完：Do you have any local wine?
順：Any local wine?

8-50 ▶ 你們有沒有 **La Rioja** 紅酒？
完：Do you have any La Rioja red wine?
順：Any La Rioja red wine?

8-51 ▶ 請問有玫瑰紅酒嗎？
完：Do you have a rose?
順：Any rose?

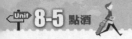
8-52 ▶ 我想點一杯紅酒。

完：I'd like to have a glass of red wine.

順：A glass of red wine, please.

8-53 ▶ 我要點一瓶紅酒。

完：I'd like to have a bottle of red wine.

順：A bottle of red wine, please.

8-54 ▶ 我要點一杯龍舌蘭酒。

完：I'd like to have a glass of tequila.

順：A glass of tequila, please.

8-55 ▶ 我要點一杯海洋微風。

完：I'd like to have a glass of Sea Breeze.

順：One Sea Breeze, please.

8-56 ▶ 我要點一杯冰涼甜心。

完：I'd like to have a Cool Sweet Heart.

順：One Cool Sweet Heart, please.

8-57 ▶ 我要點一瓶1986年份的香檳。

完：I'd like to have a bottle of champagne, 1986.

順：A bottle of champagne of 1986, please.

8-58 ▶ 你會推薦什麼酒來搭配牛排？

完：What do you recommend with the steak?

順：What's your recommendation?

8-59 ▶ 這酒是從哪裡來的？

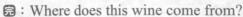
完：Where does this wine come from?

順：Where it's from?

單字片語維他命 Useful Vocabulary

🔖 **sommelier** [sɑmə`ljə] **n** 侍酒師

🔖 **dry** [draɪ] **a** 無果味的；不甜的

🔖 **aperitif** [ə,pɛrɪ`tif] **n** 開胃酒

🔖 **brandy** [`brændɪ] **n** 白蘭地酒

🔖 **tequila** [tə`kilə] **n** 龍舌蘭酒

🔖 **vodka** [`vɑdkə] **n** 伏特加酒

🔖 **wine** [waɪn] **n** 葡萄酒；水果酒

🔖 **cocktail** [`kɑk,tel] **n** 雞尾酒；調酒

🔖 **wine list** 酒單

🔖 **red wine** 紅酒

A good traveler has no fixed
plans, and is not intent on arriving.

★　★　★　★　★

好的旅人沒有固定計畫，
也不對抵達目的地過於熱切。

MP3 053

救急情境演練 Situation

A: Could you recommend something for us?
你可以為我們推薦嗎？

B: This is the recommendation by our chef.
這是我們主廚推薦的。

A: Beside this?
除了這個以外呢？

B: This appetizer is the most popular.
這道開胃菜是最多人點的。

A: What's your most famous main course?
你們最著名的主菜是什麼？

B: Beef ribs.
牛肋排。

A: Roasted?
是烤的嗎？

B: No. It's pan-fried.
不，是煎的。

A: What's the soup of the day?
今天是什麼湯？

B: Borsch.
羅宋湯。

A: What's the choice of vegetable?
有什麼青菜嗎？

B: Spinach and cabbage.
菠菜和包心菜。

KEY SENTENCES
關鍵句 (完→完整句・順→順口句)

8-60 ▸ 有什麼開胃菜？
完：What appetizers do you have?
順：What appetizers?

8-61 ▸ 今天的特餐是什麼？
完：What do you have for today's special?
順：What is today's special?

8-62 ▸ 今天有什麼湯？
完：What's the soup of the day?
順：Soup of the day, please?

8-63 ▸ 你可以為我們推薦嗎？
完：Would you recommend something?
順：Please recommend.

8-64 ▸ 麻煩你，我要點蘑菇湯和馬鈴薯沙拉。
完：I'd like to order mushroom soup and potato salad, please.
順：This and this, please.（用手指菜單）

8-65 ▸ 麻煩你，我要一份德國豬腳加酸菜。
完：I'd like one pig's knuckles with sauerkraut, please.
順：One pig's knuckles with sauerkraut, please.

8-66 ▸ 麻煩你，我要點羅宋湯。

完：I'd like to order a Borsch.
順：A Borsch, please.

8-67 ▶ 我可以把薯條換成洋蔥圈嗎？

完：Can I have onion rings instead of French fries?
順：Change French fries to onion rings, OK?

8-68 ▶ 我可以把鮭魚換成龍蝦嗎？

完：Can I have lobster instead of salmon?
順：Change salmon to lobster, OK?

8-69 ▶ 我可以把甜點改成水果嗎？

完：Can I have some fruit instead of dessert?
順：Change dessert to fruit, OK?

8-70 ▶ 這樣就可以了。

完：That's all for me.
順：That's all.

單字片語維他命 Useful Vocabulary

🔻 **salad** [`sæləd] **n** 沙拉

🔻 **appetizer** [`æpə, taɪzə] **n** 開胃菜

🔻 **pan-fried** [`pæn, fraɪd] **a** 煎的

🔻 **roasted** [`rostɪd] **a** 烤的

🔻 **Borsch** [borʃ] **n** 羅宋湯

🔻 **recommendation** [, rɛkəmɛn`deʃən] **n** 推薦

🔻 **cheddar clam soup** 巧達乳酪蛤蜊湯

🔻 **main course** 主菜

🔻 **onion soup** 洋蔥湯

🔻 **vegetable soup** 蔬菜湯

Travel NEWS ✈

　　提防旅途中的三隻手；記得將護照、較大金額鈔票放在隱藏袋裡面，建議謹慎斜背胸前。

MP3 054

救急情境演練 Situation

A: Your food looks delicious.
你的食物看起來很好吃。

B: Wanna try it?
要不要試試？

A: Yes, please give me a bit of it.
好，請給我一小塊。

B: Is it enough?
這樣夠嗎？

A: Smaller.
小一點。

B: This is delicious, too. Do you want to try this one?
這個也很好吃，你要不要試試這一個？

A: Yes, please give me a bit of it, too.
好，也請給我一小塊吧。

B: It would be much better if you add some black pepper on it.
加一點黑胡椒更美味喔。

A: Could you tell me how to eat this?
你可以告訴我這道菜要怎麼吃嗎？

B: You have to use the chopsticks.
你要用筷子夾。

A: My order hasn't come yet.
我的餐點還沒有來。

B：Let's call the waiter.
把服務生叫過來。

（完 →完整句 · 順 →順口句）

8-71 ▶ 你能告訴我怎麼吃這道菜嗎？

完：Could you tell me how to eat this?
順：How to eat this?

8-72 ▶ 給我一雙筷子好嗎？

完：May I have a pair of chopsticks?
順：Chopsticks, please?

8-73 ▶ 遞鹽巴給我好嗎？

完：Could you pass me the salt?
順：Salt, please?

8-74 ▶ 我的牛排要淋上黑胡椒醬。

完：I want the steak with black pepper gravy.
順：Black pepper gravy, please.

8-75 ▶ 牛排太生了。

完：The steak is too rare.
順：It's too rare.

8-76 ▶ 這份肉太熟了。

完：I think the meat is overdone.
順：It's overdone.

8-77 ▶ 能再給我一些麵包嗎？

完：May I have some more bread, please?

順：More bread, please?

8-78 ▶ 幫我催一下我的餐點好嗎？

完：Would you hurry up with my order?

順：Hurry up, please?

8-79 ▶ 這不是我點的東西。

完：This is not what I ordered.

順：It's not mine.

8-80 ▶ 請再給我一枝叉子。

完：Please give me one more fork.

順：An extra fork, please.

8-81 ▶ 我飽了，我要留一點胃給甜點。

完：I'm full. I want to leave some room for the dessert.

順：Enough. Leave some room for dessert.

Don't listen to what they say.
Go see.

★ ★ ★ ★ ★

別光聽人家怎麼說，出發去看看吧。

單字片語維他命 Useful Vocabulary

- **knife** [naɪf] **n** 刀
- **fork** [fɔrk] **n** 叉
- **chopsticks** [`tʃɑp, stɪks] **n** 筷子
- **gravy** [`grevɪ] **n** 肉汁
- **sauce** [sɔs] **n** 醬汁;調味醬
- **tasty** [`testɪ] **a** 可口的
- **delicious** [dɪ`lɪʃəs] **a** 美味的
- **rare** [rɛr] **a** 半熟的;很嫩的
- **well-done** [`wɛl, dʌn] **a** 全熟的
- **overdone** [, ovə`dʌn] **a** 過熟的

救急情境演練 Situation

A: Should I tip?
我要給小費嗎？

B: Yes, you have to tip in both Europe and the United States.
要，在歐美都得付小費。

A: It seems it's not necessary in Japan only.
好像只有日本不需要。

A: How much should I tip?
我應該要給多少小費啊？

B: It's about 15% to 20% of the bill in the United States and Canada.
美加這一帶，約為消費總額的百分之十五到百分之二十。

A: It's lesser than that in Taiwan.
比臺灣少吧。

B: 10% of the bill is the approved service charge in Taiwan.
臺灣是公定一成服務費。

A: By the way, Dominican Republic is the country that has the highest service charge.
順道一提，多明尼加是全球服務費最高的國家。

B: May I have the check, please?
請給我帳單好嗎？

A: Here you are.

這是您的帳單。

B : I think there's a mistake in it. We didn't order this one.
我想帳單打錯了，我們沒有點這道菜。

A : Excuse me. I'll check it for you.
抱歉，我幫您查對一下。

KEY SENTENCES
關鍵句
（完→完整句・順→順口句）

8-82 ▶ 我好飽。
完 : I'm very full.
順 : Full.

8-83 ▶ 請給我薄荷糖好嗎？
完 : Would you bring me some mints, please?
順 : Mints, please?

8-84 ▶ 請給我濕紙巾好嗎？
完 : Would you bring me some wet towels, please?
順 : Wet towels, please?

8-85 ▶ 請給我帳單好嗎？
完 : Would you show me the bill, please?
順 : Bill, please?

8-86 ▶ 我們要分開付。
完 : We'd like to pay separately.
順 : Separate, please.

8-87 ▶ 我請客。

完：It's on me.
順：My treat.

8-88 ▶ 可否再檢查一遍帳單？

完：Could you check the bill again?
順：Check the bill again, please?

8-89 ▶ 可以用美國運通卡付帳嗎？

完：May I pay with American Express?
順：American Express, OK?

8-90 ▶ 不用找零了。

完：You may keep the change.
順：Keep it.(用手示意)

單字片語維他命 Useful Vocabulary

🔖 **tip** [tɪp] **v** 給小費

🔖 **tea** [ti] **n** 茶

🔖 **mint** [mɪnt] **n** 薄荷糖

🔖 **floss** [flɔs] **n** 牙線

🔖 **toothpick** [`tuθ͵pɪk] **n** 牙籤

🔖 **mouthwash** [`mauθ͵wɑʃ] **n** 漱口水

🔖 **ashtray** [`æʃ͵tre] **n** 菸灰缸

🔖 **necessary** [`nɛsə͵sɛrɪ] **a** 必需的

🔖 **wet towel** 濕紙巾

🔖 **keep the change** 不用找零

🔊 MP3 056

救急情境演練 Situation

Ⓐ : Would you like here or to go?
請問您要內用還是外帶？

Ⓑ : To go.
我要外帶。

Ⓐ : What do you need?
您需要點些什麼？

Ⓑ : I want a family set meal.
我要一份全家福套餐。

Ⓐ : Do you want to buy a big Coke, too?
需要加購大瓶可口可樂嗎？

Ⓑ : How much money to add?
要加多少錢？

Ⓐ : US 5 dollars.
五塊錢美金。

Ⓑ : Add one more big Coke, please.
麻煩多加一瓶大瓶可口可樂。

Ⓐ : Anything else?
還要點別的嗎？

Ⓑ : No, that's all.
不用，這樣就好了。

Ⓐ : It's 95 dollars in total.
總共是九十五元。

Ⓑ : Please give me more straws.
請多給我幾根吸管。

KEY SENTENCES
關鍵句🔑

（完 →完整句・順 →順口句）

8-91 ▶ 您要點什麼？

完：What can I get for you?

順：What do you want?

8-92 ▶ 請給我二號餐。

完：Meal Number Two, please.

順：Number two, please.

8-93 ▶ 我要一份兒童餐。

完：I want a children's meal.

順：Children's meal, please.

8-94 ▶ 我要一籃炸雞和一瓶可口可樂。

完：I'll take the chicken basket and a bottle of Coke.

順：Chicken basket and Coke, please.

8-95 ▶ 我的炸雞要原味、不要辣味。

完：I want original taste, not hot one for the fried chicken.

順：Original taste, please.

8-96 ▶ 可以多給我幾包胡椒粉嗎？

完：May I have more pepper?

順：More pepper, please?

8-97 ▶ 可以多給我幾包蕃茄醬嗎？

完：May I have more ketchup?

順：More ketchup, please?

8-98 ▶ 我的五號餐少了塊炸雞。

完：A fried chicken is missing for my Meal No. 5.

順：No fried chicken for my Meal No. 5.

8-99 ▶ 我的一號餐少了一份薯條。

完：A French fries is missing for my Meal No. 1.

順：No French fries for my Meal No. 1.

單字片語維他命 Useful Vocabulary

- **straw** [strɔ] **n** 吸管
- **mayonnaise** [ˌmeəˋnez] **n** 美乃滋醬
- **ketchup** [ˋkɛtʃəp] **n** 蕃茄醬(= catchup)
- **Coke** [kok] **n** 可口可樂(= Coca-Cola)
- **French fries** 薯條
- **original taste** 原味
- **hot taste** 辣味
- **fried chicken** 炸雞
- **children's meal** 兒童餐
- **family set meal** 全家福套餐

　　出國在外,「吃」是首要的民生大計。既然來到國外,不妨放膽嘗試異國風味食物,豐富你的味覺經驗。在此分享歐洲旅遊的飲食心得。

　　歐洲的物價高,加上旅程中若想找家鄉味來解饞,荷包肯定會大失血;有時還會遇到令人大失所望的情況,因此,有許多旅歐的背包客寧願去速食店解決三餐。但各地區的價碼不同,從歐元換算回台幣其實也不便宜,為了要吃得經濟實惠,建議背包客們可以到市集或是超市購買當地食材,回青年旅社或是有附設廚房的旅館自行烹飪。以當地食材為首選的好處是新鮮、便宜,尤其是水果,只要新鮮,離好吃便八九不離十了。同時,到當地市場採買,也能夠親近當地居民的生活,這何嘗不是一種旅遊驚喜呢!

　　至於飲水方面,很多歐洲國家的水都可以生飲,對國人來說,可能會有些不習慣,若不放心或想自己泡茶來喝,可以詢問旅館是否有煮開水的服務;有些人的腸胃比較敏感,可以購買瓶裝水來喝。歐洲的水分很多種,有些水裡有氣泡,若不想喝到氣泡水,在選購時要看清楚標示,以免買錯。

Part. 9

購 物 篇

Unit 9-1 營業場所和營業時間
Unit 9-2 樓層詢問
Unit 9-3 顧客服務中心：店內服務
Unit 9-4 顧客服務中心：店內設施
Unit 9-5 詢問尺寸
Unit 9-6 詢問顏色
Unit 9-7 詢問商品
Unit 9-8 詢問店員意見
Unit 9-9 修改
Unit 9-10 詢問價格
Unit 9-11 決定購買
Unit 9-12 決定不買
Unit 9-13 詢問維修
Unit 9-14 換退貨
＊「血拼」筆記

Guide
book

MP3 057

救急情境演練 Situation

Ⓐ : When does the department store open?
請問百貨公司幾點開門？

Ⓑ : 11:00 in the morning.
早上十一點。

Ⓐ : When does it close?
幾點打烊呢？

Ⓑ : 9:00 at night.
晚上九點。

Ⓐ : How about the opening hours on holidays?
假日營業時間呢？

Ⓑ : From 10:30 a.m. to 10:00 p.m..
從早上十點半營業到晚上十點。

Ⓐ : It's quite a long opening hours.
營業時間很長嘛。

Ⓑ : That's why you can enjoy shopping fully.
所以你可以盡情地購物喔。

Ⓑ : The anniversary celebration is from Jan. 27 to Feb. 3.
週年慶是從一月二十七日到二月三日。

Ⓑ : Anything you want to buy?
你有想買的東西嗎？

Ⓐ : Perhaps a coat and a pair of boots.
可能會買大衣和靴子吧。

B : I want to buy some bottles of essence.
　　我想買幾瓶精華液。

關鍵句 🔑　（完 →完整句 · 順 →順口句）

9-01 ▶ 幾點營業？
完 : What time do you open?
順 : When to open?

9-02 ▶ 幾點打烊？
完 : What time do you close?
順 : When to close?

9-03 ▶ 營業時間是幾點？
完 : What are your opening hours?
順 : Working hours, please?

9-04 ▶ 星期日有營業嗎？
完 : Are you open on Sundays?
順 : Open on Sundays?

9-05 ▶ 假日有營業嗎？
完 : Are you open on holidays?
順 : Open on holidays?

9-06 ▶ 每天營業嗎？
完 : Are you open every day?
順 : Open every day?

9-07 ▶ 那家店在哪裡？

完：Where is that store located?

順：Where is that store?

單字片語維他命 Useful Vocabulary

- **essence** [`ɛsn̩s] **n** 精華液
- **mascara** [mæs`kærə] **n** 睫毛膏
- **blush** [blʌʃ] **n** 腮紅
- **warehouse** [`wɛr, haʊs] **n** 批發店
- **supermarket** [`supə, mɑrkɪt] **n** 超級市場
- **eye shadow** 眼影
- **lip stick** 唇膏；口紅
- **lip gloss** 唇蜜
- **shopping mall** 購物商場
- **department store** 百貨公司

Go forth on your path, as it exists only through your walking.

★ ★ ★ ★ ★

起程吧，你的旅程只存於足下。

◀》 MP3 058

救急情境演練 Situation

A : Where is the children's clothes section?
童裝部在哪裡？

B : It's on the 7th floor.
在七樓。

A : Where's the stationery?
文具部在哪裡？

B : In the merchandise area, 10th floor.
在十樓商品區。

A : Are there any special sells today?
今天有特賣會嗎？

B : There's a show of American food on the 12th floor.
十二樓有美國食品展。

A : Are there free samples?
有免費樣品嗎？

B : Sure, you can go and see it.
當然有，您可以去看看。

A : Where can I buy rings?
我能到哪裡買戒指？

B : You may go to the 6th floor, the jewelry district.
您可以到六樓的珠寶區選購。

A : Where are the sports goods?
運動用品在哪邊？

B: Just right there.
就在那兒。

KEY SENTENCES
關鍵句 （完 →完整句・順 →順口句）

9-08 ▶ 鞋子賣場在哪層樓？

完：Which floor is the shoe department on?
順：Shoe department, which floor?

9-09 ▶ 哪裡有賣化妝品？

完：Where do you sell cosmetics?
順：Cosmetics, please?

9-10 ▶ 男裝部在幾樓？

完：Which floor is men's wear department on?
順：Which floor for the men's wear department?

9-11 ▶ 運動用品在哪裡？

完：Where are the sports goods?
順：Sporting goods, please?

9-12 ▶ 文具拍賣會在哪裡？

完：Where's the stationery sale?
順：Stationery sale, please?

9-13 ▶ 我在哪裡可以買到戒指？

完：Where can I buy rings?
順：Ring section, please?

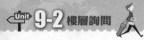

9-14 ▶ 我在哪裡可以買到這城市的地圖？

完：Where can I find the maps of this town?

順：Where to buy town maps?

單字片語維他命 *Useful Vocabulary*

◣ **stationery** [`steʃənˌɛrɪ] **n** 文具

◣ **cosmetics** [kɑz`mɛtɪks] **n** 化妝品

◣ **special sell** 特賣會

◣ **sampling activity** 試吃活動

◣ **jewelry district** 珠寶區

◣ **bedding department** 寢具部

◣ **ladies' wear department** 女裝部

◣ **men's wear department** 男裝部

◣ **children's clothes section** 童裝部

◣ **underground delicacy street** 地下美食街

Travel NEWS ✈

　　到外交部領事事務局網站查看最新的《出國旅行安全須知》：http://www.boca.gov.tw/mp?mp=1。

264

救急情境演練 Situation

A : Where can I keep my personal items?
請問哪裡可以寄放私人物品？

B : At the desk in the basement.
地下一樓服務臺。

A : Excuse me. Is there a stroller?
請問有嬰兒車嗎？

B : You can apply for it at the desk on the first floor.
可以到一樓服務臺申請。

A : I need to broadcast.
我需要廣播。

B : Please fill in this form.
請填寫單子。

A : I want to exchange parking coupon.
我要兌換停車券。

B : Please give me your receipts.
請給我您的發票。

A : Do you have any delivery service?
你們有宅配服務嗎？

B : At the desk outside the supermarket.
在超市外的那個櫃檯。

A : Where can I get this fixed?
去哪裡才能修理東西？

B：Just around the corner of the basement.
就在地下室的轉角處。

（完 →完整句・順 →順口句）

9-15 ▶ 服務臺在哪裡？
完：Where's the information counter?
順：Information counter, please?

9-16 ▶ 有宅配服務嗎？
完：Do you have delivery service?
順：Delivery service, please?

9-17 ▶ 在哪裡可以修理這個？
完：Where can I get this fixed?
順：Where to fix this?

9-18 ▶ 能告訴我哪裡有手推車嗎？
完：Can you tell me where the trolley is?
順：Trolley, please?

9-19 ▶ 哪裡可以寄放包包？
完：Where can I check my bags?
順：Where to put them?(用手示意)

9-20 ▶ 我要兌換集點券。
完：I want to exchange the reward card.
順：Exchange the reward card, please.

9-21 ▶ 我想買禮券。

完：I'd like to buy gift vouchers.

順：Gift vouchers, please.

單字片語雜他命 Useful Vocabulary

🔖 **basket** [`bæskɪt] **n** 籃子

🔖 **trolley** [`trɑlɪ] **n** 推車

🔖 **check** [tʃɛk] **v** 寄放

🔖 **broadcast** [`brɔd͵kæst] **v** 廣播

🔖 **stroller** [`strolɚ] **n** 摺疊式嬰兒車

🔖 **basement** [`besmənt] **n** 地下室

🔖 **delivery service** 宅配服務

🔖 **parking coupon** 停車券

🔖 **elevator operator** 電梯服務人員

🔖 **floor introduction** 樓層介紹

*Curiosity is the best learning tool
one can posses.*

★ ★ ★ ★ ★

人所能擁有最好的學習工具就是好奇。

救急情境演練 Situation

Ⓐ : Where's the emergency exit?
逃生門在哪裡？

Ⓑ : Beside the restroom.
在廁所旁邊。

Ⓐ : Where's the restroom?
廁所在哪裡？

Ⓑ : At the end of this corridor.
這條走道走到底。

Ⓐ : Is there a smoking area?
這裡有吸菸區嗎？

Ⓑ : Just behind the glass window.
玻璃窗後面就是。

Ⓐ : Is the non-smoking area ahead?
前面是禁菸區嗎？

Ⓑ : Yes, it's the non-smoking area.
是的，這區是禁菸區。

Ⓐ : Where's the escalator?
手扶梯在哪裡？

Ⓑ : In your right side.
在您的右手邊。

Ⓐ : Is there a restaurant in this shopping center?
這間購物中心有餐廳嗎？

Ⓑ : In the basement.
在地下一樓。

KEY SENTENCES
關鍵句🔑

（完→完整句 · 順→順口句）

9-22 ▶ 這層樓有洗手間嗎？

完：Is there a restroom on this floor?

順：Any restroom on this floor?

9-23 ▶ 這家賣場有餐廳嗎？

完：Is there a restaurant in this shopping center?

順：Any restaurant here?

9-24 ▶ 這裡有用餐的地方嗎？

完：Is there any place to eat here?

順：Any place to eat here?

9-25 ▶ 電梯在哪裡？

完：Where's the elevator?

順：Elevator, please?

9-26 ▶ 手扶梯在哪裡？

完：Where's the escalator?

順：Escalator, please?

9-27 ▶ 寄物區在哪裡？

完：Where is the storage area?

順：The storage area, please?

9-28 ▶ 兒童遊戲區在哪裡？

完：Where is the children's playground?

順：Children's playground, please?

單字片語維他命 Useful Vocabulary

🔖 **locker** [`lɑkɚ] **n** 儲物櫃

🔖 **restroom** [`rɛst‚rum] **n** 廁所

🔖 **escalator** [`ɛskə‚letɚ] **n** 電扶梯

🔖 **elevator** [`ɛlə‚vetɚ] **n** 電梯；升降機

🔖 **ATM** 自動提款機(= Automated Teller Machine)

🔖 **water dispenser** 飲水機

🔖 **nursing room** 哺乳室；育嬰室

🔖 **storage area** 寄物區

🔖 **smoking area** 吸菸區

🔖 **non-smoking area** 非吸菸區

Look at the stars lighting up
the sky: no one of them stays in the
same place.

★ ★ ★ ★

看看天空閃亮的繁星：沒有一顆是停留在
相同位置上的。

MP3 061

救急情境演練 Situation

A : Is there size L?
請問有L號的嗎？

B : Yes, it is.
有，這件就是。

A : It still seems too small.
好像還是太小了。

B : There's also size XL.
還有XL號的。

A : Do you have a larger one?
還有更大的嗎？

B : I'm sorry. This is the largest.
抱歉，這是最大的了。

A : Sorry, I'm too fat. I'll see other products.
不好意思，我太胖了，我再看看其他的商品。

B : It's OK.
沒關係。

A : Do you have any bags that are bigger than this one?
你有比這個更大的包包嗎？

B : Yes. What color do you like?
有，你喜歡什麼顏色？

A : Brown.
咖啡色。

B : Wait a second, please.
請稍候。

KEY SENTENCES
關鍵句 （完→完整句・順→順口句）

9-29 ▸ 這件毛衣有大一點的尺寸嗎？
完 : Do you have this sweater in bigger size?
順 : Bigger size?(用手示意)

9-30 ▸ 我不知道我的英吋尺寸。
完 : I don't know my size in inches.
順 : No idea in inches.

9-31 ▸ 我不曉得我的尺寸。
完 : I don't know what size I am.
順 : What's my size?

9-32 ▸ 可以幫我量一下尺寸嗎？
完 : Could you take my measurements?
順 : Measure my size, please?

9-33 ▸ 可以試穿嗎？
完 : Can I try it on?
順 : Try it, OK?

9-34 ▸ 我可以試穿褲子看合不合身嗎？
完 : May I put these pants on to see how they fit?
順 : Can I put them on?

9-35 ▶ 可否幫我量一下我的腳？

完：Could you measure my foot?

順：Measure my foot, please?

單字片語維他命 Useful Vocabulary

- **size** [saɪz] **n** 尺寸；大小
- **inch** [ɪntʃ] **n** 英吋
- **fit** [fɪt] **v** 合身
- **sleeve** [sliv] **n** 袖子
- **color** [`kʌlɚ] **n** 顏色
- **style** [staɪl] **n** 款式
- **measure** [`mɛʒɚ] **v** 測量
- **put sth. on** 試穿…
- **wait a second** 稍候
- **take sb's measurements** 幫…量尺寸

Travel NEWS

為維護自身安全，不要在機場隨意替人拿取或看顧行李、也不要幫人夾帶行李過海關，以免被捲入非法事件。

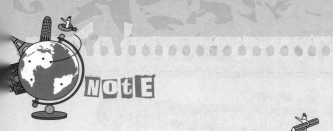

MP3 062

救急情境演練 Situation

A：Do you have this jacket in black?
請問這件夾克有黑色的嗎？

B：Yes, should I show it to you?
有的，需要拿給您看看嗎？

A：Yes, please.
好的，麻煩你。

B：This is the only one left.
只剩這件了。

A：Do you have other color?
還有其他顏色嗎？

B：There're also white and brown.
還有白色跟咖啡色。

A：Are there only 3 colors?
只有三種顏色嗎？

B：Yes, there're only 3 colors.
是的，只有三種顏色。

A：I want the black one.
我要黑色那件。

B：All right. Need anything else?
好，還需要別的嗎？

A：I need a brown belt, too.
我還要一條棕色的皮帶。

B：It's totally 850 dollars.
總共是八百五十元。

KEY SENTENCES
關鍵句

（完 →完整句・順 →順口句）

9-36 ▶ 這個有藍色的嗎？
完：Do you have this in blue?
順：Have blue ones?

9-37 ▶ 有紅色的嗎？
完：Do you have a red one?
順：Have red ones?

9-38 ▶ 有其他顏色嗎？
完：Do you have any other colors?
順：Have other colors?

9-39 ▶ 你們有白色的褲子嗎？
完：Do you have any white color pants?
順：Any white pants?

9-40 ▶ 我較喜歡暗色系。
完：I prefer dark colors.
順：Dark colors, please.

9-41 ▶ 我較喜歡亮色系。
完：I prefer light colors.
順：Light colors, please.

9-42 ▶ 我較喜歡暖色系。
完：I prefer warm colors.
順：Warm colors, please.

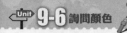

單字片語維他命 Useful Vocabulary

- **purple** [`pɝpl̩] **a** 紫色的
- **vermeil** [`vɝmɪl] **a** 朱紅色的
- **pink** [pɪŋk] **a** 粉紅色的
- **orange** [`ɔrɪndʒ] **a** 橘黃色的
- **maize** [mez] **a** 玉米黃的
- **nude** [njud] **a** 象牙黃的
- **beige** [beʒ] **a** 米色的
- **khaki** [`kɑkɪ] **a** 卡其色的;土黃色的
- **indigo** [`ɪn͵dɪɡo] **a** 靛藍色的
- **spearmint** [`spɪr͵mɪnt] **a** 松石綠的

The wise man's home is the universe.

★ ★ ★ ★ ★

智者之家座落於宇宙間。

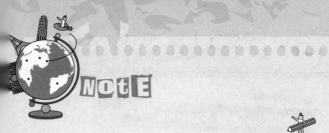

🔊 MP3 063

救急情境演練 Situation

A : Is this style of jacket still available?
請問還有這款外套嗎？

B : This is out of stock.
這已經缺貨了。

A : Is there similar one?
有類似的嗎？

B : Do you want to see this style?
您要不要看這一款？

A : Is this the new arrival of this season?
這是本季的新貨嗎？

B : This is the new product that just arrived.
這是剛到的新品。

A : Is it limited?
有限量嗎？

B : There're only 100 of them in the world.
全球只有一百件。

A : Does this jacket need dry cleaning?
這件夾克需要乾洗嗎？

B : No, it doesn't.
不，它不用乾洗。

A : Is that shirt one hundred percent cotton?
那件襯衫是純綿的嗎？

B : Yes, it is.
是，它是純綿的。

KEY SENTENCES
關鍵句 🔑

(完 →完整句・順 →順口句)

9-43 ▶ 我能看你們的目錄嗎？

完：Can I see your catalogue?

順：Catalogue, please?

9-44 ▶ 有絲巾嗎？

完：Do you have silk scarves?

順：Silk scarves, please?

9-45 ▶ 有尖領襯衫嗎？

完：Do you have a shirt with the peaked collar?

順：Peaked collar shirt, please?

9-46 ▶ 有低腰牛仔褲嗎？

完：Do you have low-waist jeans?

順：Low-waist jeans, please?

9-47 ▶ 請給我看架子上的皮包。

完：Please show me that purse on the shelf.

順：That purse, please. (用手示意)

9-48 ▶ 我能試戴這條項鍊嗎？

完：May I try the necklace on?

順：May I? (用手示意)

9-49 ▶ 這可以用洗衣機洗嗎？

完：Is it machined washable?

順：Wash by machine, OK?

單字片語維他命 Useful Vocabulary

- **catalogue** [`kætəlɔg] **n** 目錄
- **shrink** [ʃrɪŋk] **v** 縮水
- **waterproof** [`wɔtɚ, pruf] **a** 防水的
- **leather** [`lɛðɚ] **n** 皮革
- **cotton** [`katŋ] **n** 棉布
- **silk** [sɪlk] **n** 絲織品
- **linen** [`lɪnən] **n** 亞麻布
- **wool** [wʊl] **n** 羊毛織品
- **cashmere** [`kæʃmɪr] **n** 喀什米爾羊毛
- **peaked collar** 尖領

NotE

🔊 MP3 064

救急情境演練 Situation

A：Do I look good in this dress?
我穿這件洋裝好看嗎？

B：I think it's kind of old-fashioned.
我覺得有點老氣。

A：How about this shirt?
那這件襯衫呢？

B：Not bad.
還不錯。

A：I like it quite a bit.
我蠻喜歡的。

B：You can try it on.
您可以試穿看看。

A：Where can I try it on?
我可以在哪裡試穿？

B：Please go to the dressing room to try it on.
請到更衣間來試穿。

A：The sleeves are too long for me.
袖子太長了。

B：We may shorten them for you.
我們會為您改短。

A：What color would you recommend for me?
你要推薦什麼顏色給我？

B：You can choose yellow and blue ones.
您可以選黃色和藍色這兩件。

KEY SENTENCES
關鍵句 🔑

（完→完整句・順→順口句）

9-50 ▶ 看起來如何？

完：How does it look?

順：Look good?

9-51 ▶ 我可以照一下鏡子嗎？

完：May I look in a mirror?

順：Where's a mirror?

9-52 ▶ 你認為我適合什麼顏色？

完：What color would you recommend for me?

順：For me, what color is better?

9-53 ▶ 我穿這件洋裝看起來如何？

完：How does this dress look on me?

順：How is it on me?

9-54 ▶ 你建議哪一個牌子？

完：Which brand do you recommend?

順：Which is better?

9-55 ▶ 我想這個款式的裙子還會流行好幾年。

完：I think this kind of skirt will stay in fashion for a few more years.

順：It's going to be in fashion for a few more years.

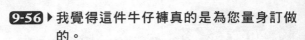
9-56 ▶ 我覺得這件牛仔褲真的是為您量身訂做的。

完：I feel like the jeans were made for you.
順：They suit you very much.

單字片語維他命 Useful Vocabulary

🔖 **old-fashioned** [`old`fæʃənd] **a** 過時的

🔖 **shorten** [`ʃɔrtn̩] **v** 縮短；改短

🔖 **sew** [so] **v** 縫製

🔖 **trousers** [`trauzəz] **n** 長褲

🔖 **brand** [brænd] **n** 商標；牌子

🔖 **slim** [slɪm] **a** 苗條的；纖細的

🔖 **waist** [west] **n** 腰；腰部

🔖 **hip** [hɪp] **n** 臀部；屁股

🔖 **thigh** [θaɪ] **n** 大腿

🔖 **crotch** [krɑtʃ] **n** 褲檔

Travel NEWS

　　萬一在旅行途中發生車禍受傷了，要立刻向當地警方報案、做筆錄，取得證明並確認肇事者身份，同時迅速通知我國駐當地的領事館或辦事處，請求協助。

MP3 065

救急情境演練 Situation

A: I want to modify the length. Is there an extra charge?
我想修改長度，需要另外收費用嗎？

B: No.
不用。

A: Can I take it today?
我今天可以拿嗎？

B: Yes. It only takes few minutes.
可以，只花一下子時間。

A: My waist is a bit wide.
我的腰圍有點寬。

B: I'll measure the waistline for you.
我為您量一下腰圍。

A: Please stitch my name on the waist.
請幫我在腰部縫上我的名字。

B: No problem. But you have to pay extra charges.
沒問題，但你必須要多付額外費用。

A: Then, how much is it?
那要多少錢？

B: 100 dollars.
一百元。

A: How long should I wait?
我需要等多久？

B：You can come to take it about 30 minutes later.

您大約三十分鐘後過來拿。

KEY SENTENCES

關鍵句 （完 →完整句 · 順 →順口句）

9-57 ▶ 你可以幫我把長度改短嗎？

完：Can you make the length shorter?

順：Make it shorter, OK?

9-58 ▶ 請幫我放長一點。

完：Could you make them a little bit longer, please?

順：A little longer, please?

9-59 ▶ 現在可以幫我改長度嗎？

完：Could you adjust the length right now?

順：Adjust it now, OK?

9-60 ▶ 可以幫我把腰圍改窄嗎？

完：Could you make the waist tighter?

順：Tighter, please?

9-61 ▶ 可否幫我放寬？

完：Could you make it wider?

順：Wider, please?

9-62 ▶ 改這個要多久時間？

完：How long will it take to do that?

順：When will it be finished?

9-63 ▶ 請幫我在袖口繡上我的名字。

完：Please stitch my name on the sleeves.

順：Stitch my name on them, please. (用手示意)

單字片語維他命 Useful Vocabulary

🔻 **wide** [waɪd] **a** 寬鬆的

🔻 **stitch** [stɪtʃ] **v** 縫紉

🔻 **modify** [ˋmɑdə͵faɪ] **v** 修改

🔻 **seam** [sim] **n** 接縫

🔻 **hem** [hɛm] **v** 鑲邊

🔻 **thimble** [ˋθɪmb!] **n** 頂針

🔻 **button** [ˋbʌtn̩] **n** 釦子

🔻 **Velcro** [ˋvɛlkro] **n** 魔鬼氈

🔻 **pincushion** [ˋpɪn͵kuʃən] **n** 針插

🔻 **tape measure** 皮尺

NotE

MP3 066

救急情境演練 Situation

A: How mush is this pair of shoes?
請問這雙鞋多少錢？

B: US 128 dollars.
美金一百二十八元。

A: Is tax-included?
含稅嗎？

B: No, tax is not included.
不，未含稅。

A: Do you have any products on sale?
有特價商品嗎？

B: These products have a discount.
這些商品有打折。

A: What's the discount rate now?
現在打幾折？

B: 30% off.
打七折。

A: May I use your gift vouchers?
我可以用你們的禮券嗎？

B: Sorry, the discount items cannot be paid by gift vouchers.
抱歉，折扣商品不能用禮券。

A: By checks?
付支票可以嗎？

B：Follow me to the counter, please.
請跟我到櫃檯。

KEY SENTENCES
關鍵句 （完 →完整句 · 順 →順口句）

9-64 ▶ 這個多少錢？
完：How much is this one?
順：How much is it? (用手示意)

9-65 ▶ 這件外套標價多少？
完：What's the price of this jacket?
順：How much is it? (用手示意)

9-66 ▶ 這個和紅色的同價嗎？
完：Is this the same price as the red one?
順：Same price as the red one? (用手示意)

9-67 ▶ 有促銷活動嗎？
完：Do you have any promotion now?
順：Any promotion?

9-68 ▶ 如果我買五個，可不可以打折？
完：If I buy five, can I have a discount?
順：Discount for five?

9-69 ▶ 我有那件商品的折價券。
完：I have coupons for that.
順：Coupons are here.

9-70 ▶ 有折扣嗎？

完：Is there any discount?

順：Any discount?

單字片語維他命 Useful Vocabulary

🖎 **price** [praɪs] **n** 價格

🖎 **discount** [`dɪskaʊnt] **n** 折扣

🖎 **promotion** [prə`moʃən] **n** 促銷

🖎 **coupon** [`kupɑn] **n** 折價券

🖎 **tax-included** [ˌtæksɪn`kludɪd] **a** 含稅的

🖎 **gift voucher** 禮券

🖎 **lucky bag** 福袋

🖎 **bar code** 條碼

🖎 **point card** 集點卡

🖎 **buy one get one free** 買一送一

Travel NEWS

　　雖然國人表示肯定時是以點頭示意，但在印度人回答問題時，若將頭歪一邊或搖頭，卻為肯定的意思，可別會錯了意。

NOtE

MP3 067

救急情境演練 Situation

A : I want this style of shirt.
我要這種款式的襯衫。

B : Do you need anything else?
還需要其他的嗎？

A : Yes, one in each color.
要，每種顏色各一件。

B : Should I wrap them together?
要包在一起嗎？

A : I want to wrap them separately.
我要分開包裝。

B : Are they gifts?
是送禮嗎？

A : Yes, please make the wrapping look better.
對，麻煩幫我包好看一點。

B : I'll wrap them prettily for you.
我會幫你包裝得很漂亮的。

A : As I want to bring it back to London, please wrap it carefully.
我要帶回倫敦，請小心包裝。

B : Certainly.
一定會的。

A : How much is it?
多少錢？

B：3,750 dollars.
　　三千七百五十元。

（完 →完整句 · 順 →順口句）

9-71 ▸ 請給我這個。

完：I'll take this, please.
順：This one, please.

9-72 ▸ 請給我五個。

完：I need five of this, please.
順：Five, please.

9-73 ▸ 請給我兩件紅色和一件黑色的毛衣。

完：I'll take two red sweaters and a black one,
　　please.
順：Two red and one black, please.

9-74 ▸ 我要送人的，請幫我包裝漂亮一點。

完：This is a gift for someone. Please make it
　　more beautiful.
順：It's a gift. Make it beautifully, please.

9-75 ▸ 我付現金。

完：I'll pay by cash.
順：By cash.

9-76 ▸ 好！成交！

完：OK! Let's shake on it!

順：OK! I'll buy it!

9-77 ▶ 好，我要買這雙靴子。

完：OK. I'll take this pair of boots.

順：OK. I'll take them.

單字片語維他命 Useful Vocabulary

🔙 **gift** [gɪft] **n** 禮物

🔙 **present** [`prɛzn̩t] **n** 贈品

🔙 **shirt** [ʃɜt] **n** 襯衫

🔙 **blouse** [blauz] **n** 女用襯衫

🔙 **sweater** [`swɛtɚ] **n** 毛線衣

🔙 **jacket** [`dʒækɪt] **n** 夾克

🔙 **jeans** [dʒinz] **n** 牛仔褲

🔙 **hat** [hæt] **n** (有邊的)帽子

🔙 **hood** [hud] **n** 風帽；兜帽

🔙 **beanie** [`binɪ] **n** 室內無邊便帽

🔊 **MP3 068**

救急情境演練 Situation

A : This is not my favorite style.
這不是我喜歡的款式。

B : You can try on this one.
您可以試穿這一款。

A : It's not suitable for me.
跟我不搭。

B : Oh, I think it's suitable for you.
喔，我覺得跟您很適合。

A : I look like kind of fat.
我看起來有點胖。

B : No, you are thin.
您太客氣了，您很瘦的。

A : It's too expensive. I'll think about it.
太貴了，我再想想。

B : There are cheaper ones here.
這裡有比較便宜的。

A : I don't like this color.
我不喜歡這種顏色。

B : How about this one?
這個怎麼樣？

B : It really fits your shoes.
這跟您的鞋真搭配。

A : I'll think it over.
我考慮一下。

9-78 ▶ 我考慮一下。

完：I'll think it over.

順：Let me think.

9-79 ▶ 不，謝謝，那不是我想要的。

完：No, thanks. That's not what I had in mind.

順：Thanks. Not what I want.

9-80 ▶ 我不喜歡這種款式。

完：I don't like this model.

順：Not this model.

9-81 ▶ 我只是看看。

完：I'm just looking.

順：Looking only.

9-82 ▶ 我還沒決定要不要買。

完：I haven't yet decided to buy it.

順：Not yet decided.

9-83 ▶ 這雙鞋我穿起來不太舒服。

完：It's uncomfortable for me to wear the shoes.

順：I didn't find them comfortable.

9-84 ▶ 我沒有太多預算。

完：I only have a low budget.

順：My budget is low.

單字片語維他命 Useful Vocabulary

- **model** [`mɑdl̩] **n** 樣式；款式
- **suitable** [`sutəbl̩] **a** 適當的
- **fat** [fæt] **a** 肥胖的
- **thin** [θɪn] **a** 瘦的
- **match** [mætʃ] **v** 搭配
- **casual** [`kæʒuəl] **n** 便服
- **favorite** [`fevərɪt] **a** 特別喜愛的
- **think about** 考慮
- **think over** 仔細考慮
- **go along with** 和…搭配

Travel NEWS

　　國人常會摸摸小朋友的頭，以表讚許，不過，緬甸人認為摸頭是一件不禮貌的事，在緬甸別隨便摸小孩的頭。

304

NotE

MP3 069

救急情境演練 Situation

A : I want the shoes fixed.
我要修鞋子。

B : This brand is out of stock.
這個廠牌已經斷貨了。

A : Can you fix them?
那可以維修嗎？

B : If you don't mind, I can fix them by other brands for you.
如果您不介意，我以其他廠牌為您維修。

A : Please fix them for me then.
那麻煩為我修理。

A : It's OK as long as they look like similar.
只要看起來相似就可以了。

B : Rest assured that I'll make you satisfied.
放心，我會做到讓您滿意。

A : There are components here.
這些是零件。

B : I'll take a look at them.
我來看一下。

B : It snapped in two.
它折成兩半了。

B : You may pay extra charges for the new components.
你可能要多花錢買新零件了。

B : Please take a rest. It'll be OK soon.
請您稍事休息，馬上好。

KEY SENTENCES

關鍵句 🔑　（完 →完整句・順 →順口句）

9-85 ▶ 這部相機壞掉了。
完 : This camera is out of function.
順 : It doesn't work.

9-86 ▶ 我要修理這個。
完 : I'd like to have this fixed.
順 : Fix this, please. (用手示意)

9-87 ▶ 我的電腦無法開機，請幫我維修。
完 : My PC cannot boot up, please fix it for me.
順 : It cannot boot up, please fix it.(用手示意)

9-88 ▶ 我的硬碟出了些問題，可以幫我救回檔案嗎？
完 : My hard drive has some problems. Can you help me recover the files?
順 : It has been changed, help me, please?

9-89 ▶ 修理費用可能會比買新的還貴。
完 : The cost of repairing may be much more than buying a new one.
順 : It's more expansive than buying a new one.

9-90 ▸ 保固期已經過了。

完：The warranty has expired.

順：It's expired.

9-91 ▸ 我們可以幫您換鞋跟。

完：We can change the heels for you.

順：It's OK to change the heels.

單字片語維他命 Useful Vocabulary

▸ **fix** [fɪks] **V** 修理

▸ **snap** [snæp] **V** 突然折斷

▸ **repair** [rɪ`pɛr] **V** 修補

▸ **adjust** [ə`dʒʌst] **V** 校準

▸ **component** [kəm`ponənt] **n** 零件

▸ **take a look** 看看；看一下

▸ **take a rest** 休息一下

▸ **make sb. satisfied** 讓…滿意

▸ **boot up** 啟動；(電腦)開機

▸ **warranty period** 保固期

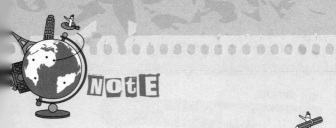

MP3 070

救急情境演練 Situation

A: This is defective.
這有瑕疵。

B: Can I have a look for you?
我幫您看看好嗎？

A: Can I exchange?
可以換貨嗎？

B: I'll check to see if there is one in stock.
我幫您查看是否有現貨。

A: If not, can I have a refund?
如果沒有，可以退貨嗎？

B: There is one, but it needs some time.
有貨，但需要一些時間。

A: How long is it?
需要多久時間？

B: It needs 3 days.
需要三天時間。

A: So long?
要等那麼久啊？

B: Excuse me. We have to order the stock from another store.
抱歉，我們要從別家店訂貨過來。

A: Well, how much is it?
那要多少錢呢？

Ⓑ：Free.
免費。

KEY SENTENCES
關鍵句🔑　（完→完整句・順→順口句）

9-92 ▶ 這不能使用。
完：This doesn't work.
順：It's dead.

9-93 ▶ 這個用一天就壞了。
完：This stopped working after one day.
順：It's worked only for one day.

9-94 ▶ 我從盒子裡拿出來時，它就已經壞掉了。
完：This was broken when I took it out of the box.
順：It's broken already.

9-95 ▶ 有一片不見了。
完：There is one piece missing.
順：One is missing.

9-96 ▶ 麻煩你，我想換另外一個。
完：I'd like to have another one, please.
順：Another one, please.

9-97 ▶ 我要換大一號的尺寸。
完：I want to change to a bigger size.
順：Bigger size, please.

9-98 ▶ 我要換小一號的尺寸。

完：I want to change to a smaller size.

順：Smaller size, please.

9-99 ▶ 麻煩你，我想退款。

完：I'd like to get a refund, please.

順：Refund, please.

單字片語維他命 Useful Vocabulary

📍 **refund** [`rɪˌfʌnd] **n** 退款金額

📍 **work** [wɜk] **v** 起作用；行得通

📍 **storage** [`storɪdʒ] **n** 庫存量

📍 **warranty** [`wɔrəntɪ] **n** 保證書

📍 **compensation** [ˌkɑmpənˋseʃən] **n** 補償

📍 **broken** [`brokən] **a** 損壞的；破碎的

📍 **defective** [dɪˋfɛktɪv] **a** 有缺陷的；不完美的

📍 **toll-free call** 免付費電話

📍 **customer service** 客戶服務

📍 **maintenance department** 維修部

背包客旅遊筆記 BON VOYAGE!

　　有些人出國就是為了要購物(shopping)。各國的購物節活動，通常會在夏天和冬天登場，各商家會打折以提高旅客買氣。

　　以下分享幾處知名的購物節活動。首先要介紹距離很近的「香港」，香港旅遊局每年都會吸引人潮到香港消費，暑假為高峰，例如二零一二年的「香港夏日盛會」，就要從六月二十二日一直展開至八月三十一日，期間各商家準備好各項優惠及超值商品等候血拼族光顧。此外，如果要買便宜又好的東西，要把握每年十一月底至聖誕節前夕最優惠的冬日購物節活動，除了各大商場打七、八不等的折扣，有些品牌甚至會下殺到五折呢！

　　而國人愛去的日本，每年夏季的七夕、盂蘭盆節時分也有大拍賣，以及冬季的新年初賣，想抽新年福袋的話，叫十萬个要錯過！

　　喜歡往歐洲跑的血拼客，則不會忘記英國一年兩次大減價的時機，除了夏季的購物節活動外，最具特色的就是從十二月二十六日到一月中，剛好在節禮日(Boxing Day)後的折扣活動，(為了要刺激消費，有點像是美國感恩節後的「黑色星期五」瘋狂採購)，各大品牌都紛紛打折，甚至會下殺到對半折扣。

　　另外，近年來，南韓積極推動的首爾購物

節也吸引許多遊客的注意,而二零一二年夏季的首爾購物節,也要在六月二十九日至七月二十九日時舉辦,想必血拼族都摩拳擦掌、蓄勢待發了吧!

許多人會專程到「outlet store」,也就是過季商品店去血拼。那兒聚集了許多過季的名牌商品,以低於正品許多的價格賣出。雖說是過季商品,但品質仍不錯,只要精挑細選,絕對可以買到物超所值的商品,讓你滿載而歸。

接著來分享與購物相關的字彙。不管到哪裡購物,消費者最在乎的就是價格了。因此,折扣(discount)是大家最關心的問題。英語中「打折」的表示方式剛好與中文相反,在中文裡講的「打八折」,在英文裡則是指減去的折扣數,因此是「20 percent off」(扣除百分之二十)。

再來要學學英語中關於拍賣(sale)的花招語。血拼族最喜歡的不外乎是on sale(拍賣)、free gift(贈品)、drawing(摸彩)、buy one get one free(買一送一)、clearance sale(清倉大拍賣)、all items under $10(所有商品十元以下)、two for fifty dollars(兩件五十元)等。這些在拍賣或促銷時常見的標語,可隨時讓消費者知道哪裡有便宜的好貨可撈,所以愛採購的你,眼睛可得擦亮一點喔!

Part. 10

觀光篇

Unit 10-1 詢問遊覽行程

Unit 10-2 詢問遊覽內容

Unit 10-3 詢問遊覽費用

Unit 10-4 旅途用餐

Unit 10-5 變更行程

＊ 生態旅遊筆記

🔊 MP3 071

救急情境演練 Situation

A: I want to join a local tour.
我要參加本地的觀光行程。

B: This is the brochure for our local tours.
這是我們本地的觀光行程手冊。

A: How much is the cost?
費用怎麼算?

B: It's US$ 120 for one day.
一天一百二十元美金。

A: What is included?
包含什麼?

B: It includes lunch, dinner and fees for transport and a tour guide.
午餐、晚餐、交通跟導遊費用。

A: Do I need to tip the tour guide?
還需要給導遊小費嗎?

B: No, it is included.
不用,已經包含在裡面了。

A: Do you have a night tour?
你們有夜間行程嗎?

B: Our "Night Market Tour" is famous.
我們的「夜市之旅」很出名。

A: How much is it?
要多少錢?

🅱 : Those who check in on our Facebook have 20% discount.

有上我們臉書打卡的旅客可以打八折。

KEY SENTENCES
關鍵句 （完 →完整句・順 →順口句）

10-01 ▶ 請問有觀光手冊嗎？

完 : Do you have a pamphlet on sightseeing?

順 : Sightseeing pamphlet, please?

10-02 ▶ 請問有半日遊嗎？

完 : Do you have any half-day tours?

順 : Any half-day tours?

10-03 ▶ 請問上午有出團嗎？

完 : Do you have a tour in the morning?

順 : Any morning tour?

10-04 ▶ 我要參加夜間行程。

完 : I'd like to join a night tour.

順 : A night tour, please.

10-05 ▶ 請問有古蹟之旅嗎？

完 : Are there any tours of historic sights?

順 : Any tours of historic sights?

10-06 ▶ 請問有遊湖之旅嗎？

完 : Do you have any lake tours?

順 : Any lake tours?

10-07 ▶ 請問有滑雪之旅嗎？

完：Do you have any ski tours?

順：Any ski tours?

10-08 ▶ 請問有潛水之旅嗎？

完：Do you have any diving tours?

順：Any diving tours?

10-09 ▶ 請問有衝浪之旅嗎？

完：Do you have any surfing tours?

順：Any surfing tours?

10-10 ▶ 有小孩喜歡的行程嗎？

完：Do you have a tour that children would enjoy?

順：Any tour for children?

10-11 ▶ 這個團會參觀什麼古蹟嗎？

完：What historical sites does the tour go?

順：What historical sites shall we visit?

10-12 ▶ 我們會去自由女神像嗎？

完：Will we visit the Statue of Liberty?

順：Will we see the Statue of Liberty?

10-13 ▶ 一日遊會提供午餐嗎？

完：Does your one-day tour include lunch?

順：Does it include lunch?

10-14 ▶ 這個城市有沒有什麼必去景點？

完：Are there any must-see places in the city?
順：Any must-see places in the city?

單字片語維他命 Useful Vocabulary

- **cost** [kɔst] **V** 花費
- **pamphlet** [`pæmflɪt] **n** 手冊；小冊子
- **tour guide** 導遊
- **camp field** 營地
- **local tour** 本地觀光團
- **optional tour** 自費行程
- **bicycle tour** 自行車之旅
- **ski tour** 滑雪之旅
- **diving tour** 潛水之旅
- **night tour** 夜間行程

Travel NEWS ✈

國人常用食指示意、或指出人來，但在馬來西亞以食指指人是一件不禮貌的事，最好以姆指來代替。

救急情境演練 Situation

A: Can you suggest some tourist attractions?
你可以建議旅遊景點嗎？

B: This is our brochure.
這是我們的手冊。

A: Can you recommend the nearest one?
可以推薦最近的地方嗎？

B: This is the nearest hot spring area.
這是最近的溫泉區。

A: Is the transport convenient?
交通方便嗎？

B: There's a bus to there.
有公車到達。

A: How about the frequency of the bus?
公車班次多嗎？

B: One every 15 minutes.
每十五分鐘一班車。

A: Is there a Chinese-speaking guide?
有會說中文的導遊嗎？

B: Yes. You have to pay an extra fee, though.
有，不過你得多付錢。

A: Where do we get the bus?
我們要去哪裡搭巴士？

B: By the City Hall.
在市政府附近搭乘。

KEY SENTENCES
關鍵句 (完→完整句・順→順口句)

10-15 ▶ 有什麼值得一看的地方嗎？

完：What do you get to see?

順：What to see?

10-16 ▶ 可以告訴我這趟行程的路線嗎？

完：Would you tell me the route of this tour?

順：What's the route?

10-17 ▶ 這趟行程中有自由活動時間嗎？

完：Do we have any free time during the tour?

順：Any free time?

10-18 ▶ 有會說中文的導遊嗎？

完：Is there a Chinese-speaking guide?

順：Any Chinese-speaking guide?

10-19 ▶ 我可以只參加這個團的第一部份嗎？

完：Can I take the first part of the tour only?

順：First part only, OK?

10-20 ▶ 這些行程有何不同？

完：What's the difference among these tours?

順：What's the difference among them?(用手示意)

10-21 ▶ 需要付導遊小費嗎？

完：Should I tip the tour guide?

321

順 : Need to tip the tour guide?

10-22 ▶ 遊樂園什麼時候開門？

完 : What time does the amusement park open?

順 : The opening time, please?

10-23 ▶ 通行券包括所有設施嗎？

完 : Does the pass include everything?

順 : Does it include all?

10-24 ▶ 那是內戰紀念碑嗎？

完 : Is that a memorial of Civil War?

順 : The memorial of Civil War?

10-25 ▶ 到了西班牙廣場會有自由活動時間嗎？

完 : Will I have free time when I get to Piazza di Spagna?

順 : Have free time at Piazza di Spagna?

10-26 ▶ 有很多適合拍照的地點嗎？

完 : Are there lots of good spots to take pictures?

順 : Good spots for photos?

單字片語雜他命 Useful Vocabulary

- **route** [rut] **n** 路線
- **suggest** [sə`dʒɛst] **v** 建議
- **transport** [`træns. pɔrt] **n** 運輸；交通
- **frequency** [`frikwənsɪ] **n** 頻率；次數
- **monument** [`mɑnjəmənt] **n** 紀念碑
- **get off** 動身
- **get on** 登上(交通工具)
- **get back** 回來
- **hot spring** 溫泉
- **tourist attraction** 旅遊景點

救急情境演練 Situation

A: Do you have any meals on special offer today?
請問今天有特惠餐點嗎？

B: This is the meal on special offer today.
這是今日特餐。

A: Is there other choice?
有其他選擇嗎？

B: You can choose A, B or C.
有A、B、C三種可以選擇。

A: What's the difference?
有什麼差別？

B: Main courses are different, others are the same.
主菜不同，其他都相同。

A: Is there service charge?
要服務費嗎？

B: It needs 5% service charge.
需要百分之五的服務費。

A: Is there any student discount?
學生有優惠嗎？

B: Excuse me. There's no discount for students.
抱歉，學生沒有優惠。

A: Is there any discount for children?
小朋友會打折嗎？

B：Yes, there's 15% discount for children.
　　有的，小朋友打八五折。

KEY SENTENCES

關鍵句　（完→完整句・順→順口句）

10-27 ▶ 兩個人要多少錢？

完：How much is it for two people?

順：How much for two?

10-28 ▶ 全包含在內嗎？

完：Is everything included?

順：All included?

10-29 ▶ 學生有折扣嗎？

完：Is there any student discount?

順：Any discount for student?

10-30 ▶ 小孩有折扣嗎？

完：Is there any discount for children?

順：Any discount for children?

10-31 ▶ 殘障者有折扣嗎？

完：Is there any discount for the handicapped?

順：Any discount for a handicapped?

10-32 ▶ 這費用包含些什麼？

完：What's included in the price?

順：What's included in it?

10-33 ▶ 含午餐嗎？

完：Is lunch included?

順：With lunch?

10-34 ▶ 含入場費嗎？

完：Are admission fees included?

順：With admission fees?

10-35 ▶ 含稅金和小費嗎？

完：Are tax and tips included?

順：With tax and tips?

10-36 ▶ 含保險費用嗎？

完：Is insurance included?

順：Including insurance?

10-37 ▶ 有包含紀念品嗎？

完：Are the souvenirs included?

順：Including the souvenirs?

10-38 ▶ 有包含證書嗎？

完：Is the certificate included?

順：Including the certificate?

10-39 ▶ 有包含機票嗎？

完：Is the flight ticket included?

順：Including the flight ticket?

10-40 ▶ 有包含材料費用嗎？

完：Are material fees included?

順：Including material fees?

單字片語雜他命 Useful Vocabulary

- **mother-to-be** [ˌmʌðətuˈbi] **n** 孕婦
- **handicapped** [ˈhændɪˌkæpt] **a** 有生理缺陷的；殘障的
- **DIY** 自己動手做(=Do It Yourself)
- **senior citizen** 銀髮族
- **admission fee** 入場費
- **profound traveling** 深度旅遊
- **meals on special offer** 特惠餐點
- **happy hour** 酒吧優惠時間
- **Ladie's Night** 淑女之夜優惠
- **Gentlemen's Night** 紳士之夜優惠

◄)) MP3 074

救急情境演練 Situation

A : I'm very hungry.
我好餓喔。

B : We're going to a restaurant.
我們現在要去餐廳。

A : What is today's lunch?
今天的午餐是什麼呢？

B : It's French cuisine.
是法國菜。

A : But I eat vegetarian food today.
可是我今天吃素耶。

B : I'll prepare it for you specially.
我會為您特別準備的。

A : May I have my food without spring onion, garlic and leek?
我的餐點可以不加蔥、蒜和韭菜嗎？

B : OK. I'll tell the chef.
好的，我會吩咐主廚

A : Neither butter, thank you.
也不要牛油，謝謝你。

B : Certainly.
沒問題。

A : You are thoughtful.
你真體貼。

B : This is what I should do.
這是我應該作的。

KEY SENTENCES
關鍵句

（**完** →完整句・**順** →順口句）

10-41 ▶ 請問午餐是幾點？

完 : Excuse me. What time is lunch?
順 : When is lunch?

10-42 ▶ 請問我們會在哪裡吃午餐？

完 : Where will we have lunch?
順 : Lunch, where?

10-43 ▶ 請問這是自費行程嗎？

完 : Is this a trip at my expense?
順 : At my expense?

10-44 ▶ 我們吃的餐點是什麼？

完 : What are the meals we are eating?
順 : What are the meals?

10-45 ▶ 我們可以自己挑選餐點嗎？

完 : Can we choose meals by ourselves?
順 : Choose meals on our own?

10-46 ▶ 我需要一份素食餐。

完 : I need a vegetarian meal.
順 : A vegetarian meal.

10-47 ▶ 我要吃早齋。

完：I'd like to have a vegetarian breakfast.

順：Vegetarian breakfast, please.

10-48 ▶ 我對蛋過敏。

完：I have an allergy to eggs.

順：I'm allergic to eggs.

10-49 ▶ 我對海鮮過敏。

完：I have an allergy to seafood.

順：I'm allergic to seafood.

10-50 ▶ 我對牛奶過敏。

完：I have an allergy to milk.

順：I'm allergic to milk.

10-51 ▶ 我對花生過敏。

完：I have an allergy to peanuts.

順：I'm allergic to peanuts.

10-52 ▶ 我對草莓過敏。

完：I have an allergy to strawberries.

順：I'm allergic to strawberries.

單字片語維他命 Useful Vocabulary

- **garlic** [`gɑrlɪk] **n** 蒜
- **leek** [lik] **n** 韭
- **butter** [`bʌtɚ] **n** 牛油
- **lard** [lɑrd] **n** 豬油
- **cuisine** [kwɪ`zin] **n** 菜餚
- **dressing** [`drɛsɪŋ] **n** 沙拉醬汁
- **thoughtful** [`θɔtfəl] **a** 體貼的；考慮周到的
- **considerate** [kən`sɪdərɪt] **a** 體諒的；體貼的
- **spring onion** 蔥
- **vegetarian dish** 素菜；齋菜

(🔊) **MP3 075**

救急情境演練 Situation

A: I'm sorry. I have to work overtime this Wednesday.
很抱歉，我這個星期三必須加班。

B: It's a shame.
真是遺憾。

A: Can we change it to some other time?
我們可以改約其他時間嗎？

B: OK.
好的。

A: I'm free this Sunday.
我週日有空。

B: So am I.
我也有空。

A: Then, we'll change the time to the noon on Sunday.
那我們改約星期天中午吧。

B: OK, see you at noon on Sunday.
好的，週日中午見。

A: Can I get a rain check on dinner?
晚餐可以延期嗎？

B: Why?
為什麼？

A: I made an appointment with my dentist.
我和牙醫有約了。

B：Hmm, that's OK.
嗯，好吧。

KEY SENTENCES
關鍵句 （完 →完整句・順 →順口句）

10-53 ▶ 我們可以改期嗎？
完：Can we change the date?
順：Change the date, OK?

10-54 ▶ 我們不能去了，可以退款嗎？
完：We can't go. Can we get a refund?
順：Refund, OK?

10-55 ▶ 我可以退票嗎？
完：Can I have a refund for this ticket?
順：Can I have a refund?

10-56 ▶ 我可更改搭機時間嗎？
完：Can I change the flight time?
順：Can I change it?

10-57 ▶ 我可以更改心理醫師的門診時間嗎？
完：Can I change the appointment with my shrink?
順：Can I change the appointment?

10-58 ▶ 我想更改會面時間。
完：I want to change the meeting time.
順：Change the meeting time, please.

10-59 ▶ 聚餐可以改到下週五嗎？

完：Can you change the meal gathering to next Friday?

順：Can you change it to next Friday?

10-60 ▶ 我們的會議延期了。

完：Our meeting has been postponed.

順：It has been postponed.

單字片語雜他命 Useful Vocabulary

🔻 **overtime** [ˋovɚˌtaɪm] **n** 加班

🔻 **shame** [ʃem] **n** 憾事；遺憾

🔻 **get a rain check** 延期另約

🔻 **make an appointment with sb.** 和⋯有約

🔻 **meal gathering** 聚餐

🔻 **team-building event** 團隊默契培養活動

🔻 **honeymoon trip** 蜜月旅行

🔻 **field trip** 校外教學

🔻 **senior trip** 畢業旅行

🔻 **rotary island travel** 環島旅行

　　「生態旅遊」(ecotourism)，是指具有環境責任感，以保育自然環境與延續當地住民福祉為最終目標的旅遊方式，是近年來的旅遊趨勢。依照我國行政院永續發展委員會《生態旅遊白皮書》的說明，在推動生態旅遊時需整合「基於自然」、「環境教育與解說」、「永續發展」、「喚起環境意識」及「利益回饋」等五個面向，才能顯現生態旅遊的精神。此外，生態旅遊通常具有以下幾項原則：

　　1. 必須採用低環境衝擊之營宿與休閒活動方式。

　　2. 必須限制到此區域之遊客量(不論是團體大小或參觀團體數目)。

　　3. 必須支持當地的自然資源與人文保育工作。

　　4. 必須儘量使用當地居民之服務與載具。

　　5. 必須提供遊客以自然體驗為旅遊重點的遊程。

　　6. 必須聘用了解當地自然文化之解說員。

　　7. 必須確保野生動植物不被干擾、環境不被破壞。

　　8. 必須尊重當地居民的傳統文化及生活隱私。

　　最近發展出的旅遊行程，不只聚焦在各地

的著名景點上，有些背包客甚至會在旅途中關心當地的自然與人文環境，而選擇參加「觀星」、「賞鳥」、「賞鯨」、「浮潛」等親近自然的行程。

為了尊重當地的居民與環境，別忘了遵守以下原則：

1. 不食用瀕危生物。雖說出國可以讓自己的味蕾冒冒險，但還是要提醒你：別觸法，才是地球好公民喔！

2. 留下足跡、而非垃圾。出外旅遊，也是國人道德被檢視的時候，別讓外國人笑我們髒啊！

3. 不討價還價。別用「凱子」心態看待當地居民的手工藝品，如果真的不滿意價錢，可以到別家購買，犯不著殺價殺得面紅耳赤、買到以後還沾沾自喜，把血拼的事情留到大賣場去做吧！

4. 尊重當地居民作息。手持相機的我們，在按下快門前，請先思考五秒鐘：如果自己是當地居民，是否真的想被拍下吃飯、甚至是洗澡等隱私呢？

5. 不拿應該留在原地的物品。有些人出國時，喜歡撿拾砂石之類的物品帶回家，如果每個旅人都這樣做的話，日後美景就不復存在了；大方點，讓每個旅人都能欣賞到這樣美麗的景觀！

Part. 11

交通篇

Unit 11-1　問路

Unit 11-2　搭計程車

Unit 11-3　搭公車

Unit 11-4　搭地鐵

Unit 11-5　搭火車

Unit 11-6　租車

Unit 11-7　加油

Unit 11-8　汽車故障

＊ 美國公路筆記

MP3 076

救急情境演練 Situation

A: Excuse me. Is there any tourist center nearby?
請問這附近有遊客中心嗎？

B: I'm sorry. I don't know.
不好意思，我不太清楚。

A: Thank you anyway.
還是謝謝你。

B: You're welcome. You can ask other pedestrians.
不客氣，你可以再問問其他的行人。

A: Is there any tourist center in this station?
這車站有遊客中心嗎？

B: In the lobby on the first floor.
在一樓大廳。

A: How to get there?
怎麼過去？

B: Take the escalator right there and go up, and then you can see it.
搭前面的手扶梯上去，你就可以看見了。

A: Is this the counter of tourist center?
這是遊客中心的櫃檯嗎？

B: No. It's on your left.
不，它在你的左手邊。

A: Thank you.

謝謝你。

B：Any time.
不客氣。

關鍵句 （完→完整句・順→順口句）

11-01 ▶ 附近有百貨公司嗎？

完：Is there a department store nearby?
順：Any department store nearby?

11-02 ▶ 附近有醫院嗎？

完：Is there a hospital in the area?
順：Any hospital here?

11-03 ▶ 最近的地鐵站在哪裡？

完：Where's the closest subway station?
順：The closest subway station, please?

11-04 ▶ 它是在紅綠燈的這邊嗎？

完：Is it on this side of the traffic light?
順：This side?(用手示意)

11-05 ▶ 這是去華盛頓廣場正確的方向嗎？

完：Is this the right direction for Washington Square?
順：This way to Washington Square?

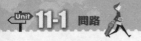

單字片語雜他命 Useful Vocabulary

- **pedestrian** [pə`dɛstrɪən] **n** 行人
- **museum** [mju`zɪəm] **n** 博物館
- **station** [`steʃən] **n** 車站
- **stadium** [`stedɪəm] **n** 體育館；運動場
- **plaza** [`plæzə] **n** 步行區
- **square** [skwɛr] **n** 廣場
- **landmark** [`lænd‚mɑrk] **n** 地標
- **fountain** [`fauntn̩] **n** 噴泉
- **statue** [`stætʃu] **n** 雕像
- **shopping street** 商店街

 MP3 077

救急情境演練 Situation

A: How far is it to Times Square?
請問到時代廣場有多遠？

B: Quite a distance.
有點距離喔。

A: How can I get there?
請問我要怎麼過去呢？

B: By bus.
搭公車。

A: How long does it take?
要花多久時間？

B: About 10 minutes.
大約十分鐘。

A : Where should I take it?
　　我要去哪裡搭乘呢？

B : The bus stop is right there.
　　公車站牌就在那兒。

A : To which station?
　　是到哪一站？

B : Time Square.
　　時代廣場站。

A : Thank you very much.
　　很謝謝你。

B : Don't mention it.
　　不客氣。

KEY SENTENCES

關鍵句 **🔑** (完 →完整句・順 →順口句)

11-06 ▶ 走路可以到嗎？
完 : Can I walk there?
順 : On foot, OK?

11-07 ▶ 多遠呢？
完 : How far is it?
順 : How far?

11-08 ▶ 中央車站離這裡遠嗎？
完 : Is there Central Station far from here?
順 : Central Station far away?

11-09 ▶ 走到公園要多久？

完：How long will it take to walk to the park?
順：How long to the park?

11-10 ▶ 到百貨公司還有幾段？

完：About how many blocks is it to the department store?

順：How many blocks to the department store?

單字片語維他命 Useful Vocabulary

❥ **distance** [`dɪstəns] **n** 距離

❥ **block** [blɑk] **n** 街區；段

❥ **lane** [len] **n** 巷

❥ **alley** [`ælɪ] **n** 弄

❥ **hitchhike** [`hɪtʃ,haɪk] **n** 搭便車旅行

❥ **on foot** 步行

❥ **traffic circle** 圓環

❥ **hitch a ride** 搭便車

❥ **thumb a lift** 要求搭便車

❥ **show sb. along the way** 順路帶⋯過去

🔊 **MP3 078**

救急情境演練 Situation

A：Excuse me, I'm lost.
　　不好意思，我迷路了。

B：Please tell me where you want to go?
請告訴我你要去哪？

A：Could you tell me how to get to Ritz Hotel?
能告訴我怎麼到麗池飯店嗎？

B：It's very easy. Take this way and you'll get there.
很簡單，走這條路就會到了。

A：How far?
要走多遠？

B：Go straight until you hit the first traffic light.
直走，到你遇見第一個紅綠燈為止。

B：I'll lead you the way, follow me!
我帶你去吧，跟我走！

A：Thank you. You're so kind.
謝謝，您人真好。

B：Cross the street, and you can see Ritz Hotel.
穿過街口，你就可以看到麗池飯店了。

A：Ah, I'm appreciative of your help!
啊，真感謝您的幫助！

B：You're welcome.
不用客氣。

A：Good bye!
再見！

KEY SENTENCES
關鍵句 🔑
(完→完整句 · 順→順口句)

11-11 ▸ 請問迪士尼樂園怎麼去？

完：How do I get to Disney World?

順：Disney World, please?

11-12 ▸ 請問去尼斯最好的方式是什麼？

完：What's the best way to get to Nice?

順：Best way to Nice, please?

11-13 ▸ 請問去達拉斯的交流道出口在哪裡？

完：Where's the turnoff for Dallas?

順：Dallas' turnoff, please?(用手指地圖)

11-14 ▸ 請問這是98號公路嗎？

完：Is this Route 98?

順：Route 98?(用手指地圖)

11-15 ▸ 請問這條路是去舊金山嗎？

完：Does this road go to San Francisco?

順：To San Francisco?(用手指地圖)

344

單字片語維他命 Useful Vocabulary

- **turnoff** [`tɜn, ɔf`] **n** 交流道出口
- **railroad** [`rel, rod`] **n** 平交道；鐵路
- **freeway** [`frɪ, we`] **n** 高速公路
- **highway** [`haɪ, we`] **n** 幹道；公路
- **the locals** 當地人
- **road travel** 公路旅行
- **toll station** 收費亭
- **ask for directions** 問路
- **highway patrol** 高速公路巡警(美)
- **zebra crossing** 斑馬線；行人穿越道

🔊 MP3 079

救急情境演練 Situation

A：Oops, we're lost!
糟糕，我們迷路了！

B：How about reading the map?
要不要看一下地圖？

B：Where are we now?
我們人在哪裡？

A：I think we should ask passersby.
我想我們問一下路人吧。

A：Excuse me. Where are we?
不好意思，請問這是哪裡？

C：Queens Boulevard.
皇后大道。

345

A : Could you point where I am on the map?
可以指出我在地圖的哪裡嗎？

C : Here.
這裡。

A : Could you show me where Time Square is on the map?
可否指出時代廣場在地圖上的位置？

C : Right here.
就在這裡。

A : Could you tell us how to get back to Crown Hotel?
請問我們要怎麼回到皇冠飯店呢？

C : Just go 2 blocks, and you'll see it.
只要走過兩個街區，你就會看到了。

KEY SENTENCES

關鍵句 （完→完整句・順→順口句）

11-16 ▶ 可否指出我在地圖的哪裡？

完 : Could you show me where I am now on the map?

順 : Where am I?(用手指地圖)

11-17 ▶ 可否指出倫敦塔橋在地圖的哪裡？

完 : Could you show me where the Tower Bridge is on the map?

順 : Where is Tower Bridge? (用手指地圖)

11-18 ▶ 我迷路了。

完：I think I am lost.
順：I'm lost.

11-19 ▶ 我在找克里斯多飯店。

完：I'm looking for the Cristal Hotel.
順：Cristal Hotel, please?(用手指地圖)

11-20 ▶ 請問我該如何回到城市飯店？

完：Could you tell me how to get back to the City Hotel?
順：City Hotel, please? (用手指地圖)

單字片語維他命 Useful Vocabulary

🔖 **passerby** [`pæsə͵ baɪ] **n** 過往行人

🔖 **direction** [də`rɛkʃən] **n** 方向

🔖 **compass** [`kʌmpəs] **n** 羅盤

🔖 **east** [ist] **n** 東方

🔖 **west** [wɛst] **n** 西方

🔖 **south** [sauθ] **n** 南方

🔖 **north** [nɔrθ] **n** 北方

🔖 **orientation** [͵ orɪɛn`teʃən] **n** 定位

🔖 **sense of direction** 方向感

🔖 **direction finder** 測向器

347

MP3 080

救急情境演練 Situation

A : Do you mean turn at the next intersection?
你是說在下一個路口轉彎嗎?

B : Yes, that's right.
是的,沒錯。

A : Turn right or left?
請問是右轉還左轉?

B : Turn left.
左轉。

A : Excuse me. Could you repeat it again?
不好意思,可以再說一次嗎?

B : Turn left at the intersection.
路口左轉。

A : I'm sorry. My English is poor.
不好意思,我的英文很爛。

B : It's OK.
沒關係。

A : Go straight and then turn left?
先直走,然後再左轉嗎?

B : That's right!
就是那樣!

A : Thank you very much.
很謝謝你。

B : You're welcome.
不客氣。

關鍵句 （完 →完整句 · 順 →順口句）

11-21 ▶ 直走嗎？

完：Should I go straight?
順：Go straight?

11-22 ▶ 它是在第21街嗎？

完：Is it on Twenty-first Street, isn't it?
順：On Twenty-first Street?

11-23 ▶ 先直走，然後再左轉嗎？

完：Go straight and then turn left?
順：Go straight and then left?

11-24 ▶ 我走過兩個街口，然後再右轉嗎？

完：I walk two blocks and then turn right?
順：Two blocks and turn right?

11-25 ▶ 我不懂你的意思，可以再說一次嗎？

完：I can't get it, can you repeat it again?
順：Sorry, can you repeat it again?

單字片語雜他命 Useful Vocabulary

- **straight** [stret] **a** 直的
- **turn** [tɜn] **v** 轉彎；轉向
- **curve** [kɜv] **n** 彎道
- **shortcut** [`ʃɔrt͵kʌt] **n** 捷徑；近路
- **intersection** [͵ɪntə`sɛkʃən] **n** 道路交叉口
- **state of road** 路況
- **traffic sign** 交通號誌
- **traffic cone** 交通錐
- **forked road** 岔路
- **S curve** S形彎道

((♪)) MP3 081

救急情境演練 Situation

A: Thank you. It's lucky that I got your help.
謝謝您，還好有您的協助。

B: You're welcome.
不客氣。

A: Without your help in time, I really wouldn't know how to do.
要不是您及時幫忙，我真的不知道該怎麼辦。

B: It's just a piece of cake. Never mind.
這只是小事一樁，別太在意。

A: This is a small gift for you.
這是送您的小禮物。

B: You're so welcome.

你太客氣了。

A：I hope you like it.
希望您會喜歡。

B：Thanks, I like it very much.
謝謝，我很喜歡。

A：May I have your E-mail? I'll guide you when you visit my hometown.
可以給我您的電子信箱嗎？您造訪我家鄉時，我來為您導覽。

B：You're so kind!
你好客氣啊！

A：Your E-mail, please?
您的電子信箱是？

B：My E-mail is: aloha@gmail.com.
我的電子信箱是：aloha@gmail.com。

KEY SENTENCES
關鍵句 （完 →完整句・順 →順口句）

11-26 ▸ 謝謝您的幫忙。
完：Thanks for your help.
順：Thanks.

11-27 ▸ 謝謝您撥冗。
完：Thanks for your time.
順：Thanks.

11-28 ▸ 非常感謝您的幫忙。
完：I appreciate your help.

順：Very appreciate.

11-29 ▶ 您真是幫了我一個大忙。

完：You really did me a big favor.

順：It's a big favor.

11-30 ▶ 沒有您，我真不知該怎麼辦。

完：Without you, I really wouldn't know what to do.

順：Without you, how can I do!

11-31 ▶ 還好有您來解圍。

完：It's lucky that I got your help.

順：It's lucky for you help me out.

11-32 ▶ 可以給我您的電子信箱嗎？

完：May I have your E-mail?

順：Your E-mail, please?

11-33 ▶ 可以給我您的地址嗎？

完：May I have your address?

順：Your address, please?

11-34 ▶ 可以給我您的臉書帳號嗎？

完：May I have your Facebook account?

順：Your Facebook account, please?

單字片語維他命 Useful Vocabulary

- **thank** [θæŋk] **V** 感謝
- **appreciate** [əˋpriʃɪ,et] **V** 感謝；感激
- **appreciation** [ə,priʃɪˋeʃən] **n** 感謝
- **encouragement** [ɪnˋkɝɪdʒmənt] **n** 鼓勵
- **support** [səˋport] **V** 支持
- **hometown** [ˋhomˋtaʊn] **n** 家鄉
- **help out** 解圍
- **do sb.'s favor** 幫…的忙
- **a piece of cake** 小事一樁
- **keep in touch with** 和…保持聯絡

Travel NEWS ✈

進入清真寺前必須脫鞋，非教徒必須先得到寺方的准許才可以進入；對於正在寺中祈禱的教徒，儘量不拍攝他們的照片，更不能由前方穿過。

🔊 MP3 082

救急情境演練 Situation

A : Please take me to the airport.
麻煩載我到機場。

B : OK.
好的。

A : Please open the trunk.
請開後車箱。

B : I'll take your luggage for you.
我幫你拿行李。

A : How much time will it take to arrive?
要多久才會到？

B : About 3 hours.
大概要三個鐘頭。

A : So long?
要那麼久啊？

B : You may take a nap. I'll wake you up when we arrive at the airport.
您可以打個盹，到機場時我會叫醒你。

A : Thanks. I really need to take a nap.
謝啦，我真的需要小睡一下。

B : Excuse me, sir. We are now at the airport.
先生，不好意思，我們到達機場了。

A : Oh, how much is it?
喔，多少錢？

B：3,000 dollars.
　　三千元。

KEY SENTENCES
關鍵句 （完 →完整句・順 →順口句）

11-35 ▸ 請載我到這個地址。
完：Please drive me to this address.
順：This address, please. (用手指)

11-36 ▸ 請開慢一點。
完：Please drive a little bit slowly.
順：Slow down, please.

11-37 ▸ 請在下一個紅綠燈右轉。
完：Please turn right at the next traffic light.
順：Turn right at next traffic light.

11-38 ▸ 請讓我在希爾頓飯店下車。
完：Please drop me off at the Hilton Hotel.
順：Drop me at Hilton, please.

11-39 ▸ 麻煩為我提行李。
完：Please kindly take my luggage for me.
順：Help me with my luggage, please.

11-40 ▸ 請把冷氣調小一點好嗎？
完：Could you turn down the air conditioner, please?
順：Turn down the air conditioner, please?

11-41 ▶ 我們到達火車站了。

完：We are now at the train station.

順：We're at train station.

單字片語維他命 Useful Vocabulary

➤ **address** [əˋdrɛs] **n** 地址

➤ **taxi** [ˋtæksɪ] **n** 計程車(美)

➤ **cab** [kæb] **n** 計程車(英)

➤ **taxi / cab company** 計程車行

➤ **taxi driver** 計程車司機

➤ **taxi meter** 計程車錶

➤ **wake sb. up** 把⋯叫醒

➤ **hire a taxi / cab for sb.** 替⋯叫計程車

➤ **traffic light** 紅綠燈

➤ **pick sb. up** (開車)接人

救急情境演練 Situation

A：Which bus should I take to get to the School of Visual Arts?
請問我要搭幾路公車到視覺藝術學院？

B：This one will do.
這班公車就是。

A：Where should I get off?
我要在哪裡下車？

B：4 more bus stops to go.
還有四站。

A：Do I have to transfer?
需要轉車嗎？

B：No, just get off the bus.
不用，下車就是。

A：How many coins does it take?
需要多少硬幣？

B：One dollar.
一塊錢。

A：I would like to go to the British Museum, which stop should I get off?
我想去大英博物館，我該在哪一站下車呢？

B：Two more stops will do.
再過兩站就到了。

A：Thanks!
謝謝！

B：Any time.
　　不客氣。

（完 →完整句 · 順 →順口句）

11-42 ▶ 這是往大英博物館的公車嗎？

完：Is this the right bus to the British Museum?

順：Is it to the British Museum?(用手示意)

11-43 ▶ 這班公車有到中央公園嗎？

完：Does this bus go to Central Park?

順：To Central Park?(用手示意)

11-44 ▶ 請問你有公車路線圖嗎？

完：Do you have a bus route map?

順：A bus route map, please?

11-45 ▶ 請問我可以在哪裡搭**219**號公車？

完：Excuse me. Where can I catch a No. 219 Bus?

順：Where to catch No. 219?

11-46 ▶ 請問下一站是火車站嗎？

完：Excuse me. Is the next stop the train station?

順：Next stop for train station?

11-47 ▶ 我可以使用一日券嗎？

完：May I use the one-day pass?

順：One-day pass, OK?

單字片語維他命 Useful Vocabulary

- **handrail** [`hænd,rel] **n** 扶手
- **baluster** [`bæləstə] **n** 欄杆
- **sensor** [`sɛnsə] **n** 感應器
- **timetable** [`taɪm,tebḷ] **n** 時刻表
- **itinerary** [aɪ`tɪnə,rɛrɪ] **n** 旅程；路線
- **GPS** 全球衛星定位系統 (= Global Positioning System)
- **recharge card** 儲值卡
- **tourist bus** 觀光巴士
- **get on / off the bus** 上 / 下公車
- **bus route map** 公車路線圖

Tourists don't know where they've been, travelers don't know where they're going.

★ ★ ★ ★

觀光客不知他們到過哪裡；旅行者不知他們將去何方。

🔊 MP3 084

救急情境演練 Situation

A: Where is this train bound?
請問這是開往哪裡的地下鐵？

B: For Soho.
蘇活區。

A: Excuse me. Which platform should I go to?
請問，我該到哪個月臺去搭車？

B: You should go to the platform 4.
你要到4號月臺。

A: Which floor should I go to?
我要到第幾層？

B: You have to go to the second floor underground.
你必須到地下二樓。

A: How should I get there?
我該怎麼過去？

B: Take that stair, and go down will do.
走那個階梯下去就可以了。

A: How long does it take?
要搭多久的車呢？

B: About 30 minutes.
大概要花半小時吧。

A: Thank you.
謝謝你。

B: Any time.
舉手之勞啦。

KEY SENTENCES
關鍵句 🔑

（完 →完整句・順 →順口句）

11-48 ▶ 請問售票亭在哪裡？
完：Where's the ticket office?
順：Ticket office, please?

11-49 ▶ 我要買張一日券。
完：I'd like to have a one-day pass.
順：A one-day pass, please.

11-50 ▶ 可以給我一張地鐵路線圖嗎？
完：May I have a subway route map?
順：A subway route map, please?

11-51 ▶ 要搭哪一條線到市政府呢？
完：Which line goes to City Hall?
順：Which line to City Hall?

11-52 ▶ 到「大教堂」有幾站？
完：How many stops are there to Cathedral?
順：How many stops to Cathedral?

11-53 ▶ 這是要往百老匯的車嗎？
完：Is this bound for Broadway?
順：To Broadway, OK?(用手示意)

11-54 ▶ 這是要往中央公園的車嗎？

完：Is this bound for Central Park?

順：To Central Park, OK?(用手示意)

單字片語維他命 Useful Vocabulary

🔖 **underground** [`ʌndə. graʊnd] **n** 地下鐵(英)

🔖 **tube** [tjub] **n** 地下鐵(英)

🔖 **subway** [`sʌb. we] **n** 地下鐵(美)

🔖 **spur** [spɜ] **n** 支線

🔖 **platform** [`plæt. fɔrm] **n** 月臺

🔖 **automat** [`ɔtə. mæt] **n** 自動售票機

🔖 **free pass** 免費票

🔖 **ticket office** 售票亭

🔖 **waiting line** 候車線

🔖 **barrier-free environment** 無障礙空間

MP3 085

救急情境演練 Situation

A: I want two train tickets to New York.
我要兩張到紐約的火車票。

B: When?
什麼時候的？

A: 21:00.
二十一點的火車。

B: I'm sorry, it's full.
不好意思，已經沒有位子了。

A: Is there any other train tonight?
那今晚還有其他班次嗎？

B: There is one at 23:00.
還有一班二十三點的車。

A: Hmm, we'll take this one.
嗯，那我們搭這一班。

B: OK, I'll reserve the seats for you.
好的，我為您劃位。

A: Is there a restaurant car in this train?
這班列車上有餐車嗎？

B: Yes, besides the bed seats, there's also a restaurant car in this train.
有的，這班列車除了有臥舖外，也附有餐車。

A: How much is it?
要多少錢？

B : USD 600.
美金六百元。

（完 →完整句・順 →順口句）

11-55 ▶ 可以給我兩張到米蘭的車票嗎？

完 : Would you give me two tickets to Milan, please?

順 : Two for Milan, please?

. . . .

11-56 ▶ 可以給我一張到巴塞隆納的單程票嗎？

完 : Would you give me a one-way ticket to Barcelona, please?

順 : One-way ticket to Barcelona, please?

. . . .

11-57 ▶ 到紐約的最後一班火車幾點出發？

完 : What time does the last train to New York leave?

順 : When is the last train to New York?

. . . .

11-58 ▶ 有快車到尼斯嗎？

完 : Is there any Express to Nice?

順 : Any Express to Nice?

. . . .

11-59 ▶ 我要用歐洲火車週遊券訂一張火車票到羅馬。

完 : I'd like to book a train ticket to Rome by Europass.

順 : To Rome by Europass, OK?

. . . .

11-60 ▶ 可以給我一張時刻表嗎？

完：May I have a timetable?

順：A timetable, please?

單字片語維他命 Useful Vocabulary

- **feeder** [`fidə] **n** 支線
- **express** [ɪk`sprɛs] **n** 快車
- **Europass** [`juro͵pæs] **n** 歐洲火車週遊券
- **conductor** [kən`dʌktə] **n** 列車服務員
- **branch line** 支線
- **platform ticket** 月臺票
- **sightseeing train** 觀光列車
- **bed seat** 臥鋪
- **dinning car** 餐車
- **check-in gate** 驗票閘門

◄)) MP3 086

救急情境演練 Situation

🅰 : I want to rent a car.
   我要租車。

🅱 : What kind of car do you need?
   您需要哪款車？

🅰 : A BMW convertible.
   一輛寶馬的敞棚車。

🅱 : Do you have an international driver's license?
   請問您有國際駕照嗎？

🅰 : These are my passport and international driver's license.
   這是我的護照跟國際駕照。

🅱 : Please fill in this form.
   請填這份資料。

🅰 : Should I sign here?
   在這裡簽名嗎？

🅱 : Yes, there are vehicle registration and related documents of the car.
   是的，這是行照跟車子的相關資料。

🅰 : Please send a car to my hotel.
   請派車到我的飯店來。

🅱 : From this evening?
   從今天傍晚開始租借嗎？

🅰 : Yes, for three days.
   是的，租三天。

B : All right.
　　好的。

KEY SENTENCES
關鍵句 🔑 　（完 →完整句 ・ 順 →順口句）

11-61 ▶ 這是我的國際駕照。

完 : Here is my international driver's license.

順 : My license.

11-62 ▶ 我要租三天的車。

完 : I want to rent a car for three days.

順 : Three days, please.

11-63 ▶ 我要租一個星期的吉普車。

完 : I want to rent a jeep for one week.

順 : A jeep for one week, please.

11-64 ▶ 我週末要用車。

完 : I need a car for the weekend.

順 : A car for the weekend, please.

11-65 ▶ 請派輛車到我住的飯店。

完 : Please send a car to my hotel.

順 : Send a car to my hotel, OK?

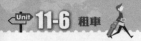
單字片語維他命 Useful Vocabulary

➤ **rent** [rɛnt] **V** 租用

➤ **leaseholder** [`lis,holdə] **n** 租賃人

➤ **automobile** [`ɔtəmə,bɪl] **n** 汽車

➤ **beetle** [`bitl̩] **n** 金龜車

➤ **jeep** [dʒip] **n** 吉普車

➤ **convertible** [kən`vɝtəbl̩] **n** 有活動摺篷的汽車

➤ **take on lease** 租用

➤ **four-wheel drive vehicle** 四輪傳動車

➤ **vehicle registration** 行照

➤ **international driver's license** 國際駕照

🔊 MP3 087

救急情境演練 Situation

Ⓐ : What kind of car do you have?
請問你們有什麼車款？

Ⓑ : This is the list for all the kinds of cars we have.
這是所有車款的資料。

Ⓐ : How many people can sit in an SUV?
休旅車最多可坐幾人？

Ⓑ : 12.
12人。

Ⓐ : Is there a lengthened sedan?
有加長型轎車嗎？

Ⓑ : We have a Rolls-Royce and a Lincoln.

我們有勞斯萊斯跟林肯。

A : A Benz or a BMW?
賓士或寶馬呢？

B : We have Benz, too.
我們也有賓士車。

A : I would rather have a car with automatic transmission.
我比較喜歡自排車。

B : Any other requirements?
還有其他需求嗎？

A : I'd like to rent an SUV in olive yellow.
我想租一輛秋香色的休旅車。

B : OK, follow me, please.
好的，請跟我來。

KEY SENTENCES
關鍵句 （完 →完整句 · 順 →順口句）

11-66 ▶ 我要租一輛小型車。
完 : I'd like to rent a small-sized car.
順 : Small size, please.

11-67 ▶ 我要一輛中型車。
完 : I'd like to have a mid-size car.
順 : Mid-size, please.

11-68 ▶ 你們有跑車嗎？
完 : Do you have any sports cars?
順 : Any sports cars?

11-69 ▶ 我比較喜歡自排車。

完：I would rather have a car with an automatic transmission.

順：With automatic transmission, please.

11-70 ▶ 我要租一輛手排車。

完：I'd like to rent a car with a manual shift.

順：With a manual shift, please.

單字片語維他命 Useful Vocabulary

◥ **sedan** [sɪ`dæn] **n** 轎車

◥ **limousine** [`lɪməˌzin] **n** 豪華大轎車

◥ **SUV** 運動型休旅車 (= Sport Utility Vehicle)

◥ **low beam** 近光燈

◥ **high beam** 遠光燈

◥ **fog light** 霧燈

◥ **tail light** 尾燈

◥ **turn signal** 方向燈

◥ **manual shift** 手動排檔

◥ **automatic transmission** 自動排檔

🔊 MP3 088

救急情境演練 Situation

A : Let me see the documents of the car, please.
請讓我看一下車子的資料。

B : There is the related document of our car.
這是我們車子的相關資料。

A : I want a sports car.
我要跑車。

B : Take a look at the photos of them, please.
請參看跑車相片。

A : I want a 2-door sports car.
我要兩門的跑車。

B : These are some 2-door convertible sports cars.
這幾輛都是兩門的敞篷跑車。

A : What're the features?
有何麼特徵？

B : It starts very fast and is very stable.
啟動非常快速，而且很穩定。

A : How many miles per gallon does it get?
一加侖油可以跑幾英哩？

B : 300 miles.
三百英哩。

A : Does it have ABS'?
有防鎖死煞車系統嗎？

B : Yes, it does.
有的。

KEY SENTENCES
關鍵句 🔑

（完 →完整句・順 →順口句）

11-71 ▶ 它是兩門車、還是四門車？
完：Is it a two-door or a four-door car?
順：Two-door or four-door?

11-72 ▶ 一加侖油可以跑幾英哩？
完：How many miles per gallon does it get?
順：How many miles per gallon?

11-73 ▶ 有安全氣囊嗎？
完：Does it have air bags?
順：Have air bags?

11-74 ▶ 有防鎖死煞車系統嗎？
完：Does it have ABS?
順：Have ABS?

Bon Voyage!

單字片語維他命 Useful Vocabulary

- **gallon** [`gælən] **n** 加侖
- **mileage** [`maɪlɪdʒ] **n** 行駛哩數
- **turbocharger** [`tɜbo,tʃardʒə] **n** 渦輪增壓器
- **ABS** 反鎖死煞車系統(= Against deadlock Brakes System)
- **sports car** 跑車
- **air bag** 安全氣囊
- **sun visor** 遮陽板
- **steering wheel** 方向盤
- **instrument panel** 儀表板
- **vehicle guidance system** 行車導引系統

🔊 MP3 089

救急情境演練 Situation

Ⓐ : I want to rent a car.
我要租車。

Ⓑ : How much is your budget?
請問您的預算是？

Ⓐ : I want a cheaper SUV for six people.
我要便宜一點的六人座休旅車。

Ⓑ : What do you think about this one?
這一款您覺得如何？

Ⓐ : How about the fee?
費用怎麼算？

Ⓑ : USD 120 per day.

一天一百二十元美金。

A : Does that cover insurance?
包含保險費用嗎？

B : No, this one doesn't.
不，這款車沒有包含。

A : How about this silver one?
那這輛銀色的呢？

B : Yes, it does.
有，這輛有包含保險費用。

A : OK, I'll take this one.
好的，我要租這輛休旅車。

B : Please fill in this form.
請填寫這份資料。

KEY SENTENCES
關鍵句

（完→完整句‧順→順口句）

11-75 ▶ 可以給我看租車價目表嗎？

完：May I see the rent chart?
順：Rent chart, please?

11-76 ▶ 有包含碰撞險嗎？

完：Does that include collision insurance?
順：Include collision insurance?

11-77 ▶ 含稅嗎？

完：Does that include tax?
順：Include tax?

11-78 ▶ 有包含油錢嗎？

完：Does that include the gas?

順：Include the gas?

11-79 ▶ 租車保證金是多少錢？

完：What's the deposit for the car?

順：How much is the deposit?

單字片語維他命 Useful Vocabulary

🔖 **budget** [`bʌdʒɪt] **n** 預算

🔖 **contract** [`kɑntrækt] **n** 契約

🔖 **navigation** [ˌnævə`geʃən] **n** 導航

🔖 **rent chart** 租車價目表

🔖 **airport pick-up** 機場接送

🔖 **compulsory insurance** 強制險

🔖 **car damage insurance** 車體損失險

🔖 **burglary insurance** 竊盜險

🔖 **automobile liability insurance** 汽車責任險

🔖 **third person injured liability insurance**
第三者受傷責任險

MP3 090

救急情境演練 Situation

A: Can I return the car at other locations?
我可以在異地還車嗎？

B: Yes, you can.
可以的。

A: I want to return it to L.A..
我想在洛杉磯還車。

B: I'll find the return location for you.
我為您找一下還車地點。

A: Please find some locations near the airport.
麻煩找離機場近一點的地方。

B: Yes, there is one just near the airport.
有的，在機場附近剛好有個還車地點。

A: Could you write down the address and the phone number for me?
可以抄地址和聯絡電話給我嗎？

B: OK, please wait for a moment.
好的，請您等一下。

A: If I have some trouble, to whom should I call?
如果有故障，我該打給誰呢？

B: You may call any of our office. We'll send our technicians to help you.
您可以打電話給任何一家分公司，我們會派技師過去協助。

A: Do you have roadside assistance?
你們有道路救援服務嗎？

B：Yes, we do.
　　有的。

關鍵句 （完 →完整句 · 順 →順口句）

11-80 ▶ 有分店名單嗎？

完：Do you have a list of your other offices?

順：List of offices, please?

11-81 ▶ 如果有故障，我該找誰呢？

完：If I have some trouble, to whom should I call?

順：Whom to call when I got some trouble?

11-82 ▶ 我可以在多倫多還車嗎？

完：May I leave the car in Toronto?

順：Drop off in Toronto, OK?

11-83 ▶ 請問有各駐點的服務電話嗎？

完：Do you have service phone numbers of all locations?

順：Have service phone numbers of all locations?

11-84 ▶ 你們有道路救援服務嗎？

完：Do you have roadside assistance?

順：Have roadside assistance?

11-85 ▶ 你們有附帶腳踏車嗎？

完：Do you equip with the bicycle additionally?

順：With the bicycle additionally?

單字片語維他命 Useful Vocabulary

- **location** [loˋkeʃən] **n** 地點
- **quotation** [kwoˋteʃən] **n** 估價
- **car type** 車款
- **branch store** 分店
- **business extension** 分店
- **service item** 服務項目
- **coupon code** 優惠券代碼
- **roadside assistance** 道路救援
- **personal protection plan** 人身保護方案
- **lost damage waiver** 竊盜與碰撞免負擔減免

A ship in a harbor is safe, but
that's not what ships are built for.

★ ★ ★ ★ ★

船隻停泊在港灣是安全的，
但那並非建造船隻的目的。

救急情境演練 Situation

Ⓐ : I want to fuel up.
我要加油。

Ⓑ : What kind of gasoline?
要加什麼油呢？

Ⓐ : Unleaded gasoline 95.
九五無鉛汽油。

Ⓑ : How much do you want to fuel up?
要加多少？

Ⓐ : Please fill it up.
請加滿。

Ⓑ : We have a free car washing service.
我們有免費洗車服務。

Ⓐ : Please wash my car, too.
也麻煩幫我洗車。

Ⓑ : Yes, we'll wash your car right away.
好的，我們馬上幫您洗車。

Ⓐ : Do you have the map of southern California?
有南加州的地圖嗎？

Ⓑ : Yes, we do.
有。

Ⓐ : I need one.
我要一份。

Ⓑ : Here you are.
這是南加州的地圖。

KEY SENTENCES

關鍵句 （完 →完整句 · 順 →順口句）

11-86 ▶ 一般無鉛汽油，請加滿。

完：Please fill it up with regular unleaded.

順：Tank up the regular unleaded, please.

11-87 ▶ 請加十美元高級汽油。

完：Ten dollar's worth of premium, please.

順：Premium for ten dollars, please.

11-88 ▶ 請幫我檢查一下機油好嗎？

完：Would you check the engine oil, please?

順：Check the engine oil for me, please?

11-89 ▶ 請幫我檢查一下冷卻水好嗎？

完：Would you check the water, please?

順：Check the water for me, please?

11-90 ▶ 請幫我檢查一下電瓶好嗎？

完：Would you check the battery, please?

順：Check the battery for me, please?

11-91 ▶ 請幫我洗車好嗎？

完：Would you wash my car, please?

順：Wash car for me, please?

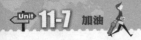
11-92 ▶ 請幫我打蠟好嗎？

完：Would you wax my car, please?

順：Wax car for me, please?

單字片語維他命 Useful Vocabulary

🔖 **wax** [wæks] **V** 上蠟

🔖 **LPG car** 瓦斯動力車(= Liquefied Petroleum Gas)

🔖 **hybrid car** 油電混合動力車

🔖 **gas station** 加油站(美)

🔖 **petrol station** 加油站(英)

🔖 **fuel up** 加油

🔖 **gas up** 加油

🔖 **car wash** 洗車

🔖 **engine oil** 機油

🔖 **unleaded gasoline** 無鉛汽油

Travel NEWS

　　尊重穆斯林國家的規範，不任意拍攝當地女子照片，也不要搭訕當地女性；女性旅人也應多注意自己的衣裝與言行，儘量避免穿著背心短褲。

NotE

🔊 MP3 092

救急情境演練 Situation

A : My car is smoking!
我的車冒煙了！

B : Hurry to pull over and check it.
趕快停在路邊查看一下。

A : I'll open the hood and check it first.
我先打開引擎蓋檢查一下。

B : Found the problem?
找出問題了嗎？

A : No. The smoke is too big.
沒有，煙太大了。

B : Let's call the "roadside assistance."
我們打電話叫「道路救援」吧。

A : I don't know whom to call.
我不知道要打給誰。

B : You can try the travel guide in the car.
你可以試試車上那本旅遊指南。

A : Which part should I check?
我該查哪個部份呢？

B : Try "FAQ."
試試「常用問答集」。

A : Ah! "Roadside Assistance Center!"
啊！有「道路救援中心」！

B : Call the customer service!
快打給客服人員！

388

KEY SENTENCES
關鍵句

（完→完整句・順→順口句）

11-93 ▶ 我的車爆胎了。

完：I've got a flat tire.

順：Flat tire.

11-94 ▶ 我車子的散熱器過熱。

完：The radiator is overheated.

順：Radiator's too hot.

11-95 ▶ 我車子的風扇皮帶斷了。

完：My fan belt is broken.

順：Fan belt is broken.

11-96 ▶ 我的車沒辦法發動。

完：I can't get my car started.

順：It can't start.

11-97 ▶ 我的汽車雨刷不會動。

完：My windshield wipers don't work.

順：Windshield wipers are dead.

11-98 ▶ 我的儀表板有問題。

完：There's something wrong with my instrument board.

順：The instrument board is broken-down.

11-99 ▶ 我的油門踏板有問題。

完：There's something wrong with my gas

pedal.

順：The gas pedal is not working.

單字片語維他命 Useful Vocabulary

- **radiator** [`redɪˌetə] **n** 散熱器；冷卻器
- **dashboard** [`dæʃˌbɔrd] **n** 擋泥板
- **FAQ** 常用問答集(= Frequently Asked Question)
- **get a flat tire** 爆胎
- **windshield wiper** 雨刷
- **door lock** 車門鎖
- **spark plug** 火星塞
- **brake pedal** 煞車踏板
- **gas pedal** 油門踏板
- **pull over** 把車開到路邊

Bon voyage!

背包客旅遊筆記 BON VOYAGE！

　　想要在國外租車旅遊，要先在國內各監理單位申請國際駕照。國際駕照會將五種駕駛車種記錄在同一本上，包括汽、機車駕照資料。各監理單位可同時申請兩種或以上車種駕照，只要先準備好個人駕照、身分證、護照影本、兩張兩吋照片，以及兩百五十元的手續費，申請當天就可取得。國際駕照自核准日起的有效期限是三年，過期可再更新。不過，一旦國內駕照被吊銷或停用時，國際駕照也就失效了，因此，要保持良好駕駛習慣喔！以下是各監理所的網址：

1. 臺北市區監理所暨士林監理站：http://tpcmv.thb.gov.tw/Mp.aspx。

2. 臺北市區監理所金門監理站：http://www.kmvs.gov.tw/default.aspx。

3. 臺北市區監理所連江監理站：http://www.matsu-mv.gov.tw/。

4. 臺北區監理所：http://www.tmvso.gov.tw/。

5. 新竹區監理所：http://www.hmv.gov.tw/。

6. 臺中區監理所：http://www.tmv.gov.tw/。

7. 嘉義區監理所：http://www.cyi.gov.tw/。

8. 高雄市區監理所暨苓雅監理站：http://khcmv.thb.gov.tw/。

9. 高雄區監理所(屏東、旗山、臺東、澎湖站及恆春分站)：http://www.komv.gov.tw/cht/index.

php?。

接下來介紹美國的各種公路名稱。首先，
「interstate highway」是州際公路，也就是州
與州之間互相往來的道路；「expressway」是
高速公路；「four-lane expressway」是四線道
的高速公路，有時會與一般道路交會；另外，
「freeway」也是高速公路的一種，但會從交流道
(ramp)進出。在高速公路上會遇到「tollgate」，
收費站；而「toll road」則是指收費道路。

美國的高速公路都非常地寬，因此，駕駛人
往往一不留神就會超過最高速限(speed limit)，美
國的公路警察(highway police)總是神出鬼沒、會
突然出現在超速的車旁，所以為了別吃罰單(get a
ticket)，還是小心為上。

常在警察廣播電臺報路況時，聽到「紐澤西
護欄(New Jersey Concrete Safety Shape
Barrier，或稱New Jersey Median Barrier，簡稱
Jersey barrier)」這個交通裝置名詞嗎？這項交通
裝置是由美國紐澤西州首先開發，作為高速公路
分隔之用。

紐澤西護欄的特色是下方斜凸出來的形狀，
可減少車輛擦撞時鈑金等部份受損的機會。由於
效果很好，因此逐步普及到加州、美國各地與世
界各地使用。而在道路施工時使用的暫時性紐澤
西護欄，常被稱為「K-rails」。

Part. 12

電信聯絡篇

Unit 12-1 國際電話

Unit 12-2 國內電話

Unit 12-3 郵局

＊ 手機漫遊筆記

))) **MP3 093**

救急情境演練 Situation

A : I'd like to make an international call to Taipei, Taiwan.
我要打一通國際電話到臺灣臺北。

B : May I know whom you are trying to reach?
請問您想找哪一位呢？

A : I'd like to call Mr. Chen.
我要找陳先生。

B : Your name, please?
您的大名是？

A : Mark Wang.
王馬克。

B : Excuse me. What's the country code for Taiwan?
請問臺灣的國際代碼是幾號？

A : The country code is 886.
國碼是886。

A : The area code is 2 and the number is 3456-8901.
區碼是2，電話號碼是：3456-8901。

B : Wait a second, please.
請稍候。

B : I'm sorry. The line is busy now.
不好意思，目前忙線中。

A : Thank you anyway.

還是謝謝你。

B：You are welcome.
不客氣。

KEY SENTENCES
關鍵句 （**完**→完整句・**順**→順口句）

12-01 ▶ 我想打國際電話到臺灣。

完：I'd like to make an international phone call to Taiwan.

順：International phone call to Taiwan, please.

12-02 ▶ 我想打對方付費的電話。

完：I'd like to make a collect phone call.

順：Collect phone call, please.

12-03 ▶ 請告訴我對方的號碼及姓名。

完：Please tell me the person's phone number and name.

順：Phone number and name, please.

12-04 ▶ 我想打越洋電話到雪梨。

完：I want to place an oversea call to Sidney.

順：Oversea call to Sidney, please.

12-05 ▶ 印度的國際代碼是幾號？

完：What's the country code for India?

順：Country code for India, please?

12-06 ▶ 巴西的國際代碼是幾號？

完：What's the country code for Brazil?
順：Country code for Brazil, please?

12-07 ▶ 要如何撥打國際電話？

完：How can I make an international phone call?

順：International phone call, please?

12-08 ▶ 電話佔線中。

完：The line is busy.

順：It's busy now.

12-09 ▶ 沒有人接聽電話。

完：Nobody answers the phone.

順：There's no answer.

12-10 ▶ 請問哪裡有賣電話卡？

完：Excuse me. Where can I buy a telephone card?

順：Telephone card, please?

12-11 ▶ 要如何使用這張電話卡打電話？

完：How can I make a phone call with this card?

順：How to call with this card?

12-12 ▶ 這附近有公用電話嗎？

完：Is there any pay phone nearby?

順：Any pay phone nearby?

12-13 ▶ 我可以用這具電話嗎？

完：Can I use this phone?
順：This phone, OK?(用手示意)

單字片語維他命 Useful Vocabulary

🔸 **transoceanic** [ˌtrænsoʃɪˈænɪk] **a** 越洋的

🔸 **star key** 米(*)字鍵

🔸 **pound key** 井(#)字鍵

🔸 **area code** 區碼

🔸 **country code** 國碼

🔸 **time difference** 時差

🔸 **telephone card** 電話卡

🔸 **web phone** 網路電話

🔸 **video phone** 視訊電話

🔸 **collect phone call** 對方付費電話

Travel NEWS

　　雖然國人在交談時會注視著對方，表示禮貌，但與衣索比亞當地人交談時，不要目不轉睛地注視著對方，否則會被認為是災禍或死神將至。

MP3 094

救急情境演練 Situation

A: Hello, may I speak to Jack?
喂，我可以和傑克說話嗎？

B: He's in the meeting. May I take a message for you?
他在開會，要我幫您留言嗎？

A: Would you have him call back to me? I am Ivan Liu.
你能請他回電話給我嗎？我是劉艾文。

B: How can he get in contact with you, Mr. Liu?
劉先生，他要怎麼跟您聯絡呢？

A: Could you ask him to call me at Hilton Hotel, Room 621?
可否請他打電話到希爾頓飯店的621號房找我？

B: It's no problem. I'll get him to call you back.
沒問題，我會請他回電給您。

A: By the way, my cell-phone number is 0952-461297.
對了，我的手機號碼是：0952-461297。

B: Ivan Liu, 0952-461297?
是劉艾文，電話0952-461297嗎？

A: That's right.
是的。

A: Oh, please tell him to call back after 6:00 in

the evening, thank you.
喔,麻煩他在下午六點過後回電,謝謝。

Ⓑ: Yes, I'll remind him.
好的,我會提醒他。

Ⓐ: Thank you.
謝謝你。

KEY SENTENCES
關鍵句 🔑

(完 →完整句 · 順 →順口句)

12-14 ▸ 我是王大衛,請問理察‧勒溫先生在家嗎?
完: This is David Wang. May I speak to Mr. Richard Lewin?
順: It's David Wang. Mr. Richard Lewin, please?

12-15 ▸ 可否請丹‧戴爾接電話?
完: May I speak to Dan Dale?
順: Dan Dale, please?

12-16 ▸ 請問是誰打來的?
完: May I know who is calling?
順: Who's calling, please?

12-17 ▸ 他不在家。
完: He's not at home.
順: Not at home.

12-18 ▸ 她現在不在座位上。

完：She's away from her desk.
順：Not at desk.

12-19 ▶ 這裡沒有這個人。

完：There's nobody here by this name.
順：We have no one by this name.

12-20 ▶ 需要我幫您留言嗎？

完：Shall I take a message for you?
順：Leave a message?

12-21 ▶ 等他回來後再回電給您，好嗎？

完：After he is back, I'll ask him to call you back, OK?
順：Tell him to call you back, OK?

12-22 ▶ 你能請他回電給我嗎？

完：Could you have him to get back to me?
順：Ask him to call me back, OK?

12-23 ▶ 我可以留言嗎？

完：May I leave a message?
順：Message, please?

12-24 ▶ 您要等一下嗎？

完：Would you like to be on hold?
順：Hold on, please?

12-25 ▶ 請幫我轉分機112。

完：Please transfer this call to extension 112.
順：Extension 112, please.

12-26 ▶ 我聽不太清楚您說的話。

完：I can't hear you very well.

順：Not clear.

12-27 ▶ 您可以說慢一點嗎？

完：Could you speak a little bit slowly?

順：Slowly, please?

12-28 ▶ 您可以說大聲一點嗎？

完：Could you speak louder?

順：Louder, please?

12-29 ▶ 對不起，我打錯電話了。

完：Sorry, I have the wrong number.

順：Sorry, wrong number.

12-30 ▶ 請告訴我希爾頓飯店的電話號碼。

完：Please give me the phone number for the Hilton Hotel.

順：Phone number for Hilton, please.

12-31 ▶ 我打電話來是要和王先生約開會的時間。

完：I'm calling to set up a meeting with Mr. Wang.

順：Call to set up meeting with Mr. Wang.

12-32 ▶ 我週一上午有空。

完：I have an opening on Monday morning.

順：Monday morning is OK.

12-33 ▶ 請問他的行動電話是幾號？

完：What's the number of his mobile phone?

順：His mobile phone number, please?

12-34 ▶ 我喜歡你的來電答鈴。

完：I love your answer tone.

順：Your answer tone's cool.

12-35 ▶ 你的手機有藍芽裝置嗎？

完：Does your mobile phone have Bluetooth?

順：Does it have Bluetooth?

12-36 ▶ 你開車的時候應該使用免持聽筒裝置。

完：You should use the speakerphone function when driving.

順：Use the speakerphone when you're driving.

12-37 ▶ 我們應遵守行動電話禮儀。

完：We should comply with the mobile phone etiquette.

順：We must obey the mobile phone etiquette.

單字片語維他命 Useful Vocabulary

- **transfer** [træns`fɜ] **v** 轉接
- **operator** [`ɑpə,retə] **n** 總機
- **extension** [ɪk`stɛnʃən] **n** 分機
- **answer tone** 來電答鈴
- **ring tone** 電話鈴聲
- **voice mailbox** 語音信箱
- **telephone secretary** 電話秘書
- **answering machine** 電話答錄機
- **have the wrong number** 打錯電話
- **be away from sb.'s desk** …離開座位；…不在座位上

Bon Voyage!

◀)) MP3 095

救急情境演練 Situation

A : I'd like to send some international mail to Taiwan.
我想寄國際郵件到臺灣。

B : Do you want the express mail or the ordinary mail?
您要寄快捷郵件、還是一般郵件？

A : What's the difference?
請問有什麼差別？

B : The express mail takes only 3 days to Taiwan; the ordinary mail takes 7 days.
快捷郵件到臺灣只要三天，一般郵件要七天。

A : How about the price?
價錢呢？

B : The difference is USD 10 for every 100 grams.
一百公克差十元美金。

A : Please send it by ordinary mail.
請幫我寄一般郵件。

B : OK, I'll do it right away.
好的，我立刻為您辦理。

A : I also need some stamps.
我還要幾張郵票。

B : How many of them?
要多少張？

🅐 : Four five-dollar stamps, five one-dollar stamps and one ten-dollar stamp.
五元郵票四張、一元郵票五張,還有十元郵票一張。

🅑 : Here you are.
這是您的郵票。

KEY SENTENCES
關鍵句

（完 →完整句·順 →順口句）

12-38 ▸ 請問郵局在哪裡?
完 : Excuse me. Where's the post office?
順 : Post office, please?

12-39 ▸ 我想寄這個包裹到臺灣。
完 : I'd like to mail this parcel to Taiwan.
順 : Taiwan, please.

12-40 ▸ 請把這些寄到臺灣。
完 : Please mail these to Taiwan.
順 : Taiwan, please.

12-41 ▸ 請給我一封航空郵簡。
完 : Please give me one aerogram.
順 : One aerogram, please.

12-42 ▸ 我要五張一元的郵票。
完 : I need five one-dollar stamps.
順 : Five one-dollar stamps, please.

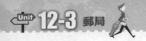

12-43 ▶ 我要買兩張到臺灣的郵票。

完：I would like to buy two stamps for Taiwan.

順：Two stamps for Taiwan, please.

12-44 ▶ 我想寄掛號郵件。

完：I want to send this by registered mail.

順：Registered mail, please.

12-45 ▶ 我想寄快捷郵件。

完：I'd like to send this by express mail.

順：Express mail, please.

12-46 ▶ 我想要寄印刷品。

完：I want to send this as printed matter.

順：Printed matter, please.

12-47 ▶ 在哪裡可以買到郵票？

完：Where can I buy stamps?

順：Stamps, please?

12-48 ▶ 我不曉得這地址的郵遞區號。

完：I have no idea what the zip code is for the address.

順：I don't know the zip code for the address.

單字片語維他命 Useful Vocabulary

- **postal** [`postl̩] **a** 郵政的
- **address** [ə`drɛs] **n** 地址
- **envelope** [`ɛnvə,lop] **n** 信封
- **aerogram** [`ɛrə,græm] **n** 航空郵簡
- **mail box** 信箱；郵筒
- **postal code** 郵遞區號
- **stamped addressed envelope** 回郵信封
- **printed matter** 印刷品
- **bulk mail** 大宗郵件
- **mail baggage car** 郵件小貨車

🔊 MP3 096

救急情境演練 Situation

A : Please give me the stamps for ordinary mail.
請給我平信的郵票。

B : Is it for other state or New York City only?
要其他州的、還是只要紐約市的？

A : Stamps for ordinary mail to New York City.
要紐約市的平信郵票。

B : How many do you need?
請問您需要幾張？

A : Five, please.
請給我五張郵票。

B : There are commemorative stamps, do you need them?

您需要紀念郵票嗎？

A : Can I take a look?
我可以看一下嗎？

B : This is the commemorative stamp for Christmas.
這是聖誕節的紀念郵票。

A : Wow, there's the ice-skating rink of Central Park!
哇，是中央公園的溜冰場耶！

B : Yes, there are five patterns of them.
是的，有五款圖案。

A : I'll take them all!
我五張全要了！

B : OK. Here you are.
好的，這是您的郵票。

KEY SENTENCES
關鍵句 （完 →完整句・順 →順口句）

12-49 ▶ 寄明信片到臺灣要多少錢？

完 : How much to send a postcard to Taiwan?

順 : Postcard to Taiwan, how much?

12-50 ▶ 這個寄到臺灣要多少錢？

完 : How much is the postage for this to Taiwan?

順 : How much is it to Taiwan?

12-51 ▶ 一張到臺灣的郵票要多少錢？

完：How much does it cost a stamp to Taiwan?

順：How much is a stamp to Taiwan?

12-52 ▶ 書籍有特別費率嗎？

完：Is there a special rate for books?

順：Any special rate for books?

12-53 ▶ 海運到臺灣的包裹多少錢？

完：What's the rate for sea parcels to Taiwan?

順：Sea parcel to Taiwan, how much?

12-54 ▶ 到臺灣的郵資如何計算？

完：How to calculate the postage to Taiwan?

順：How much is the postage to Taiwan?

單字片語維他命 Useful Vocabulary

🔻 **mail** [mel] **V** 郵寄

🔻 **stamp** [stæmp] **n** 郵票

🔻 **philately** [fəˋlætlɪ] **n** 集郵

🔻 **postmark** [ˋpost, mɑrk] **n** 郵戳

🔻 **postage** [ˋpostɪdʒ] **n** 郵資；郵費

🔻 **calculate** [ˋkælkjə, let] **V** 計算

🔻 **ordinary mail** 平信

🔻 **certified mail** 掛號信

🔻 **special rate** 特別費率

🔻 **mail-order service** 郵購服務

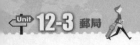
◄») MP3 097

救急情境演練 Situation

A : How long does it take to Taiwan?
這個寄到臺灣需要多久時間？

B : Do you want international express or ordinary mail?
您要寄國際快遞、還是一般郵件？

A : What's the difference?
有何差別？

B : International express takes only 3 days.
國際快遞只要三天。

A : How about ordinary mail?
一般郵件呢？

B : About 7 to 10 working days.
大約要七到十個工作天。

A : How about the price?
價格呢？

B : It's 20 US dollars every 100 grams for international express.
國際快遞一百公克二十塊美金。

B : On the other hand, it's 10 US dollars every 100 grams for ordinary mail.
一般郵件則是一百公克十塊美金。

A : Hmm, ordinary mail, please.
嗯，麻煩寄一般郵件。

B : It is 200 grams.
重量是兩百公克。

410

B: 2,000 US dollars, please.
　　總共是兩千塊美金，麻煩您。

（**完** →完整句．**順** →順口句）

12-55 ▶ 它什麼時候會到臺灣？

完: When will this get to Taiwan?
順: When to arrive at Taiwan?

12-56 ▶ 什麼方式會最快寄到？

完: What's the fastest way to send it?
順: The fastest way, please?

12-57 ▶ 一般運送要多久才會到？

完: How long will it take by surface mail?
順: How long by surface mail?

12-58 ▶ 請問海運需要多久時間？

完: How long is the shipping time by sea?
順: How long?

12-59 ▶ 請問空運需要多久時間？

完: How long is the shipping time by air?
順: How long?

12-60 ▶ 請問最快速寄到臺灣的方式是什麼？

完: What's the fastest way to deliver to
　　Taiwan?
順: What is the fastest way to Taiwan?

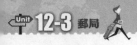

12-61 ▶ 麻煩你，我要寄國際快捷。

完：I'd like to send an international express, please.

順：International express, please.

單字片語雜他命 Useful Vocabulary

🔖 **shipping** [`ʃɪpɪŋ] **n** 海運

🔖 **scale** [skel] **n** 秤；天平

🔖 **gram** [ɡræm] **n** 公克

🔖 **kilogram** [`kɪlə͵ɡræm] **n** 公斤

🔖 **mail carrier** 郵差

🔖 **domestic mail** 國內郵件

🔖 **foreign mail** 國外郵件

🔖 **air mail** 航空郵件

🔖 **surface mail** 普通郵件

🔖 **international express** 國際快捷

(((●))) **MP3 098**

救急情境演練 Situation

🅐：I'd like to send these things to Taiwan.
我要寄這些東西到臺灣。

🅑：You can't send meat products.
肉品不能寄喔。

🅑：More than 20 kg should be separated into

412

boxes.
超過二十公斤要分箱裝。

A: Could you weigh it for me?
你可以幫我秤一下重量嗎？

B: OK, I'll weigh it for you.
好，我為您秤一下重量。

B: It's 30 kg. You have to buy 2 boxes.
共三十公斤，您需要買兩個紙箱。

A: How about these?
那這些呢？

B: They are OK, but they are overweight and you need to separate into boxes.
可以，但它們超重了，需要分裝。

A: Well, I need three more boxes.
那麼，我還要多買三個紙箱。

A: How much is it?
要多少錢呢？

B: 120 dollars, please.
一百二十元美金，麻煩您。

A: Here you are.
給你。

KEY SENTENCES
關鍵句 🔑

(**完**→完整句 · **順**→順口句)

12-62 ▶ 我可以寄水果到臺灣嗎？

完: Can I send fruits to Taiwan?

順: Fruits to Taiwan, OK?

12-63 ▶ 包裹的最大長度是多少？

完：What's the maximum length for parcel post?

順：The maximum length, please?

12-64 ▶ 寄到臺灣的航空包裹有重量限制嗎？

完：Is there a weight limit on air parcel post to Taiwan?

順：Any weight limit on parcels to Taiwan?

單字片語雜他命 Useful Vocabulary

◥ **weight** [wet] **n** 重量

◥ **width** [wɪdθ] **n** 寬度

◥ **length** [lɛŋθ] **n** 長度

◥ **letter** [`lɛtə] **n** 信

◥ **parcel** [`parsl] **n** 包裹

◥ **postcard** [`post͵kard] **n** 明信片

◥ **limitation** [͵lɪmə`teʃən] **n** 限制

◥ **love letter** 情書

◥ **customs duty** 關稅

◥ **dead letter** 無法投遞的信件

　　如果，「在臺灣接聽國際電話，還需負擔國際漫遊的費用」，那麼這位受話者必然是在臺灣持用別國的行動電話門號。

　　所謂的「國際電話」(international call)，就是「從甲國打電話到乙國」。撥碼結構是「發話地的國際冠碼=>被叫國碼=>被叫區碼=>被叫市話號碼」，或「發話地的國際冠碼=>被叫國碼=>被叫行動號碼」。如果「發話地的國際冠碼」不只一種的話，表示該國有多家行動電信業者，費率會按照所選擇撥打國際冠碼所屬的業者計價。

　　所謂「國際漫遊」，就是「拿甲國的行動門號到乙國使用」。持行動電話出國漫遊時，請記住一個原則，那就是「入境隨俗」：發話費率是依照當地行動電話費率再加上漫遊處理費用計算的；減價時段則是依照當地電信業者的規定，撥碼方式也是依照當地的撥法。因此不論撥回臺灣的是市話或行動電話，都當作是從該國打國際電話到臺灣來。

　　接電話是否該付費這一點，得要取決於各國或各家行動電信業者。以臺灣的業者來說，在臺灣單純接電話並無涉及國際漫遊，業者不會向受話方收費，但業者間會互相支付空時費、接續費等費用；而中國的業者則要發話業者向發話方收費，受話業者向受話方收費，各收各的。

　　什麼是「漫遊」(roaming)？講白一點，就是「您的行動門號在其他業者的地區還能繼續使用」。其實漫遊並不一定指國際漫遊，舉例來說，最初東信、泛亞分別只取得中區和南區GSM900的單區執照，這兩家用戶原本只能個別在中區和南區使用而已；但業者間簽訂漫遊互惠條款後，其門號在對方網路系統也能認證使用了。臺灣的漫遊，舉東信、泛亞、臺哥大為例，其用戶可在三網裡漫遊；而和信和遠傳則可在雙網裡漫遊。像中國幅員遼闊，還分成本省漫遊、省外漫遊、國際漫遊等模式(參考 http://www.chinamobile.com/10086/help/faq/ commnetanalyze/)。

　　有關我國旅客手機國際漫遊的費用，在各家行動電信業者網站上所列出的價格，已合計了漫遊處理費與稅金，計價單位是「分鐘」，所以只要直接乘以幾分鐘來計算費率即可。不過，也有些業者會註解在旅遊當地每通還要加收多少錢；因此，建議出國前先上各家行動電信業者網站看清楚收費規則。

Part. 13

意外狀況篇

Unit 13-1 遺失

Unit 13-2 遭竊

Unit 13-3 交通事故

Unit 13-4 生病受傷

* 預防時差筆記

🔊)) MP3 099

救急情境演練 Situation

A : My passport is gone!
我的護照不見了！

B : When is the last time you saw it?
您最後一次是在哪裡看見的？

A : I don't know.
我不清楚。

B : Don't worry. We will help you find it.
您不要著急，我們會協助您尋找。

A : I have to go back to Taiwan tomorrow, what can I do?
我明天就要回臺灣了，怎麼辦？

B : We will immediately inform the Taiwan Office for you.
我們馬上為您通知臺灣辦事處。

A : Please help me deal with it as soon as possible!
請趕快幫我處理！

B : Don't panic. I'll do it immediately.
您別慌張，我會立即處理。

A : Could you please see if it's been turned in?
可否幫我看看是否有人送還？

B : OK, I'll notice you if anyone find your passport.
好的，如果有人找到您的護照，我就會通知您。

Ⓐ：I appreciate your help!
　　承蒙您的協助！

Ⓑ：It's my pleasure!
　　這是我的榮幸！

KEY SENTENCES
關鍵句 （完→完整句 · 順→順口句）

13-01 ▶ 我的筆電好像不見了。
完：I think I have lost my laptop.
順：My laptop is gone.

13-02 ▶ 我的護照不見了。
完：My passport is missing.
順：My passport is gone.

13-03 ▶ 我的信用卡掉了。
完：I've lost my credit card.
順：My credit card is gone.

13-04 ▶ 我姊姊掉了旅行支票。
完：My sister lost her traveler's checks.
順：My sister's traveler's checks, lost.

13-05 ▶ 我不確定掉在哪裡。
完：I'm not sure where I left it.
順：Not sure the site.

13-06 ▶ 可能掉在我的房間。
完：I might have left it in my room.

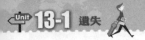

順：It maybe in my room.

13-07 ▶ 我的包包掉在計程車上了。

完：I left my bag in the taxi.

順：In the taxi.

13-08 ▶ 請問有失物招領處嗎？

完：Do you have a lost-and-found department?

順：Lost-and-found department, please?

13-09 ▶ 可否看一下是否有人送還？

完：Could you please see if it's been turned in?

順：Anybody returned it?

13-10 ▶ 那是一只紅色的小錢包。

完：That's a small red purse.

順：A small, red purse.

13-11 ▶ 它價值非凡。

完：It's very valuable.

順：Very expensive.

13-12 ▶ 麻煩你，我要掛失信用卡。

完：I'd like to report a missing credit card, please.

順：Report a missing credit card, please.

13-13 ▶ 我來這邊掛失旅行支票。

完：I'm here to report the loss of my traveler's checks.

順：Report the loss of traveler's checks, please.

13-14 ▶ 你要先到當地警察局取得失竊證明。

完：You should get a Report of Loss at a local police office first.

順：Get a Report of Loss at a local police office first.

單字片語維他命 Useful Vocabulary

🔖 **panic** [ˋpænɪk] **V** 驚慌

🔖 **bulletin** [ˋbʊlətɪn] **V** 公告

🔖 **embassy** [ˋɛmbəsɪ] **n** 大使館

🔖 **missing** [ˋmɪsɪŋ] **a** 找不到的

🔖 **valuable** [ˋvæljʊəbḷ] **a** 貴重的

🔖 **turn in** 歸還

🔖 **look for** 尋找

🔖 **lose one's head** 驚慌失措

🔖 **lost property** 招領的失物

🔖 **lost-and-found department** 失物招領處

MP3 100

救急情境演練 Situation

A : My bag was stolen!
我的包包被偷了！

B : Where did you lose it?
您是在哪裡遺失的？

A : At the restaurant. I left my seat for a while and it was gone when I returned.
在餐廳。我離開座位一會兒，回來就不見了。

B : Have any purses been turned in at the restaurant?
有人在餐廳裡撿到錢包嗎？

A : No, do you think that I should report to the police?
沒有，你認為我該向警方報案嗎？

B : Yes. You should go.
是的，您該去報案。

A : Can you help me?
你可以幫幫我嗎？

B : Sure, this is the direction to the police office.
可以，這是警察局的方向。

A : How can I get there?
我要怎麼過去呢？

B : We'll send a bellboy to escort you there.
我們會派名腳伕護送您過去。

A : Thanks a lot!

太感謝了！

B：You're welcome.
不必客氣。

KEY SENTENCES

關鍵句 🔑 （完 →完整句・順 →順口句）

13-15 ▶ 我的皮包被偷了。
完：My bag was stolen.
順：My bag, stolen.

13-16 ▶ 我的手機被搶了！
完：My mobile phone was robbed!
順：My phone, robbed!

13-17 ▶ 阻止那個男人！
完：Stop that man!
順：Stop him!

13-18 ▶ 請幫我抓住那個黑衣男！
完：Please catch that man in black for me!
順：Catch that man in black!

13-19 ▶ 不好意思，請問警察局在哪裡？
完：Excuse me. Where's the police office?
順：Police office, please?

13-20 ▶ 請報警。
完：Please call the police.
順：Police, please.

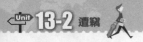
13-21 ▶ 我該怎麼找警察來？

完：How do I call the police?

順：Police, please?

13-22 ▶ 我想通報竊案。

完：I want to report a theft.

順：Theft.

13-23 ▶ 我要報失我的護照。

完：I'd like to report a stolen passport.

順：My passport was stolen.

13-24 ▶ 我的旅行支票被偷了。

完：My traveler's checks have been taken.

順：My checks were stolen.

13-25 ▶ 有人闖入我的車內。

完：Someone broke into my car.

順：Someone intruded my car.

13-26 ▶ 一定有人扒過我的口袋。

完：Someone must have picked my pocket.

順：Someone picked my pocket.

13-27 ▶ 我要下公車時，有人搶了我的錢包就跑。

完：As I was getting off the bus, someone grabbed my purse and ran away.

順：I was off bus and someone robbed my purse.

13-28 ▶ 那個強盜瘦瘦的、穿黑色夾克，三十幾歲左右。

完：The robber is very thin, in a black jacket and in his thirties.

順：Thin, in black jacket and thirties.

13-29 ▶ 我需要辦什麼手續嗎？

完：Is there any procedure that I need to do'?

順：Any procedure to do?

13-30 ▶ 能幫我取消信用卡嗎？

完：Could you cancel my credit card?

順：Cancel my credit card, please?

13-31 ▶ 我的簽證能重發嗎？

完：Can I get my visa reissued?

順：Visa reissued, OK?

單字片語雖他命 Useful Vocabulary

▼ **rob** [rɑb] **V** 搶劫

▼ **theft** [θɛft] **n** 偷竊

▼ **report** [rɪˋport] **V** 報案

▼ **arrest** [əˋrɛst] **V** 逮捕

▼ **pilferer** [ˋpɪlfərə] **n** 小偷

▼ **pickpocket** [ˋpɪk͵pɑkɪt] **n** 扒手

▼ **witness** [ˋwɪtnɪs] **n** 目擊者

▼ **nab** [næb] **V** 逮住現行犯

▼ **burglar** [ˋbɜɡlə] **V** 進行盜竊

▼ **police office** 警察局

🔊 **MP3 101**

救急情境演練 Situation

🅐 : You have to report the car accident.
你得通報車禍。

🅑 : Yes, I've dialed 911.
有,我已經打了九一一專線。

🅐 : Can you describe how it happened?
你能描述一下它是如何發生的嗎?

🅑 : I saw that car speed up from my rear view mirror.
我從後視鏡看到那輛車加速。

🅐 : Could you give me more details?
可以再給我一點細節嗎?

🅑 : Then, the car rear-ended me a moment later.
過不久,那輛車就從後面撞上來了。

🅐 : I suggest that you can make reconciliation privately.
我建議你們可以私下和解。

🅑 : I think we can discuss with each other.
我想我們可以互相討論一下。

🅐 : Do you have insurance?
你有投保嗎?

🅑 : Yes, I do.
是的,我有。

🅐 : You may call your agent to deal with the compensation.

你可以打電話叫業務員辦理賠事宜。

B：Yes, I just want to call.
嗯，我正要打去呢。

KEY SENTENCES
關鍵句（完 →完整句・順 →順口句）

13-32 ▶ 我出車禍了。
完：I've had a car accident.
順：Car accident.

13-33 ▶ 我後面的車撞到我的車。
完：The car behind of mine hit my car.
順：That car hit mine.

13-34 ▶ 他後退撞到我。
完：He backed right into me.
順：He hit me.

13-35 ▶ 我沒看見他過來。
完：I didn't see him coming.
順：I neglected him.

13-36 ▶ 那個時候是綠燈。
完：That moment was green light.
順：It was a green light.

13-37 ▶ 他紅燈未停。
完：He didn't stop for the red light.
順：He ran the red light.

13-38 ▸ 請報警。

完：Please call the police.

順：Police, please.

13-39 ▸ 有人受傷了。

完：Someone's got injured.

順：Someone's hurt.

13-40 ▸ 請叫救護車來。

完：Please call the ambulance.

順：Ambulance, please.

13-41 ▸ 我看到他被摩托車撞了。

完：I saw him was hit by a motorcycle.

順：He was hit by a motorcycle.

13-42 ▸ 他需要急救。

完：He needs first aid.

順：First aid!

13-43 ▸ 他的頭部受了重傷。

完：His head was critically injured.

順：His head hurt badly.

13-44 ▸ 我需要一名律師。

完：I need a lawyer.

順：A lawyer, please.

13-45 ▸ 請載我去急診室。

完：Please drive me to the emergency room.

順：Emergency room, please.

單字片語維他命 Useful Vocabulary

- **dial** [ˋdaɪəl] **v** 打；撥(電話)
- **injure** [ˋɪndʒɚ] **v** 受傷；損壞
- **ambulance** [ˋæmbjələns] **n** 救護車
- **collision** [kəˋlɪʒən] **n** 追撞；碰撞
- **fender-bender** [ˋfɛndɚˋbɛndɚ] **n** 小車禍；擦撞
- **speeding** [ˋspidɪŋ] **n** 行車超速
- **rear view mirror** 後視鏡
- **run the red light** 闖紅燈
- **write a ticket** 開罰單
- **make reconciliation** 達成和解協議

The real voyage of discovery consists not in seeing new landscapes, but in having new eyes.

★ ★ ★ ★

真正的探索旅程不只見識到新奇的景觀，
還包括擁有嶄新的眼界。

🔊 MP3 102

救急情境演練 Situation

A : Please tell me how you feel and what your symptoms are?
請告訴我，你感覺怎麼樣、有什麼症狀呢？

B : I have a fever and cough a lot.
我發燒了，又咳個不停。

A : OK, I will take your temperature.
好，我來量一下你的體溫。

B : Is it serious?
嚴重嗎？

A : No, it's not that serious. You need a good rest and drink more water.
不，沒那麼嚴重，你需要好好休息和多喝水。

A : Roll up your sleeve. I'll give you an injection.
捲起袖子，我要給你打個針。

B : How long will it take to get better?
什麼時候會好一點？

A : It could be one week long for you to get better.
可能要一個星期，你才會覺得好一點。

B : Can I have a medical certificate?
可以給我一份診斷證明嗎？

A : Sure. You have to pay extra 100 dollars, though.
當然可以，不過你要多付一百塊。

B : That's OK. I'll give it to my insurance agent.
不要緊，我是要給保險員的。

A : Here you are.
拿去吧。

KEY SENTENCES

關鍵句 （完 →完整句・順 →順口句）

13-46 ▶ 我想預約看診。

完 : I'd like to make an appointment to see a doctor.

順 : Appointment with doctor, please.

13-47 ▶ 我今天下午可以看診嗎？

完 : Can I come to see a doctor this afternoon?

順 : This afternoon, OK?

13-48 ▶ 我發燒了。

完 : I have a fever.

順 : Fever.

13-49 ▶ 我拉肚子了。

完 : I have diarrhea.

順 : Diarrhea.

13-50 ▶ 我好像得了流感。

完 : I think I have the flu.

順 : Flu.

13-51 ▶ 我流鼻水。

完：I have a runny nose.
順：Runny nose.

13-52 ▶ 我咳得很厲害。

完：I have a bad cough.
順：Bad cough.

13-53 ▶ 我覺得頭暈。

完：I feel dizzy.
順：Dizzy.

13-54 ▶ 我喉嚨痛。

完：I have a sore throat.
順：Sore throat.

13-55 ▶ 把他抬到擔架上。

完：Lift him up and place him on a litter.
順：Move him on a litter.

13-56 ▶ 我割到拇指。

完：I cut my thumb.
順：I cut it. (用手指出患部)

13-57 ▶ 嚴重嗎？

完：Is it serious?
順：Serious?

13-58 ▶ 斷了嗎？

完：Is it broken?
順：Broken?

13-59 ▶ 要多久才會好？

完 : How long will it take to heal?

順 : How long to heal?

13-60 ▶ 我得住院多久？

完 : How long do I have to stay in the hospital?

順 : How long should I stay in the hospital?

13-61 ▶ 每天換藥一次。

完 : Change the dressing once daily.

順 : Change it once a day.

13-62 ▶ 傷口可能有感染。

完 : The wound is probably infected.

順 : It's probably infected.

13-63 ▶ 你的狀況很穩定。

完 : You are in stable condition.

順 : Your condition is stable.

13-64 ▶ 我還可以繼續旅行嗎？

完 : Can I still travel?

順 : Travel, OK?

13-65 ▶ 可否開處方箋給我？

完 : Can I have a prescription?

順 : Prescription, please?

13-66 ▶ 可否開診斷書，好讓我申請保險理賠？

完：Will you write down your diagnosis for my insurance claim?

順：Diagnosis for my insurance claim, please?

單字片語維他命 Useful Vocabulary

- **injection** [ɪnˋdʒɛkʃən] **n** 注射
- **operation** [͵ɑpəˋreʃən] **n** 手術
- **treatment** [ˋtritmənt] **n** 治療
- **diagnosis** [͵daɪəgˋnosɪs] **n** 診斷
- **symptom** [ˋsɪmptəm] **n** 症狀；徵候
- **prescription** [prɪˋskrɪpʃən] **n** 處方；藥方
- **have a fever** 發燒
- **take sb.'s temperature** 量⋯的體溫
- **insurance claim** 保險理賠
- **medical certificate** 診斷證明；醫療證明

背包客旅遊筆記 BON VOYAGE！

時差(jet lag)，是指因飛行橫越三個以上時區時，所造成日夜節奏脫序的現象；可能會導致暈眩、睡眠障礙(失眠或嗜睡)、全身倦怠疲勞、注意力不集中、情緒不穩、興趣減少、食慾不振、反應遲鈍、思想緩慢等不適。

一般而言，往西飛較易調整時差，兒童適應時差的能力又比成人強，原因可能是兒童的睡眠行為較能適應環境改變；而老人適應時差的能力則較弱。

搭乘長途班機(long-distance flight)的旅客，最害怕因時差(time difference)所引起的「時差症候群」(jet syndrome)。相信很多人有這種難受的經驗，這種情況尤其在夏季搭機前往高緯度(high latitude)國家更為顯著，因為高緯度地區的日照時間很長(the daytime is much longer)，國人常適應不良；如果在飛機上睡不好，勢必會影響身體狀況及旅遊行程。

為了不讓遊興被時差一掃而空，以下提供幾個避免產生時差症候群的方法：

1. 出發前幾天改變睡眠習慣。根據我國與目的地的時差，提早或延後自己的睡眠時間。

2. 別在啟程前幾天的下午喝含有咖啡因的飲料(如茶、咖啡、可樂等)。

3. 出發前調整飲食型態。原則上，登機的前

三天要吃飽些,早餐及中餐要吃富含蛋白質的食物,晚餐則吃富含澱粉的食物;第二、三天則儘量吃清淡點。

4. 在飛行途中可多喝些水、果汁,但避免飲用含有酒精的飲料。

5. 到達目的地後,白天多吃含蛋白質的食物,晚餐則吃含高澱粉的食物。

6. 抵達旅遊地點後,多作些日間活動,避免太早就寢;也別在睡前飲用太多含咖啡因的飲料。

7. 如有必要,可與醫師商討服用褪黑激素或短效安眠藥,但服用這類藥物後,不能從事需要警覺性的事務。

8. 除了可以應用上述方法來克服時差困擾外,在搭機前擁有充足的睡眠、維持健康的飲食及運動習慣、在飛行中注意補充水份、抵達目的地後自我強制配合當地時間作息,也可以調整時差。

附錄

* 必殺單字

* 旅遊補充包

⊗ 十二星座

中　文	英　文	日　期
♈ 牡羊座	Aries	03 / 21～04 / 19
♉ 金牛座	Taurus	04 / 20～05 / 20
♊ 雙子座	Gemini	05 / 21～06 / 21
♋ 巨蟹座	Cancer	06 / 22～07 / 22
♌ 獅子座	Leo	07 / 23～08 / 22
♍ 處女座	Virgo	08 / 23～09 / 22
♎ 天秤座	Libra	09 / 23～10 / 23
♏ 天蠍座	Scorpio	10 / 24～11 / 22
♐ 射手座	Sagittarius	11 / 23～12 / 21
♑ 魔羯座	Capricorn	12 / 22～01 / 19
♒ 水瓶座	Aquarius	01 / 20～02 / 18
♓ 雙魚座	Pisces	02 / 19～03 / 20

數字

英　文	中文	英　文	中文
one	一	two	二
three	三	four	四
five	五	six	六
seven	七	eight	八
nine	九	ten	十
eleven	十一	twelve	十二
thirteen	十三	fourteen	十四
fifteen	十五	sixteen	十六
seventeen	十七	eighteen	十八
nineteen	十九	twenty	二十
twenty one	二十一	twenty two	二十二
thirty	三十	forty	四十
fifty	五十	sixty	六十
seventy	七十	eighty	八十
ninety	九十	hundred	百

⊗ 顏 色

英　文	中文	英　文	中文
maroon	棗紅色	pink	粉紅色
violet	紫羅蘭色	amber	琥珀黃
aqua	水綠色	coral	珊瑚紅
indigo	靛青	ivory	象牙白
khaki	卡其色	lavender	薰衣草紫
olive	橄欖綠	skyblue	天藍色
navy blue	深藍	sea green	海洋綠
light yellow	鵝黃	henna	棕紅
gold	金色	silver	銀色
bronze	古銅色	camel	駝色
cream	奶油色	lila	丁香紫
modena	深紫	mustard	芥末黃
viridity	碧綠	breen	褐綠
azure	蔚藍	ultramarine	青藍
vermeil	朱紅	garnet	石榴紅
scarlet	緋紅	aquamarine	藍寶石色

✺ 菜 單

英 文	中 文	英 文	中 文
ham	火腿	kidney	腰子
salad	沙拉	liver	肝
lobster	龍蝦	lamb	小羊肉
mushroom	磨菇	mussel	淡菜
meatballs	肉丸	omelette	煎蛋捲
pizza	披薩	noodles	麵
oyster	牡蠣	roast duck	烤鴨
ox tongue	牛舌	sausage	香腸
shrimp	蝦子	salmon	鮭魚
veal	小牛肉	cheese	起司
truffle	松露	crab	螃蟹
spaghetti	義大利麵	chicken wings	雞翅
salad	沙拉	seafood	海鮮
skewer	烤肉串	mashed patatoes	馬鈴薯泥
chicken nuggets	雞塊	fish fillet	炸魚條

◉ 飲 料

英 文	中文	英 文	中文
black tea	紅茶	green tea	綠茶
milk tea	奶茶	lemon tea	檸檬茶
Coca-Cola	可口可樂	soda	汽水
lemonade	檸檬水	mineral water	礦泉水
beer	啤酒	wine	水果酒
white wine	白酒	red wine	紅酒
sherry	雪利酒	whiskey	威士忌
brandy	白蘭地	gin	琴酒
cocktails	雞尾酒	liqueur	利口酒
rum	蘭姆酒	punch	潘趣酒
sake	日本清酒	vermouth	苦艾酒
Beaujulais	薄酒萊新酒	Mocha	摩卡咖啡
milk shake	奶昔	herbal tea	花草茶
root beer	沙士	mint tea	薄荷茶
Bloody Mary	血腥瑪麗	Screw Driver	螺絲起子

❂ 甜 點

英 文	中文	英 文	中文
apple pie	蘋果派	pumpkin pie	南瓜派
waffle	格子鬆餅	egg roll	蛋捲
puff	泡芙	custard	蛋奶凍
pudding	布丁	ice cream	冰淇淋
cookies	甜餅乾	Swiss roll	瑞士捲
jelly	果凍	crépe	可麗餅
muffin	馬芬鬆餅	fruit tart	水果塔
soufflé	舒芙蕾	cream brulee	焦糖布丁
brownie	布朗尼	macaroon	馬卡龍
tiramisu	提拉米蘇	madeleine	瑪德琳蛋糕
chiffon	戚風蛋糕	sponge cake	海綿蛋糕
cheesecake	起司蛋糕	pastry	酥皮點心
apple cinnamon roll	蘋果肉桂捲	black forest cake	黑森林蛋糕
egg-free cake	無蛋蛋糕	sundae	聖代
scone	司康餅	mousse	慕斯

🧭 紀念品

英　文	中文	英　文	中文
duty-free items	免稅品	necklace	項鍊
T-shirt	T恤衫	key chain	鑰匙圈
cell-phone charm	手機吊飾	pressed flower	壓花
magnet	磁鐵	oil painting	油畫
scarf	圍巾	stuffed toy	填充玩具
tea	茶葉	mug	馬克杯
tie	領帶	toy	玩具
handicraft	手工藝品	essential oil	精油
jade	玉石	jewelry	珠寶
carpet	地毯	embroidery	刺繡品
antique	古董	sculpture	雕塑品
pottery	陶器	china	瓷器
snow ball	雪花球	slide	幻燈片
jigsaw	拼圖	model	模型
figure	公仔玩具	pin	別針

⊗ 住　宿

英　文	中文	英　文	中文
5-star hotel	五星級飯店	budget hotel	廉價旅館
bungalow	平房	lodge	旅舍
motel	汽車旅館	apartment for lease	出租公寓
suite	套房	hostel	青年旅館
B & B (Bed and Breakfast)	民宿(一宿一泊)	guest room	客房
single room	單人房	double room	雙人房(一床)
triple room	三人房	family room	家庭房
twin beds	雙床	queen size	加大雙人床
king size	超大雙人床	extra bed	加床
extra night	續住	long stay	長住
check-in	入住	check-out	退房
high season	旺季	low season	淡季

飯店服務

英 文	中文	英 文	中文
bath salts	浴鹽	body lotion	身體乳液
cleansing oil	卸妝油	lotion / toner	化妝水
mask	面膜	hair dryer	吹風機
toilet paper	衛生紙	cotton swabs	棉花棒
razor	刮鬍刀	shaving cream	刮鬍膏
comb	梳子	cotton pad	化妝棉
aroma stress relief	芳香紓壓	toxin relief	排毒淨化
lymphatic massage	淋巴引流按摩	acupressure	指壓按摩
Thai massage	泰式按摩	foot massage	腳底按摩
hot spring	溫泉	Jacuzzi	按摩浴缸
steam bath	蒸汽浴	sauna	三溫暖

◉ 搭 機

英 文	中文	英 文	中文
passport	護照	boarding pass	登機證
gate	登機門	baggage / luggage	行李
carry-on luggage	手提行李	belongings	隨身物件
first class	頭等艙	business class	商務艙
economy class	經濟艙	international airport	國際機場
international flight	國際航線	check-in desk	報到櫃檯
domestic airport	國內機場	domestic flight	國內航線
take off	起飛	landing	降落
waiting room	候機室	metal detector	金屬探測器
baggage tag	行李標籤	luggage carousel	行李轉盤

機上小物

英 文	中文	英 文	中文
catalog / catalogue	商品型錄	manual	說明書
immigration card	入境卡	oxygen mask	氧氣罩
life jacket	救生衣	airsickness bag	嘔吐袋
poker	撲克牌	indicator	指示燈
Customs declaration card	海關申報單	headset	耳機
tissue	面紙	menu	菜單
hot water	熱水	warm water	溫水
ice water	冰水	lavatory	廁所
dining car	餐車	pillow	枕頭
perfume	香水	skin care	保養品
makeup	化妝品	souvenir	紀念品
cigar	雪茄	cigarette	菸
champagne	香檳	blanket	毯子
white spirit	白葡萄酒	tray table	餐桌托盤

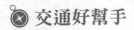 交通好幫手

英 文	中 文	英 文	中 文
MRT	捷運	MRT station	捷運站
subway	地鐵	taxi	計程車
ricksha	人力車	train	火車
helicopter	直升機	urban bus	市區巴士
bus station	公車站	train station	火車站
hot air balloon	熱氣球	cable car	纜車
taxi stand	計程車招呼站	map	地圖
travel service counter	旅遊服務處	timetable	時刻表
sailboat	帆船	gondola	貢多拉船
ferry	渡輪	monorail	單軌電車
tram	陸上電車	airplane	飛機

✲ 汽車種類

英　文	中文	英　文	中文
Mercedes-Benz	賓士	BMW	寶馬
Rolls-Royce	勞斯萊斯	Porsche	保時捷
Lotus	蓮花	Austin	奧斯汀
Lincoln	林肯	Volkswagen	福斯
Audi	奧迪	Jaguar	捷豹
Saab	薩博	Honda	本田
Mitsubishi	三菱	Ford	福特
Toyota	豐田	Opel	歐寶
Volvo	富豪	Suzuki	鈴木
Ferrari	法拉利	Chrysler	克萊斯勒
Alfa Romeo	愛快羅密歐	GM	通用汽車
Hyundai	現代汽車	Nissan	日產
Mazda	馬自達	Renault	雷諾

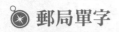 郵局單字

英　文	中文	英　文	中文
mailbag	郵袋	commemorative stamps	紀念郵票
delivery	投遞	international parcel	國際包裹
air mail	航空信	mail tracking number	郵件追蹤號碼
mailbox	信箱	package / parcel	包裹
POB (Post Office Box)	郵政信箱	postmark	郵戳
international EMS	國際快捷	bulk mail	大宗郵件
registered mail	掛號郵件	e-post	電子化便利郵局
ordinary mail	普通郵件	express mail	快遞郵件
express counter	快速窗口	scale	磅秤

◎ 國際電話怎麼撥？

1. 從國外撥回臺灣：該國國際冠碼＋臺灣國碼 (886)＋區域號碼(去0)＋用戶電話號碼。

例如從加拿大撥回高雄市：011＋886＋7＋ xxx-xxxx；撥打行動電話：去掉電話號碼 的第一個0即可，例如：011＋886＋932- xxxxxx。

2. 從臺灣撥往國外：臺灣國際冠碼(002)＋該國 國碼＋區域號碼 (去0)＋用戶電話號碼。

＊亞洲

國家地區	冠碼	國碼	國家地區	冠碼	國碼
中國大陸 China	00	86	南韓 South Korea	001	82
臺灣 Taiwan	002	886	科威特 Kuwait	00	965
香港 Hong Kong	001	842	巴基斯坦 Pakistan	00	92
印度 India	00	91	澳門 Macao	00	853
馬爾地夫 Maldives	00	960	馬來西亞 Malaysia	00	60
印尼 Indonesia	001	62	菲律賓 Philippines	00	63

伊朗 Iran	00	98	沙烏地阿拉伯 Saudi Arabia	00	966
伊拉克 Iraq	00	964	新加坡 Singapore	001	65
以色列 Israel	00	972	巴布亞紐內亞 Papua New Guinea	05	675
日本 Japan	001	81	尼泊爾 Nepal	00	977
所羅門群島 Solomon Is.	00	677	葉門 Yemen	001	66
斯里蘭卡 Sri Lanka	00	94	土耳其 Turkey	00	90
泰國 Thailand	001	66	越南 Vietnam	00	84

＊歐　洲

國家地區	冠碼	國碼	國家地區	冠碼	國碼
葡萄牙 Portugal	00	351	義大利 Italy	00	39
西班牙 Spain	00	34	盧森堡 Luxembourg	00	352
瑞典 Sweden	009	46	摩納哥 Monaco	00	377

瑞士 Switzerland	00	41	荷蘭 Netherlands	00	31
英國 U.K.	00	44	挪威 Norway	095	47
德國 Germany	00	49	波蘭 Poland	00	48
俄羅斯 Russia	810	7	羅馬尼亞 Romania	00	40
匈牙利 Hungary	00	36	奧地利 Austria	00	43
冰島 Iceland	00	354	比利時 Belgium	00	32
愛爾蘭 Ireland	00	353	丹麥 Denmark	00	45
馬爾他 Malta	00	356	芬蘭 Finland	00	358
希臘 Greece	00	30	法國 France	00	358

*美　洲

國家地區	冠碼	國碼	國家地區	冠碼	國碼
阿根廷 Argentina	00	54	厄瓜多 Ecuador	00	593
美國 U.S.A.	011	1	墨西哥 Mexico	00	32

加拿大 Canada	011	1	烏拉圭 Uruguay	00	598
智利 Chile	00	56	祕魯 Peru	00	51
哥倫比亞 Colombia	60	57	瓜地馬拉 Guatemala	00	502
多明尼加 Dominican Rep.	011	1809	哥斯大黎加 Costa Rica	00	506
巴拿馬 Panama	00	507	薩爾瓦多 El Salvador	00	503
宏都拉斯 Honduras	00	504	巴西 Brazil	00	55
尼加拉瓜 Nicaragua	00	505			

＊大洋洲

國家地區	冠碼	國碼	國家地區	冠碼	國碼
澳洲 Australia	0011	61	關島 Guam	011	1671
帛琉 Palau	011	680	紐西蘭 New Zealand	00	64
斐濟 Fiji	05	679			

*非 洲

國家地區	冠碼	國碼	國家地區	冠碼	國碼
摩洛哥 Morocco	00	212	坦尚尼亞 Tanzania	00	255
奈及利亞 Nigeria	009	234	阿爾及利亞 Algeria	00	213
南非 South Africa	09	27	埃及 Egypt	00	20
肯亞 Kenya	000	254			

國人旅外救急小幫手

1. 國人若在國外遇到急難事件,可立即撥打各駐外館處的緊急聯絡電話;若一時未能與駐外館處取得聯繫,當事人可直接或由其國內親友聯絡「外交部緊急聯絡中心」。

2. 國內的免付費「旅外國人緊急服務專線」是:0800-085-095(後六碼諧音「您幫我、您救我」);自海外撥打的付費電話為:當地國碼+886-800-085095,二十四小時均有專人接聽服務。外交部緊急聯絡中心另增設「旅外國人急難救助全球免付費專線」,電話是:800-0885-0885(後八碼諧音:「您幫幫我、您幫幫我」),可直接聯絡求援(目前因電信技術問題,開放以下二十二個國家/地區)。

* 全球免付費專線電話一覽表

001-010-800-0885-0885 0033-010-800-0885-0885 日本	001-800-0885-0885 新加坡
0011-800-0885-0885 澳洲	00-800-0885-0885 瑞典
001-800-0885-0885 泰國	00-800-0885-0885 義大利
014-800-0885-0885 以色列	00-800-0885-0885 英國
00-800-0885-0885 比利時	011-800-0885-0885 美國
00-800-0885-0885 法國	00-800-0885-0885 荷蘭
011-800-0885-0885 加拿大	00-800-0885-0885 德國
00-800-0885-0885 阿根廷	001-800-0885-0885 南韓
00-800-0885-0885 瑞士	00-800-0885-0885 紐西蘭
001-800-0885-0885 香港	00-800-0885-0885 馬來西亞
00-800-0885-0885 菲律賓	00-800-0885-0885 澳門

◎ 各國駐臺機構(以各機構公佈資訊為準)

＊大洋洲

澳洲辦事處
Australian Office
臺北市信義區松高路9-11號統一國際大樓二十七至二十八樓
(02)8725-4100
http://www.australia.org.tw/tpeichinese/home.html

紐西蘭商工辦事處
New Zealand Commerce and Industry Office
臺北市信義區松智路1號九樓
(02)2720-5228
http://www.nzcio.com

夏威夷觀光局
The Hawaiian Islands
臺北市中山區松江路152號八樓之10
(02)2537-6372
http://www.gohawaii.com/tw/

關島觀光局臺灣辦事處
Guam Visitors Bureau
臺北市信義區信義路五段7號三十七樓
(02)8758-2969
關島專線：(02)2578-1849

帛琉共和國大使館
Embassy of the Republic of Palau
臺北市士林區天母西路62巷9號五樓
(02)2876-5415

諾魯共和國大使館
Embassy of the Republic of Nauru

臺北市士林區天母西路62巷9-1號十一樓
(02)2876-1950

索羅門群島大使館
Embassy of Solomon Islands
臺北市上林區天母西路62巷9號七樓
(02)2873-1168
http://www.solomons.org.tw/

斐濟駐華貿易暨觀光代表處
Fiji Trade and Tourism Representative Office
臺北市信義區基隆路一段333號國貿大樓三十二樓3212室
(02)2757-9596
http://www.fiji.org.tw/

＊美　洲

加拿大駐臺北貿易辦事處
Canadian Trade Office in Taipei
臺北市信義區松智路1號六樓
(02)8723-3000
http://www.canada.org.tw

美國在臺協會—臺北辦事處
American Institute in Taiwan, Taipei Office
臺北市大安區信義路三段134巷7號
(02)2162-2000
http://ait.org.tw/

美國在臺協會—高雄辦事處
American Institute in Taiwan, Kaohsiung Office
高雄市新興區中正三路2號中正大樓五樓
(07)238-7744
http://kaohsiung.ait.org.tw/

美國各州政府駐臺辦事處協會
（ASOA）American State Offices Association
臺北市信義區信義路五段5號世貿展覽一館七樓C區06室
(02)2725-2499
http://www.asoa-taiwan.org/

墨西哥商務簽證文件暨文化辦事處
Mexican Trade Services Documentation and Cultural Office
臺北市信義區基隆路一段333號國貿大樓十五樓1501室
(02)2757-6566
http://portal.sre.gob.mx/taiwan

巴拿馬共和國大使館
Embassy of the Republic of Panama
臺北市中山區松江路111號六樓
(02)2509-9189

薩爾瓦多共和國大使館
Embassy of the Republic of El Salvador
臺北市士林區天母西路62巷9號二樓
(02)2876-3606

瓜地馬拉共和國大使館
Embassy of the Republic of Guatemala
臺北市士林區天母西路62巷9-1號三樓
(02)2875-6952

多明尼加共和國大使館
Embassy of the Dominican Republic
臺北市士林區天母西路62巷9號六樓
(02)2875-1357

聖克里斯多福及尼維斯大使館
Embassy of Saint Christopher and Nevis

臺北市士林區天母西路62巷9-1號五樓
(02)2873-3252

宏都拉斯共和國大使館
Embassy of the Republic of Honduras
臺北市士林區天母西路62巷9號九樓
(02)2875-5507

巴拉圭共和國大使館
Embassy of the Republic of Paraguay
臺北市士林區天母西路62巷9-1號七樓
(02)2873-6310~1
http://www.embapartwroc.com.tw

秘魯駐臺北商務辦事處
Commercial Office of Peru in Taipei
臺北市信義區基隆路一段333號國貿大樓二十四樓2411室
(02)2757-7017
http://peru.org.tw

阿根廷商務文化辦事處
Argentina Trade and Cultural Office
臺北市信義區基隆路一段333號國貿大樓十五樓1512室
(02)2757-6556
http://www.argentina.org.tw/

貝里斯大使館
Embassy of Belize
臺北市士林區天母西路62巷9號十一樓
(02)2876-0894
http://www.facebook.com/pages/Tienmu-Taiwan/
Embassy-of-Belize-ROC-Taiwan/366305679020

智利商務辦事處
Chilean Trade Office

臺北市信義區信義路五段5號世貿展覽一館七樓7B06~07室
(02)2723-0329
http://www.chile-trade.com.tw

海地共和國大使館
Embassy of the Republic of Haiti
臺北市士林區天母西路62巷9-1號八樓
(02)2876-6718

* 歐　洲

英國貿易文化辦事處
British Trade and Cultural Office
臺北市信義區松高路9-11號統一國際大樓二十六樓
(02)8758-2088
http://ukintaiwan.fco.gov.uk/zh/

瑞典貿易委員會臺北辦事處
Exportradet Taipei, Swedish Trade Council
臺北市信義區基隆路一段333號國貿大樓十一樓1101室
(02)2757-6573
http://www.swedishtrade.se/taiwan

瑞士商務辦事處
Trade Office of Swiss Industries
臺北市信義區基隆路一段333號國貿大樓三十一樓3101室
(02)2720-1001
http://www.swiss.org.tw/

芬蘭商務辦事處
Finland Trade Center
臺北市信義區基隆路一段333號國貿大樓十五樓1511室
(02)2722-0764
http://www.finpro.fi/taiwan

法國在臺協會
French Office in Taipei
臺北市松山區敦化北路205號十樓1003室
(02)3518-5151
http://www.france-taipei.org/

荷蘭貿易暨投資辦事處
Netherlands Trade and Investment Office
臺北市松山區民生東路三段133號雅適建設大樓五樓
(02)2713-5760
http://www.ntio.org.tw

德國在臺協會
German Institute Taipei
臺北市信義區信義路五段7號101大樓三十三樓
(02)8722-2800
http://www.taipei.diplo.de/

奧地利臺北辦事處
Austrian Office Taipei
臺北市松山區敦化北路167號十樓
(02) 8175-3283
http://www.bmeia.gv.at/tw/vertretung/taipeh

捷克經濟文化辦事處
Czech Economic and Cultural Office
臺北市信義區基隆路一段200號七樓B室
(02)2722-5100
http://www.mzv.cz/taipei

斯洛伐克經濟文化辦事處
Slovak Economic and Cultural Office, Taipei
臺北市信義區基隆路一段333號國貿大樓十二樓1203室
(02)8780-3231
http://www.mzv.sk/taipei

匈牙利貿易辦事處
Hungarian Trade Office
臺北市中山區敬業一路97號美孚頂級商業辦公大樓三樓
(02)8501-1200
http://hungary.org.tw/

西班牙商務辦事處
Spanish Chamber of Commerce
臺北市中山區民生東路三段49號十樓B1室
(02)2518-4905~7

丹麥商務辦事處
The Trade Council of Denmark, Taipei
臺北市松山區敦化北路205號十二樓1207室
(02)2718-2101
http://tradecouncil.taipei.um.dk/

比利時臺北辦事處
Belgian Office, Taipei
臺北市松山區民生東路三段131號六樓601室
(02)2715-1215
http://www.beltrade.org.tw/

盧森堡臺北辦事處
Luxembourg Trade and Investment Office, Taipei
臺北市北投區奇岩路201巷8弄5號
(02)2891-6647
http://www.investinluxembourg.tw/

義大利經濟貿易文化推廣辦事處
Italian Economic, Trade and Cultural Promotion Office
臺北市信義區基隆路一段333號國貿大樓十八樓1809室
(02)2345-0320
http://www.italy.org.tw/

*亞 洲

行政院大陸委員會
Mainland Affairs Council
臺北市中正區濟南路一段2之2號十五樓
(02)2397-5589
http://www.mac.gov.tw/mp.asp?mp=1

香港旅遊發展局
Hong Kong Tourism Board
臺北市信義區松仁路89號十二樓E室
(02)8789-2080
http://www.discoverhongkong.com/tc/

莫斯科臺北經濟文化合作協調委員會駐臺北代表處
Representative Office in Taipei for the Moscow-Taipei
Coordination Commission on Economic and Cultural
Cooperation
臺北市信義區信義路五段2號十五樓
(02)8780-3011
http://www.mtc.org.tw/

印度—臺北協會
India-Taipei Association
臺北市信義區基隆路一段333號國貿大樓2010~12室
(02)2757-6112~3
http://www.india.org.tw/

駐臺北印尼經濟貿易代表處
Indonesian Economic and Trade Office to Taipei
臺北市內湖區瑞光路550號倫飛大樓六樓
(02)8752-6170
http://kdei-taipei.org/id/

駐臺北越南經濟文化辦事處
Vietnam Economic and Cultural Office in Taipei

臺北市中山區松江路65號三樓
(02)2516-6626

日本交流協會—臺北事務所
Interchange Association (Japan), Taipei Office
臺北市松山區慶城街28號通泰商業大樓
(02)2713-8000
http://www.koryu.or.jp/

日本交流協會—高雄事務所
Interchange Association (Japan), Kaohsiung Office
高雄市苓雅區和平一路87號九～十樓
(07)771-4008
http://www.koryu.or.jp/kaohsiung/ez3_contents.nsf/Top

駐臺北韓國代表部
Korean Mission in Taipei
臺北市信義區基隆路一段333號國貿大樓十五樓1506室
(02)2758-8320~5
http://taiwan.mofat.go.kr/

馬尼拉經濟文化辦事處
Manila Economic and Cultural Office
臺北市中山區長春路176號十一樓
(02)2508-1719
http://www.meco.org.tw/

馬來西亞友誼及貿易中心
Malaysian Friendship and Trade Centre, Taipei
臺北市松山區敦化北路102號三和塑膠大樓八樓
(02)2713-2626
http://www.kln.gov.my/perwakilan/taipei

馬來西亞觀光局在臺辦事處
Tourism Malaysia

臺北市松山區敦化北路170號八樓C室
(02)2514-9704
http://www.promotemalaysia.com.tw/default.aspx

新加坡駐臺北商務辦事處
Singapore Trade Office in Taipei
臺北市大安區仁愛路四段85號九樓
(02)2772-1940
http://www.singaporetradeoffice.gov.sg

汶萊貿易旅遊代表處
Brunei Darussalam Trade and Tourism Office
臺北市中山區建國北路一段80號六樓
(02)2506-3767

泰國貿易經濟辦事處
Thailand Trade and Economic Office
臺北市中山區松江路168號十二樓
(02)2581-1979
http://www.tteo.org.tw/

駐臺北土耳其貿易辦事處
Turkish Trade Office in Taipei
臺北市信義區基隆路一段333號國貿大樓十九樓1905室
(02)2757-6115

*非　洲

南非聯絡辦事處
Liaison Office of the Republic of South Africa
臺北市松山區敦化北路205號十三樓1301室
(02)8175-8588
http://www.southafrica.org.tw/

布吉納法索大使館
Embassy of Burkina Faso
臺北市士林區天母西路62巷9-1號六樓
(02)2873-3096

史瓦濟蘭王國大使館
Embassy of the Kingdom of Swaziland
臺北市士林區天母西路62巷9號十樓
(02)2872-5934

奈及利亞駐華商務辦事處
Nigeria Trade Office in Taiwan, R.O.C.
臺北市信義區信義路五段5號世貿展覽一館七樓7D06室
(02)2720-2669

聖多美普林西比民主共和國大使館
Embassy of Democratic Republic of Sao Tome and
Principe
臺北市士林區天母西路62巷9-1號十樓
(02)2876-6824

＊中　東

駐臺北以色列經濟文化辦事處
Israel Economic and Cultural Office in Taipei
臺北市信義區基隆路一段333號國貿大樓二十四樓2408室
(02)2757-9692
www.iseco.org.tw/

約旦商務辦事處
The Jordanian Commercial Office
臺北市士林區忠誠路二段110號一樓
(02)2871-7712

沙烏地阿拉伯商務辦事處
Saudi Arabian Trade Office
臺北市士林區天母西路62巷9號四樓
(02)2876-1444

. . . .

阿曼王國駐華商務辦事處
Commercial Office of the Sultanate of Oman-Taiwan
臺北市信義區信義路五段5號世貿展覽一館7G05室
(02)2722-0684
www.omantaiwan.org/

. . . .

國際機場網頁連結

＊我國

✈ 臺北松山國際機場
http://www.tsa.gov.tw/
✈ 臺灣桃園國際機場
http://www.taoyuan-airport.com/chinese/index.jsp
✈ 臺中航空站
http://www.tca.gov.tw/
✈ 高雄國際航空站
http://www.kia.gov.tw/

＊中、港、澳

✈ 上海機場集團
http://www.shanghaiairport.com/
✈ 北京首都國際機場
http://www.bcia.com.cn/
✈ 香港國際機場
http://www.hongkongairport.com/chi/
✈ 澳門國際機場
http://www.macau-airport.com/site/php/zh/main.php

*日本

✈ 成田國際機場
http://www.narita-airport.jp/ch2/index.html
✈ 關西國際機場
http://www.kansai-airport.or.jp/tw/index.asp
✈ 中部新特麗亞國際機場
http://www.centrair.jp/tch/index.html
✈ 福岡機場
http://www.fuk-ab.co.jp/
✈ 新千歲機場
http://www.new-chitose-airport.jp/tw/

*韓國

✈ 仁川國際機場
http://www.airport.kr/chn/airport/index.jsp
✈ 金浦國際機場
http://www.airport.co.kr/doc/gimpo/
✈ 金海國際機場
http://muan.airport.co.kr/doc/gimhae/index.jsp
✈ 濟洲國際機場
http://www.airport.co.kr/doc/jeju_chn/

*東南亞、西亞、中東

✈ 新加坡樟宜機場
http://www.changiairport.com/changi/en/index.html?__
locale=zh
✈ 馬來西亞吉隆坡國際機場
http://www.klia.com.my/
✈ 泰國素萬那普國際機場
http://www.suvarnabhumiairport.com/
✈ 泰國清邁機場
http://www.chiangmaiairportonline.com/
✈ 柬埔寨金邊國際機場
http://www.cambodia-airports.com/

✈ 印度新德里甘地國際機場
http://www.newdelhiairport.in/

✈ 印度孟買機場
http://www.mumbaiairport.com/

✈ 土耳其伊斯坦堡阿塔圖克機場
http://www.ataturkairport.com/

✈ 莫斯科國際機場
http://www.domodedovo.ru/en/

✈ 以色列臺拉維夫機場
http://www.iaa.gov.il/Rashat/he-IL/Rashot/

✈ 杜拜國際機場
http://www.dubaiairport.com/en/Pages/home.aspx

＊中西歐

✈ 愛爾蘭都柏林機場
http://www.dublinairport.com/home.aspx

✈ 英國倫敦希斯洛機場
http://www.heathrowairport.com/

✈ 荷蘭阿姆斯特丹史基浦機場
http://www.schiphol.nl/

✈ 比利時布魯塞爾機場
http://www.brusselsairport.be/en/

✈ 法國巴黎機場
http://www.aeroportsdeparis.fr/ADP/en-gb/passagers/home/

✈ 德國法蘭克福機場
http://www.frankfurt-airport.de/cms/default/rubrik/23/23311.html

✈ 德國慕尼黑機場
http://www.munich-airport.de/en/consumer/index.jsp

✈ 德國漢堡機場
http://www.ham.airport.de/en/

✈ 奧地利維也納國際機場
http://www.viennaairport.com

✖ 瑞士蘇黎世機場
http://www.flughafen-zuerich.ch/desktopdefault.aspx

✖ 瑞士日內瓦國際機場
http://www.gva.ch/en/desktopdefault.aspx

＊北歐、東歐、南歐

✖ 挪威奧斯陸機場
http://www.osl.no/

✖ 瑞典斯德哥爾摩阿爾蘭達機場
http://www.swedavia.se/arlanda/

✖ 丹麥哥本哈根機場
http://www.cph.dk/CPH/UK/MAIN/

✖ 芬蘭赫爾辛基機場
http://www.helsinki-vantaa.fi/home

✖ 捷克布拉格機場
http://www.prg.aero/en/

✖ 匈牙利布達佩斯機場
http://www.bud.hu/english

✖ 波蘭華沙蕭邦機場
http://www.lotnisko-chopina.pl/pl/pasazer

✖ 希臘雅典國際機場
http://www.aia.gr/default.asp?langid=2

✖ 義大利羅馬機場
http://www.adr.it/fiumicino

✖ 義大利米蘭機場
http://www.seamilano.eu/landing/index_en.html

✖ 義大利威尼斯馬可波羅機場
http://www.veniceairport.com/core/index.jsp?_
requestid=37300&language=en

✖ 西班牙馬德里機場
http://www.aena-aeropuertos.es/csee/Satellite/
Aeropuerto-Madrid-Barajas/es/Inicio.html

✖ 西班牙巴塞隆納機場
http://www.aena-aeropuertos.es/csee/Satellite/

Aeropuerto-Barcelona/es/
✈ 葡萄牙里斯本機場
http://www.ana.pt/portal/page/portal/ANA/AEROPORTO_
LISBOA/

＊北美洲

✈ 加拿大溫哥華機場
http://www.yvr.ca/en/Default.aspx
✈ 加拿大多倫多皮爾森國際機場
http://www.torontopearson.com/#
✈ 美國洛杉磯世界機場
http://www.lawa.org/welcomeLAWA.html
✈ 美國舊金山國際機場
http://www.flysfo.com/web/page/index.jsp
✈ 美國西雅圖機場
http://www.portseattle.org/Sea-Tac/Pages/default.aspx/
✈ 美國紐約甘迺迪國際機場
http://www.panynj.gov/airports/jfk.html
✈ 美國紐約紐華克自由國際機場
http://www.panynj.gov/airports/newark-liberty.html
✈ 美國波士頓洛根國際機場
http://www.massport.com/Pages/Default.aspx
✈ 美國華盛頓杜勒斯國際機場
http://www.metwashairports.com/dulles/dulles.htm

＊中南美洲

✈ 阿根廷國際機場
http://www.aa2000.com.ar/
✈ 智利聖地牙哥機場
http://www.aeropuertosantiago.cl/english/
✈ 秘魯利馬國際機場
http://www.lap.com.pe/lap_portal/ingles/index.asp
✈ 巴西里約國際機場
http://www.homesinrio.com/international-airport.htm

✈ 厄瓜多基多機場
http://www.quitoairport.com/index.asp?idioma=english
✈ 委內瑞拉國際機場
http://www.aeropuerto-maiquetia.com.ve/
✈ 哥倫比亞波哥大黃金城機場
http://www.bogota-dc.com/trans/aviones.htm
✈ 墨西哥墨西哥城國際機場
http://www.aicm.com.mx/home_en.php

＊非洲

✈ 埃及開羅國際機場
http://www.cairo-airport.com/
✈ 肯亞機場局
http://www.kenyaairports.co.ke/
✈ 南非約翰尼斯堡坦博國際機場
http://www.acsa.co.za/home.asp?pid=228&selAirport=jhb

＊大洋洲

✈ 澳洲雪梨機場
http://www.sydneyairport.com.au/
✈ 澳洲墨爾本機場
http://www.melbourneairport.com.au/
✈ 澳洲伯斯機場
http://www.perthairport.net.au/index.aspx
✈ 澳洲布里斯本機場
http://bne.com.au/
✈ 紐西蘭奧克蘭機場
http://www.auckland-airport.co.nz/
✈ 關島國際機場
http://www.guamairport.com/

各國國名

國名(英文)	國名(中文)	代碼	國名(英文)	國名(中文)	代碼
Albania	阿爾巴尼亞	AL	Lao	寮國	LA
Algeria	阿爾及利亞	DZ	Latvia	拉脫維亞	LV
Angola	安哥拉	AO	Luxembourg	盧森堡	LU
Anguilla	安圭拉	AI	Macao	澳門	MO
Argentina	阿根廷	AR	Macedonia	馬其頓	MK
Armenia	亞美尼亞	AM	Madagascar	馬達加斯加	MG
Aruba	阿魯巴	AW	Malawi	馬拉威	MW
Australia	澳大利亞	AU	Malaysia	馬來西亞	MY
Austria	奧地利	AT	Maldives	馬爾地夫	MV
Azerbaijan	亞塞拜然	AZ	Mali	馬利	ML
Bahamas	巴哈馬	BS	Malta	馬爾他	MT
Bahrain	巴林	BH	Mauritius	模里西斯	MU
Bangladesh	孟加拉	BD	Mauritania	茅利塔尼亞	MR
Barbados	巴貝多	BB	Mexico	墨西哥	MX
Belarus	白俄羅斯	BY	Moldova	摩爾多瓦	MD
Belgium	比利時	BE	Mongolia	蒙古	MN
Belize	貝里斯	BZ	Morocco	摩洛哥	MA
Benin	貝南	BJ	Myanmar	緬甸	MM
Bermuda	百慕達群島	BM	Namibia	納米比亞	NA
Bhutan	不丹	BT	Nauru	諾魯	NR

Bolivia	玻利維亞	BO	Nepal	尼泊爾	NP
Botswana	波札那	BW	Netherlands	荷蘭	NL
Brazil	巴西	BR	New Caledonia	新喀里多尼亞	NC
Brunei	汶萊	BN	New Zealand	紐西蘭	NZ
Bulgaria	保加利亞	BG	Niger	尼日	NE
Burkina Faso	布吉納法索	BF	Nigeria	奈及利亞	NG
Burundi	蒲隆地	BI	Norway	挪威	NO
Cambodia	柬埔寨	KH	Oman	阿曼	OM
Cameroon	喀麥隆	CM	Pakistan	巴基斯坦	PK
Canada	加拿大	CA	Panama	巴拿馬	PA
Cape Verde	維德角	CV	Papua New Guinea	巴布亞紐幾內亞	PG
Cayman	開曼群島	KY	Paraguay	巴拉圭	PY
Central African Republic	中非共和國	CF	Peru	秘魯	PE
Chad	查德	TD	Philippines	菲律賓	PH
Chile	智利	CL	Poland	波蘭	PL
China	中國	CN	Portugal	葡萄牙	PT
Colombia	哥倫比亞	CO	Qatar	卡達	QA
Congo	剛果共和國	CG	Romania	羅馬尼亞	RO
Cook	庫克群島	CK	Russian	俄羅斯	RU
Costa Rica	哥斯大黎加	CR	Rwanda	盧安達	RW

Cote d'Ivoire	象牙海岸	CI	Saint Christopher and Nevis	聖克里斯多福及尼維斯	KN
Croatia	克羅埃西亞	HR	Saint Lucia	聖露西亞	LC
Cyprus	賽普勒斯	CY	Saint Vincent and the Grenadines	聖文森及格瑞那丁	VC
Czech Republic	捷克共和國	CZ	Sao Tome and Principe	聖多美及普林西比	ST
Democratic Republic of the Congo	剛果民主共和國	CD	Saudi Arabia	沙烏地阿拉伯	SA
Denmark	丹麥	DK	Samoa	薩摩亞	
Dominican Republic	多明尼加共和國	DO	Senegal	塞內加爾	SN
Dominica	多米尼克	DM	Seychelles	塞席爾群島	SC
Ecuador	厄瓜多	EC	Switzerland	瑞士	CH
Egypt	埃及	EG	Syria	敘利亞	SY
El Salvador	薩爾瓦多	SV	Taiwan	臺灣	TW
Eritrea	厄利垂亞	ER	Tanzania	坦尚尼亞	TZ
Estonia	愛沙尼亞	EE	Thailand	泰國	TH
Ethiopia	衣索比亞	ET	Togo	多哥	TG
Fiji	斐濟	FJ	Trinidad and Tobago	千里達及托巴哥	TT
Finland	芬蘭	FI	Tunisia	突尼西亞	TN
French Polynesia	法屬玻里尼西亞	PF	Turkey	土耳其	TR

France	法國	FR	Uganda	烏干達	UG
Gabon	加彭	GA	Ireland	愛爾蘭	IE
Georgia	喬治亞	GE	Israel	以色列	IL
Germany	德國	DE	Italy	義大利	IT
Ghana	迦納	GH	Jamaica	牙買加	JM
Gibraltar	直布羅陀	GI	Japan	日本	JP
Greece	希臘	GR	Jordan	約旦	JO
Grenada	格瑞那達	GD	Kenya	肯亞	KE
Guatemala	瓜地馬拉	GT	Korea	韓國	KR
Guinea	幾內亞	GN	Kuwait	科威特	KW
Guyana	蓋亞那	GY	Ukraine	烏克蘭	UA
Haiti	海地	HA	United Arab Emirates	阿拉伯聯合大公國	AE
Honduras	宏都拉斯	HN	United Kingdom	英國	GB
Hong Kong	香港	HK	United States of America	美國	US
Hungary	匈牙利	HU	Uruguay	烏拉圭	UY
Iceland	冰島	IS	Venezuela	委內瑞拉	VE
India	印度	IN	Vietnam	越南	VN
Indonesia	印尼	ID	Yemen	葉門	YE
Iran	伊朗	IR	Zambia	尚比亞	ZM
Iraq	伊拉克	IQ	Zimbabwe	辛巴威	ZW

 各國貨幣代碼

貨幣符號	貨幣名稱
AUD	澳大利亞元
CNY	中國人民幣
EUR	歐元
GBP	英鎊
HKD	港幣
IEP	愛爾蘭鎊
IRR	伊朗里亞爾
JPY	日圓
KRW	韓圜
MYR	馬來西亞林吉特
NZD	紐西蘭元
PHP	菲律賓披索
SGD	新加坡元
SUR	蘇聯盧布
THB	泰國銖
TWD	臺幣
USD	美元

各國紀念日

月份	日期	各國紀念日
1	1	古巴解放日 斯洛伐克國慶日 蘇丹獨立日
	4	緬甸獨立日
	14	泰國國家森林保護日
	26	澳大利亞日 印度共和國日
2	4	斯里蘭卡國慶日
	5	墨西哥憲法日
	6	紐西蘭國慶日
	7	格瑞納達獨立日
	11	日本建國日 伊朗伊斯蘭革命勝利日
	18	甘比亞獨立日
	23	汶萊國慶日 蓋亞那共和國日
	25	科威特國慶日
3	2	摩洛哥獨立日
	6	迦納獨立日
	12	模里西斯獨立日
	17	愛爾蘭國慶日

月份	日期	各國紀念日
3	20	突尼西亞國慶日
	21	墨西哥熱氣球節
	23	巴基斯坦日
	25	希臘國慶日
	26	孟加拉獨立及國慶日
4	2	阿根廷馬爾維納斯(英屬福克蘭)群島戰役紀念日
	4	塞內加爾獨立日
	7	盧安達大屠殺反思日
	9	菲律賓巴丹日
	11	烏干達解放日
	16	丹麥女王日
	17	敘利亞國慶日
	18	辛巴威獨立日
	19	委內瑞拉獨立日
	25	義大利解放日
	26	坦尚尼亞聯合日
	27	獅子山共和國日 多哥獨立日
	29	日本天皇誕辰
	30	荷蘭女王日

月份	日期	各國紀念日
5	17	挪威憲法日
	20	喀麥隆國慶日
	25	阿根廷五月革命紀念日 約旦獨立日
6	1	突尼西亞勝利日
	2	義大利共和國日
	5	丹麥憲法日 塞席爾群島解放日
	6	瑞典國慶日
	7	查德國慶日
	10	葡萄牙國慶日
	12	菲律賓獨立日
	14	英國女王官方生日
	17	冰島共和國日
	23	盧森堡國慶日 挪威聖漢斯節
	24	西班牙國王陛下日
	26	馬達加斯加獨立日
	27	吉布地獨立日
	30	蘇丹救國革命節

月份	日期	各國紀念日
7	1	蒲隆地國慶日 加拿大日 盧安達獨立日
	4	美國獨立日
	5	阿爾及利亞獨立日 維德角獨立日 委內瑞拉獨立日
	6	葛摩聯邦獨立日
	9	阿根廷獨立日
	11	蒙古人民革命紀念日
	14	法國國慶日
	17	伊拉克國慶日
	20	哥倫比亞國慶日
	21	比利時國慶日
	22	波蘭國家復興節
	23	埃及國慶日
	26	古巴起義日 賴比瑞亞獨立日 馬爾地夫群島獨立日
	27	奧地利獨立日
	28	秘魯獨立日
	30	摩洛哥國慶日 萬那杜獨立日

月份	日期	各國紀念日
8	1	瑞士聯邦成立日
	2	牙買加國慶日
	3	尼日獨立日
	5	布吉納法索國慶日
	6	玻利維亞獨立日
	7	象牙海岸國慶日
	10	厄瓜多獨立日
	13	中非共和國獨立日
	14	巴基斯坦獨立日
	15	印度獨立日 剛果國慶日
	16	賽普勒斯獨立日
	17	加彭獨立日
	19	阿富汗獨立日
	20	匈牙利國慶日
	23	羅馬尼亞國慶日
	31	馬來西亞國慶日
9	1	利比亞九月革命節
	2	越南國慶日
	3	聖馬利諾國慶日
	7	巴西獨立日

月份	日期	各國紀念日
9	9	(北韓)朝鮮民主主義人民共和國日
	12	維德角國慶日 衣索比亞人民革命日
	16	墨西哥獨立日
	18	智利獨立日
	21	馬爾他獨立日
	22	馬利宣佈獨立日
	30	波札那獨立日
10	1	奈及利亞國慶日
	2	幾內亞宣佈獨立日
	5	葡萄牙共和國日
	9	烏干達獨立日
	10	斐濟國慶日
	12	西班牙國慶日 赤道幾內亞國慶日
	21	索馬利亞十月革命節
	24	聯合國日 尚比亞獨立日
	26	奧地利國慶日
	28	捷克獨立日 希臘國慶日
	29	土耳其共和國日

月份	日期	各國紀念日
11	1	阿爾及利亞革命節 菲律賓亡人節
	9	寮國獨立日
	11	安哥拉獨立日 波蘭獨立日 美國退伍軍人節
	15	比利時國王日
	17	斯洛伐克自由民主日
	18	阿曼國慶日
	19	摩納哥國慶日
	22	黎巴嫩獨立日
	26	緬甸直桑岱點燈節
	28	茅利塔尼亞獨立日
12	1	中非共和國國慶日 葡萄牙恢復獨立紀念日
	2	寮國國慶日 阿拉伯聯合大公國國慶日
	5	泰國國王加冕日
	6	芬蘭獨立日
	7	象牙海岸獨立日
	12	肯亞獨立日
	17	不丹國慶日

月份	日期	各國紀念日
12	23	日本天皇誕生日
	26	愛爾蘭聖史蒂芬節 英國節禮日
	28	尼泊爾國王生日
	30	菲律賓黎剎日

🧭 出國必備用品：

護照	簽證	緊急聯絡電話本	信用卡
備份證件影本	相片	機票	旅行計畫表
海外旅行保險單	國際駕照	各種優惠卡	防疫注射證明書
臺幣	外幣	旅行支票	地圖
急救包	生理用品	旅遊手冊	水壺
瑞士刀	轉接插頭	變壓器	電話卡
衣物	鞋襪	盥洗用具	防身用具

NOTE

國家圖書館出版品預行編目資料

背包客一定要會的英文便利句 / 張翔 編著 --初版.
---新北市：知識工場出版 采舍國際有限公司發行,
2012.08 面；公分· -- (Excellent ；50)
ISBN-978 986 271-244-3 (平裝附光碟片)

1.英語　　　　2.旅遊　　　　3.會話

805.188　　　　　　　　　　101013129

Travel around the World

背包客
一定要會的
英文便利句

知識工場・Excellent 50

背包客一定要會的英文便利句

出版者／全球華文聯合出版平台・知識工場

作　　者／張翔	印 行 者／知識工場
出版總監／王寶玲	文字編輯／何牧蓉
總 編 輯／歐綾纖	美術設計／蔡億盈

台灣出版中心／新北市中和區中山路2段366巷10號10樓
電　　話／（02）2248-7896
傳　　真／（02）2248-7758
ISBN-13 ／978-986-271-244-3
出版日期／2021年3月二十版三十八刷

全球華文國際市場總代理 ／采舍國際
地　　址／新北市中和區中山路2段366巷10號3樓
電　　話／（02）8245-8786
傳　　真／（02）8245-8718

港澳地區總經銷／和平圖書
地址／香港柴灣嘉業街12號百樂門大廈17樓
電話／（852）2804-6687
傳真／（852）2804-6409

全系列書系特約展示
新絲路網路書店
地址／新北市中和區中山路2段366巷10號10樓
電話／（02）8245-9896
網址／www.silkbook.com